KARMA TRAIN FROM KANSAS

A novel
by Dave Hughes

Prickly Pair Publishing
Chandler, Arizona, USA

Previous books in the "Gay Tales for the New Millennium" series:

Maybe Next Year
Instant Adult
Open Books, Closed Sets
If I Seem Quiet...

Watch for the final book, Maybe <u>Now</u>, in September 2024.

Visit AuthorDaveHughes.com to learn more about Dave, gain background information and insights into Dave's books and the writing process, and receive advance notice of upcoming book releases and subscriber discounts. You will receive Dave's short story, *Cruise Virgins*, free when you subscribe to his newsletter.

If you would like to contact the author, please send an email to Dave@AuthorDaveHughes.com.

Cover photo: Jat306 (licensed from depositphotos.com)
Cover design: Dave Hughes

Library of Congress Control Number: 2024906017

ISBN: 978-0-9970018-1-5

Caught on Video

Tuesday, August 9, 2016

At the Helton Grand Hotel & Suites in Kansas City, Missouri, General Manager Trevor Zimmerman was reviewing security camera footage from the previous Friday night. His weekend night manager noticed a pattern that had been occurring over the past several months. On the first Friday of each month between the hours of 8:00 and 9:00 p.m., an unusually large number of guests entered a suite near the back of the complex. Most of them didn't leave until well after midnight. And they were all men.

Trevor looked back through the hotel's reservation system. He discovered that a man named Archibald Kilgore had reserved the same suite on the first Friday of each month for at least the past year. Trevor looked ahead to future reservations. Sure enough, Archibald Kilgore had reserved that suite on the first Friday of each month for the rest of the year.

As Trevor scanned the video, he saw four men arrive shortly after 6:00 p.m. They made multiple trips in and out of the room, carrying coolers, grocery bags, a few cases of beer and sodas, and several rectangular plastic storage tubs.

Between 8:00 and 9:00 p.m., Trevor counted at least thirty men entering the suite. Nobody came or went for the next three hours. After midnight, men trickled out. Finally, at around 2:00 a.m., the four men who had arrived first hauled everything back out to their cars.

Trevor reached for his phone and called the housekeeping supervisor. "Hi, Cynthia. Trevor here. Did anyone on your staff report anything unusual while they were cleaning suite 247 last Saturday morning?"

"Oh, yeah. Wanda asked me to come over and take a look at it. It was a mess. The trash cans were overflowing with beer bottles, soda cans, potato chip bags, and stuff like that. And there was more trash all over the kitchenette. The bed sheets were stained something awful. We had to throw them away. The bathroom was a mess – water spilled everywhere. And uh… in one of the drawers in the kitchenette, there was a little bit of white powder and an empty prescription bottle for Viagra. Looks like somebody had a pretty wild party in there."

"Do you recall hearing about that before?"

"Yeah, it seems to happen about once a month. And always in that suite."

"Okay, thanks, Cynthia. I may be able to put a stop to it. Later."

"Later."

Trevor hung up the phone, then pulled out his cell phone and searched his contacts. He called his buddy who was an officer on the Kansas City police force.

"Crockett speaking."

"Hey, Rocket! It's Trevor Zimmerman. How the hell are you?"

"Hey, Trev! Doin' good, man, doin' good. Whatchu up to, bro?"

"Would you mind dropping by my hotel sometime soon? I saw something on the security camera footage I wanted to run by you. Nothing urgent."

"Sure, man. How about right after lunch, like around 1:30?"

"Sounds good. See you then."

Trevor Zimmerman and Clayton "Rocket" Crockett had been teammates on the track team at Prairie Village High School. Rocket graduated eight years ago, Trevor seven. Rocket, who was the school's star running back, received a football scholarship to attend Texas Christian University, where he majored in criminal justice. When he failed to attract the interest of any professional football teams, he returned home and joined the Kansas City police force. With his football career behind him, he dropped his nickname. His colleagues called him Clayton, or simply Clay. But to his high school buddies, he would always be Rocket.

He walked up to the reception desk in the hotel lobby at around 1:25. "May I speak with Trevor Zimmerman? He's expecting me."

Seconds later, Trevor appeared and escorted his friend back to his office. After a hearty handshake, Trevor asked, "How was lunch?"

"It was okay. Nothing special."

Trevor scanned his friend's chest. "No donut powder on your uniform. Good job!"

"Blow me, dude."

They both smiled. Trevor pulled the guest chair around to his side of the desk, so Rocket could sit next to him and see his computer screen. "Have a seat. I've got something I want to show you."

"Does it involve tawdry teachers, slutty cheerleaders, or horny housewives?"

Trevor looked confused.

"Remember the party that night at your place back when we were in high school?"

Trevor rarely thought about that. His parents had gone away for the weekend, so he invited a bunch of guys from the track team over for a party. Rocket talked him into showing a couple of porn videos from his father's hidden stash. "Jesus Christ. You haven't changed a bit. Seriously though, you might not be too far off. Take a look at this. My weekend manager told me that on the first Friday of every month, a whole bunch of guys go into this one suite. We're talking like thirty or forty. They enter between 8:00 and 9:00, and they don't start coming out until after midnight."

Trevor showed Rocket bits and pieces of the footage of the men carrying the coolers, grocery bags, and storage tubs, then fast-forwarded to the parade of men entering the room. "My housekeeping manager says they always leave the room a mess, especially the sheets, the bathrooms, and the kitchenettes. And she says there is evidence of drug use. So, I checked my records, and the same guy reserves that suite on the first Friday of every month, going back at least a year and ahead for the rest of this year."

"So, you think they're having a party every month?"

"Sure looks like it. And given the condition they leave the sheets in, I'd say it's an orgy. And did you notice? It's all guys. Not one woman."

Rocket said, "Well, gay sex isn't against the law anymore. You said they leave a mess, but do they damage anything?"

"We have to discard most of the sheets, but there's no damage unless the stains get down to the mattress. But that stuff happens sometimes anyway. It comes with the business. But remember, it looks like there's drug use. And they're cramming more people into that suite than the fire marshal allows."

"Gotcha. So, what's the guy's name who makes the reservations?"

"Archibald Kilgore."

Rocket wrote that name on his notepad. "When's his next reservation?"

"Friday, September 2nd."

"Okay, well let me talk to my supervisor and see what we can do."

Trevor said, "Thanks. I suppose I can cancel the future reservations and tell that guy he's not welcome back. But if something illegal is going on they'll just move it somewhere else."

"Yeah, I get it. Okay, man, I'll see what I can do."

They got up and shook hands. Trevor walked Rocket back out to the hotel lobby.

***

Rocket returned to police headquarters and found his supervisor, Sergeant Timothy Garlow. He relayed the information Trevor shared with him. Garlow said, "Hmmm… Do you think your friend would let us install a couple of hidden cameras in the room?"

"I don't see why not."

"Would you please call him and set up a time when we can go see the room?"

"Sure, hang on." Rocket pulled out his cell phone and called Trevor.

"Hey, Trev. Is there a time when that room is empty and we can come take a look at it?"

"Just a minute, let me check… Actually, it's available today and tomorrow. The next reservation isn't until Thursday."

"Okay, we'll be in tomorrow morning. How about 10:00?"

"Sure. See you then."

The Police Visit

Wednesday, August 10, 2016

Rocket and Sergeant Garlow arrived at the hotel and Trevor took them to suite 247. It was a two-bedroom suite designed for vacationing families or perhaps a long-term business assignment. The living room was nicely furnished with a comfortable sofa facing a large wall-mounted TV, a kitchenette, a small round dining table with four chairs, and a desk facing the wall. The bedrooms, one on each side of the living room, contained a king-size bed, a couple of armchairs near the window, and a small round table between them. A large TV was mounted on the wall opposite the bed.

Rocket said, "I can't imagine how they fit 30 or 40 people in here, doing whatever they're doing."

Garlow asked Trevor, "What's the maximum occupancy for this suite?"

"Twelve."

Garlow walked around the perimeter of all the rooms, examining the vents and fixtures. "Hmmm. I'm trying to figure out where we could hide cameras. I suppose we could put something inside the heating vents."

Rocket said, "Maybe we could hang a two-way mirror somewhere and put a camera behind that."

Garlow replied, "Yeah, that's a possibility for the bedrooms. I don't see where we could put one in the living room. Remember, we're not trying to watch them have sex. We're watching for illegal drug use. Do you think that would be taking place in the bathrooms?"

"I don't know. There or in the kitchenette. Could be anywhere, though."

Trevor said, "My staff found white powder in one of the drawers in the kitchenette, so probably there. But remember, they've been coming here for over a year. They would notice if there were mirrors that weren't there before."

Garlow said, "Good point. I don't think cameras are our answer. I think our best option is to have someone go undercover and attend the event." Garlow placed his hand firmly on Rocket's shoulder and smiled at him.

"Wait... WHAT??? No way, man! You're messin' with me, right?"

Garlow kept smiling. Trevor was grinning from ear to ear, trying to keep from laughing out loud.

"Seriously? You want me to go to a gay orgy???"

"I can't think of a better man for the job."

"Awww shit, man... Can't you get one of the gay guys on the force? Like Fields or Harrison? I'm sure there are others."

Garlow thought for a second. "No. We don't know who attends these events. If our guy knows any of the people, his cover would get blown."

Rocket said, "Among other things." They all chuckled. "But, like, I won't know how to act or what to do."

"Don't worry. You don't have to actually do anything. Just say it's your first time and you're nervous and you want to check it out for a while until you get more comfortable. Just be a wallflower. If you see drugs, signal us, then excuse yourself and leave. We'll move in and take over."

"How am I going to signal you?"

"You'll be wearing a wire."

"How will I wear a wire if I'm... Wait a minute! Am I going to have to get naked for this?"

"We have wires that look like hearing aids. They have a tiny microphone so we can hear what's going on, and you can hear what we tell you. And I imagine you could keep your underwear on. Well, probably. I don't know how these things work any better than you do."

"I don't know, man... this isn't what I signed up for."

"There are much more dangerous situations you could encounter in the line of duty. I'll make sure you get a commendation and a nice bonus. It will look good in your file."

"Yeah, but... Why me? Isn't there anyone else you can get?"

Garlow gave Rocket a playful slap on his butt. "Because you've got a cute ass."

Trevor burst out laughing.

Rocket looked sternly at Trevor. "Not a word to our friends! I'm fuckin' serious. Don't even think about it."

Trevor slid his thumb and forefinger across his lips as if he was zipping them shut.

Garlow asked Trevor, "Can you reserve a room for us nearby? Like maybe on the floor right above or below this? Not on this floor where they could see us."

"There are meeting rooms on the first floor below this. Would that work?"

"That would be perfect."

"Okay, I'll make sure the one under this room is available on September 2nd."

"Nice to meet you, Mr. Zimmerman. Thank you for your cooperation. We'll be in touch."

Garlow handed Trevor his card. They all shook hands, and Rocket and Garlow left.

Pocket Rocket

Thursday, August 11, 2016

The next morning, Sergeant Garlow called Rocket into his office.

"Hey, thanks for stopping by. Come in and have a seat. Close the door behind you." After they were seated, Garlow continued. "I found out a couple of things. First, that guy who makes the reservations, Archibald Kilgore? He works at Eternal Savior Christian Church over in Prairie Village. According to the staff page on their website, he's the Facilities Manager."

Rocket said, "I grew up in Prairie Village. Isn't that one of those right-wing churches?"

"Yeah. In fact, I dealt with their pastor on a case eight or nine years ago. I worked at the Prairie Village Police Department before I came here. His son went missing. When we investigated, it was clear he ran away from home. But that guy – Bauer, I think it was – tried to tell us homosexuals had kidnapped him."

Rocket looked shocked. "Whoa, whoa, wait a minute. That guy was one of my friends. We were on the track team together in high school. Bryan Bauer. Super nice guy. Real clean-cut. I wonder what happened to him."

"Well, he turned 18 about three months after he disappeared, so we had to close the case. I don't think he ever turned up. But that Rev. Bauer was a real nut job. I remember he bullshitted us a lot, like he was trying to hide something. We found out he was going to force his son to go to some kind of gay conversion therapy place in Alabama. Apparently, they thought he was gay, and with his dad being the pastor of that church–"

Rocket interrupted, "Yeah, I kind of thought he was gay. He had this buddy named Chris. They were like totally inseparable. I thought maybe something was going on between them."

"Yes, we interviewed him. He mentioned they were a couple. Anyway, it was heartbreaking. We felt so sorry for that kid. In fact, during our investigation, we suspected he might have been abused. If he had turned up somewhere and they made him return home, we were going to forward the case to Child Protective Services. Oh, and there was this other guy who was with Rev. Bauer when I responded to the 911 call. He was running some sort of counseling practice where he tried to convert gay people to become straight. We investigated him, too. Turns out that a minister can offer 'pastoral counseling' and skirt a lot of laws, but we busted him for running an unlicensed business and not paying taxes on it. Anyway, he was queer as a three-dollar bill. I felt like he was drooling over me the whole time I was trying to take a report on the missing kid. But back to Mr. Kilgore. It's not appropriate for us to tell the church what one of their employees does on his off-hours."

Rocket drifted off for a moment. He was adding this new information to what he remembered from high school.

Garlow continued, "Here's the other thing. One of the detectives found the website for whoever organizes these orgies. You have to apply to be invited. Sort of like a screening process, which doesn't surprise me. I'll forward the link to you. You'll need to come up with a fake name and create a fake email address, then apply to join this group. Do it from home, in case they try to trace the IP address. They're going to ask you to submit a couple of photos – one of your face and a full-body photo showing everything. Just take them with your phone into a mirror. Let me know if you need any help answering the questions. If you incur any costs, you can expense them. I'll approve it. Any questions?"

Rocket was only half paying attention. He was thinking about Bryan. And he was trying to come to grips with taking nude photos of himself and uploading them to some website for a gay orgy group. "Not now. Not yet, anyway."

"Okay. Well, go ahead and get started on that. And hey… I really appreciate you doing this. I know it's going to be kind of awkward."

"Kind of?"

***

That evening, Rocket sat down at his computer and thought, *might as well get this over with.* He opened a browser window and typed in KC-PnP.com.

He clicked the 'Must be over 18 to enter' link on the landing page. Then he was directed to a page containing information about men-only gatherings that take place one Friday night each month at an undisclosed location. Specific information would be provided after his membership was approved.

The description claimed these gatherings attracted 30 to 50 men of all ages and types for uninhibited fun, exploration, and fulfillment. Absolute discretion was required since participants come from many different occupations and relationship situations.

There was a tab at the top of the webpage labeled 'Member Area' which required a username and password to log in.

To proceed further, Rocket had to complete a short contact form.

Username: ________________

The form noted that the Username would be the name members would call each other to preserve anonymity. Rocket typed in 'Rocket.' Then he thought, *No, wait. Maybe I shouldn't use that, in case anyone who knew me in high school or followed college football recognizes me.* He decided on 'Pocket_Rocket' – a slang term that meant either a small gun in a pants pocket or an erect penis inside pants. He continued filling out the fields.

Password: ********
First name: Joe
Last name: Miller

He thought about using Schmoe, Blow, or Mama for the last name but thought better of it.

Email: _______________________________

Rocket opened a new browser tab, went to Yahoo, and created a new email address, joemiller.69@yahoo.com. He typed it into the field.

Age: 26
Height: 5'10"
Weight: 200

Next, there was a text box labeled, 'Tell us a little about you. What are you into?'

Rocket had no idea what he should say. Finally, he settled on, 'Just an average guy wanting to try group sex.'

Then he clicked the 'Submit' button.

The confirmation message said, 'Please check your email for further instructions.'

Rocket returned to the Yahoo tab and opened his new email account. A few seconds later, an email from join@KC-PnP.com appeared. He opened it.

Dear Pocket_Rocket,

We have received your request to join our exclusive group.

To complete your application, please reply to this email and attach two recent photos of you as follows:

- A headshot. This should clearly show your unobstructed face. No sunglasses, hats, or masks. You must be the only person in the picture. When you arrive at an event, your face will be compared to

> this photo to validate your identity. A selfie taken on your phone will be fine.
>
> - A full-body nude photo. A photo taken using a mirror will be fine. Show us what you got!
>
> Applications that do not include acceptable photos will be rejected. Please be honest and send recent pictures of you (taken within the past year). Do not send photos of hot men you find on the internet. If you don't match your photos, you will be denied entrance without refund and your membership will be canceled.
>
> We're looking forward to having you join us! New members make each gathering more fun.
>
> Sincerely,
>
> The Committee

Rocket picked up his phone and took a selfie. That was easy. Now for the more awkward part. He carried his phone into his bedroom and removed his clothes. He posed naked in front of the full-length mirror on his closet door. He was proud of his body. He continued going to the gym after his college football days ended. Although he had added a few pounds, he still looked muscular and well-defined. He felt comfortable being naked in a locker room since he had done it for so many years. But this … this was different.

It was inevitable that among the hundreds of men who had seen him naked in a locker room shower over the years, some of them were gay. Heck, there was Bryan and Chris back when they were on the track team. That didn't bother him. But he felt apprehensive now.

He wondered whether he should pose with an erection. The email didn't specify that. Whoever was on The Committee shouldn't object. Was a nice cock a criterion for acceptance into this group? His cock wasn't large by any means, but it was nothing to be ashamed of either. And he was definitely a 'grower.'

He decided that since he had come this far, he might as well go all the way and not leave anything to chance. His nervousness made achieving a full erection a bit of a challenge, but he persevered and succeeded long enough to snap a few good pictures of his reflection in the mirror.

He transferred the pictures from his phone to his computer, attached the headshot and most flattering full-body photo to the email, and clicked Send.

***

The next day, he received an email welcoming him into the group. The next gathering was to take place on Friday, September 2, in suite 247 at Trevor's hotel. He breathed a sigh of relief, thankful he had joined the correct group. Who knows how many other groups like this might be operating in the area? What if he had joined the wrong one?

Party 'n' Play

Friday, September 2, 2016

The day Rocket had been dreading was finally here.

In the morning, he and Sergeant Garlow visited the meeting room where the police would gather and wait for his signal to raid the party. Garlow handed him the hearing aid, which would be their communication device. Trevor took Rocket up to suite 247 to test the system. Fortunately, it was within range and worked fine.

***

That evening, Garlow drove an unmarked car and was already in the meeting room when Rocket arrived at 8:30. The other officers were instructed to arrive after 9:00 and park out of view of the windows of suite 247.

Rocket wore workout shorts, a loose-fitting tank top, and sneakers. As suggested in the email, he brought a gym bag to put his clothes in. He packed sweatpants and a sweat jacket since it would be colder when he left later that night.

The email with the details for the evening's event emphasized that attendees should arrive only between 8:00 and 9:00 p.m. Late arrivals would not be admitted. Rocket decided to arrive as close to 9:00 as possible so he could minimize the amount of time he had to be there. He assumed that by the time he arrived, things would be well underway.

At 8:50, Rocket said, "Well, I guess it's time." He grabbed his gym bag, stood up, and placed the hearing aid in his ear.

"Good luck," Garlow replied. "And I know I've said this several times before, but thank you for doing this."

Rocket forced a weak smile. "Don't mention it. Seriously."

He climbed the stairs to the second floor and walked toward the room, his anxiety building with each step. He hoped he would be able to act cool and relaxed enough that his apprehension wouldn't show. But then, who wouldn't be nervous the first time they attended an orgy with strangers?

He took a deep breath and knocked on the door as specified in the email: knock-knock … knock … knock-knock-knock.

Seconds later, a handsome older Black gentleman cracked the door open and looked at Rocket. "Yes…?"

In a low voice, Rocket said, "Hi. I'm Pocket Rocket."

The man opened the door about a foot more and waved him in. A six-foot-tall three-panel decorative room divider stood a few feet inside the door, blocking his view of the rest of the living room. The man scanned a list of names, then flipped through a few pages with headshot photos until he found Rocket's.

"I'm Black Stallion. Welcome." Black Stallion extended his hand, which Rocket shook.

Rocket started to walk around the partition, then turned back to Black Stallion. "This is my first time. Can I ask you a couple of questions about how this works?"

"I have to stay by the door until 9:00, but let me get someone else." He stepped around the partition and waved for someone to come to the door.

A pudgy, balding man sashayed forward to meet them. He was wearing an oversized rainbow-colored tie-dye shirt that reached halfway down his thigh. Rocket couldn't tell whether he was wearing anything under it. Given the circumstances, probably not. The man scanned Rocket from head to toe and grinned. "I'm Bottom Piggy – the other white meat. How may I be of … *service*?"

Rocket heard Garlow laughing in his ear. Bottom Piggy extended his hand, palm down and angled slightly downward. Rocket lightly shook it, and Bottom Piggy curtsied. Black Stallion said, "This is Pocket Rocket's first visit and he has a few questions. Would you please show him around?”

"With pleasure! *Come* this way!” He led Rocket a few steps to the kitchenette. "There’s beer and soda in the fridge. As you can see, there’s plenty of snacks if you get the munchies." He gently pulled open one of the drawers. "And in here we have a few other treats you might enjoy." Rocket saw a zip-lock sandwich bag containing powder next to a cluster of short plastic straws. There were also two prescription pill bottles.

Rocket asked, "What’s in those?"

Bottom Piggy held up one bottle and said, "This one’s PrEP…" He put the bottle back and picked up the other one. "…and this one’s Viagra." Of course, a healthy young buck like you probably doesn’t need Viagra, but it’s good for endurance." He winked and slid the drawer closed. "And of course, if you experience an erection lasting longer than four hours…" He smiled suggestively at Rocket. "Make sure it’s inside me!"

Garlow’s voice in the hearing aid said, "Woo-hoo! Now there’s an offer you *cunt* refuse!" Rocket smiled, which was good because otherwise, he would have grimaced. Then Garlow said, "Ask him where they get the meds."

Rocket asked Bottom Piggy, "Just curious… How did you get the PrEP and the Viagra?"

"Oh, one of the guys is a pharmacist. He goes by Big Pharma." He winked and added, "And believe me, he certainly is. And Black Stallion provides the crystal meth and the coke. He has sources." Rocket made a mental note to determine who Big Pharma was, so he could identify him later. He was surprised Bottom Piggy was so generous with sharing sensitive information, but it was making his job much easier. Maybe it was because Bottom Piggy was so obviously smitten by him. He hoped that wouldn’t become a problem later.

Bottom Piggy led Rocket out of the kitchenette and into the living room.

"You can come out here to take a break between rounds, or if you want to get a snack or something to drink. You can set your gym bag down anywhere you find room. Don't worry, nobody ever bothers anything. It's okay if you want to wear something while you're in here, but when you enter either of the bedrooms, you must be completely naked."

A few men were standing around talking and holding drinks. Some were wearing shorts or underwear and others were wearing nothing. A gay pornographic movie was playing on the TV, even though no action was taking place in the living room. Bottom Piggy led Rocket to the doorway of one of the bedrooms. He stood halfway in the door and Rocket leaned in to take a quick look. The room was illuminated only by a few electric candles, the light from the bathroom, and the TV that was showing a video of a large orgy. Approximately a dozen men were piled onto the king-size bed in a variety of positions, and a few more were cavorting on two air mattresses on the floor that were covered with large bed sheets.

"As you can see, this is where the action takes place – well, here and in the other bedroom. There's a sling in there." Rocket wasn't sure if that was what he thought it was, but decided against asking. He was asking enough questions already, and he could find out for himself later.

His tour guide walked back into the living room and continued, "There's lube and poppers and little clean-up towels on all the tables. There are condoms if you want to use them, but you might be the only one."

"Seriously? People aren't using condoms?"

"Most of the guys take PrEP."

"Okay, so I'm new to this group thing, and I always use condoms. You mentioned PrEP earlier. What's that?"

"It's these magical little pills that prevent you from getting HIV. You take two tablets two hours before you start fucking, then you take one tomorrow and one the next day."

"Does that really work?"

"The CDC says it's 99 percent effective, which is better than condoms. But if you whore around a lot, you should probably take it every day. I take it, and let's just say I've earned my nickname." He winked and nudged Rocket with his elbow. "And I'm still negative! It's a miracle product!"

Rocket whispered, "Is Big Pharma in there?"

Bottom Piggy walked back to the bedroom door, glanced inside, and said, "Yeah. You see that ginger guy at the foot of the bed slamming his cock into one of the party favors? That's him."

Rocket tried to process that but couldn't make sense of it. He knew drugs like meth were sometimes called party favors, but a human? "Okay, so… what's a party favor, in this context?"

"You *are* new to this, aren't you? So, each month we bring in three or four cute young twinks who are, shall we say, always ready and willing. They're our PAPBs." He immediately realized Rocket wouldn't get that, so he said, "Pass-around party bottoms. You could say they're *open* to all *comers*. They already have it, so they don't really care who does what to them."

"It?"

"HIV."

Rocket had taken everything in stride up to this point, but this was unfathomable. And sad. He frowned and started to shake his head in disgust, but stopped himself.

Garlow said, "Ask him if they're paid."

"So, those young guys… Do they do that all night long because they want to? For free?"

"Oh, they seem to enjoy it. And we make it well worth their while."

"How do you find guys who are willing to do that?"

"You'll have to ask Franklin Pierced. He finds them – probably on Grindr or Craig's List or something. He's the one with the big arm tattoo and a PA in his dick. You can't miss him."

Rocket decided not to ask what a PA was. If he saw a tattooed guy with something in his dick – whatever it might be – that would be him.

Bottom Piggy said, "And that concludes our tour. If you have any other questions, just ask anyone. Now if you'll excuse me…" With a dramatic, sweeping flourish, Bottom Piggy pulled the extra-extra-large T-shirt over his head revealing that, as Rocket suspected, he was wearing nothing underneath. He flung the shirt over a nearby gym bag and sashayed toward the bedroom with the sling. He turned, winked, and smiled suggestively. "When you're ready, you know where to find me!" Then he disappeared into the room.

Rocket decided a beer might help him relax, so he walked over to the fridge in the kitchenette. He carefully stepped around a couple of guys who were snorting a line of crystal meth. After he retrieved a beer from the fridge, he asked, "Hey, do you guys know if there's a bottle opener?"

The one who wasn't snorting at that moment reached into the drawer next to the drug drawer and handed it to him. "Thanks. Hey, just curious. What does that do for you?"

"Oh, man, it makes sex intense! You should check it out. Here, take a hit."

"Thanks, maybe later. By the way, I'm Pocket Rocket."

"Jack Hammer. I'm the guy who approved your membership application. Glad you came – or will come."

Having finished his line, the other man stood up straight. He was a few inches taller than Rocket, about 50 years old, with a full head of well-coiffed salt and pepper hair. He was handsome in a GQ sort of way. He looked vaguely familiar, but Rocket couldn't place him. "I'm Rod Long." Rocket quickly glanced down to see if his rod was, in fact, long, but he had shorts on. Rod saw him look down. For a second, Rocket felt embarrassed, but then he realized he was purporting to be a gay man, so it was probably okay. Rod smirked. "And yes, it is." The look in his eyes clearly implied an invitation.

Rocket left the kitchenette and headed out to the living room. It was ten after nine. Black Stallion had chained the door and engaged the security lock, and was now getting undressed. Rocket guessed him to be at least sixty, but he was in excellent shape and his skin was remarkably smooth. Rocket sat down in one of the chairs and turned his attention to the porn video playing on the TV. Black Stallion was the eldest participant he had seen so far, and the only Black man. Rocket wondered whether he would receive much attention or if he would be destined to watch from the sidelines. Out of the corner of his eye, Rocket saw his shorts come down. He concluded that Black Stallion was probably quite popular.

Black Stallion turned to Rocket and said, "You're a bit overdressed for the occasion."

"Yeah, I guess." Rocket removed his tank top, then leaned down and started untying his shoes. Black Stallion disappeared into the bedroom Rocket hadn't seen yet – the one with the sling. Rocket removed his shoes and socks but wasn't quite ready to part with his shorts.

He watched a four-way taking place on the screen as he sipped his beer. *Jesus, all those guys are hung like horses, too.* Rocket knew he would have to drop his shorts and venture into one of the rooms soon. Since he was no stranger to locker rooms and communal showers, he wasn't bashful about being naked around other men. In a gym locker room, he knew every guy was surreptitiously checking out every other guy, and that was okay. It was part of the environment. He did it, and every other guy did it. Anyone who said they didn't was a liar. It didn't even matter what size the other guys' dicks were, it was just something to be curious about. It wasn't like he was going to do anything with them.

The only exception had been Bryan. Rocket couldn't stop looking at his dick. It was the biggest one he had ever seen in person, except maybe for Black Stallion just now. And it was so … perfect. Perfectly proportioned, perfectly colored, perfectly shaped. And it was perfect for Bryan's tall, slender body. He suspected that Bryan knew he was frequently checking him out, because after several weeks Bryan made a habit of lingering behind after practice to run a couple of extra laps or talk to Coach Riley for a few minutes – just so he could hit the shower after everyone else had finished.

But this situation was different. The shower room at the gym wasn't a sexual situation. Well, maybe there was a tiny bit of sexual energy beneath the surface, but it was never acknowledged and nothing ever happened. Rocket never cared much about how he measured up in comparison with the other guys. But tonight, it mattered. He felt self-conscious. It was pretty dark in there, but as a new guy, he knew everyone would be checking out his dick for a totally different reason.

He looked at the guys on the screen and the guys he had seen so far this evening. He wondered, *Do gay guys have bigger dicks? Does having a bigger dick make you more likely to be gay? It certainly seemed to be the case for Bryan. On the other hand, there's Bottom Piggy. He's easily the gayest guy here, and he has... not so much. I wonder how gay guys decide who will pitch and who will catch, so to speak. Maybe the guy with the bigger dick gets to be the pitcher and the other one has to be the catcher. Does that mean I'd have to be a catcher?*

He shook his head and tried to stop thinking about that. He wasn't going to be a pitcher or a catcher with anyone so it didn't matter. His beer bottle was empty. He really wanted another one. But he knew he needed to face his fears and head into one of the bedrooms, or people would start to wonder why he wasn't. Might as well get it over with.

He heard Garlow's voice. "Are you okay? I haven't heard much lately."

There was nobody near him at the moment, so he cupped his hand over his mouth and whispered, "Yes." He heard somebody in the background say, "He can't talk with his mouth full," followed by laughter. *Bastards. Let them try being here.*

He glanced toward the kitchenette and saw three other guys hitting the crystal meth. There had been a steady stream during his stay so far. He tried to mentally keep track of each guy who was using meth, in case his boss wanted to press charges.

Rocket walked over to his gym bag and unzipped it. He stuffed his shoes, socks, and tank top into the gym bag. He took a deep breath, dropped his shorts, added them to the gym bag, and zipped it up.

He walked over to the bedroom he hadn't looked into yet – the one Bottom Piggy said had a sling. He peeked in the door and saw an assembly of poles forming a cube-shaped structure. Chains hung from each corner and connected to the four corners of a leather sling. The sling contained Bottom Piggy, whose ass was hanging over one end. His legs were elevated above his body and his ankles and wrists were secured to the chains with leather cuffs. Someone was holding a little brown bottle under his nose. Black Stallion was standing in front of his ass, vigorously pulling him back and forth using the chains to which his ankles were attached. A line had formed behind him.

Rocket turned around and headed for the other bedroom. He hoped that someday he would be able to unsee what he had just witnessed.

He entered the other bedroom and found a spot to stand along the wall near the bed, where he could watch the TV and observe most of the action taking place on the bed and the air mattresses. He stood just far enough from the action to avoid being pulled into it. He detected a harsh, pungent chemical smell in the air, like some kind of industrial solvent.

He spotted Rod Long. And yes, it certainly was. He was having his way with a cute young man he assumed was one of the party favors. In the dim light, he couldn't tell from the young man's face whether he was in ecstasy or extreme pain. The young man extended his hand toward the nightstand, and someone handed him one of the little brown bottles. He unscrewed the lid, took a long whiff up each nostril, and screwed the lid back on. He handed it back and mouthed, "Thanks." A moment later, his face looked redder but he didn't appear to be in as much pain.

Rocket glanced at Rod Long's face again. He still couldn't think who it reminded him of.

He turned his attention to the TV. The others in the room were paying little attention to the porn video since they were focused on their own sex acts, but it added to the ambiance aurally as well as visually. On the screen, much like on the bed and air mattresses in front of him, there was an orgy taking place. This one was in a spacious living room with a large sectional sofa, a couple of square ottomans, and a coffee table. It was difficult to count, but Rocket guessed there were probably

15 or 16 men in a variety of pairings and three-person clusters filling all the available space on the furnishings. The camera shots alternated among extreme close-ups, various medium and wide shots, and faces in the throes of ecstasy. At one point, several of the performers changed partners and positions, and Rocket got a better look at one of them – a tall, slender, dark blond guy with a massive, rock-hard erection.

He looked like Bryan.

Rocket did a double-take. *No, it can't be Bryan. Not the Preacher's Kid!* He was the last person Rocket would expect to ever see in porn, despite his anatomical qualifications. He watched the screen intently, hoping they would show that guy again. They did, and at that moment, the performer broke into an unmistakable smile. It was definitely Bryan. Rocket spent several minutes fixated on the video.

During a moment when they were showing someone other than Bryan, he glanced down. His dick was semi-hard. *Oh, shit! Not now! No, wait – everyone in the room has a hard-on. This is a gay orgy!* Having a hard-on helped him fit in. He was undercover, after all. Without thinking about it, he started idly fondling his dick with his right hand. Not seriously stroking it to get off, just playing with it because it felt good.

Rocket had been so focused on the video, he didn't notice until now that another guy was standing next to him. He started to reach toward Rocket's mostly-hard cock and said, "Can I give you a hand with that?"

"Uh, no thanks." Rocket stepped a few inches to his right and turned away. "Sorry."

The other guy was surprised to get 'no' for a response, but he said nothing and went away.

Rocket glanced around the room to see if anyone was watching him and his erection. He spotted Rod Long. Someone tapped Rod on the shoulder, whispered something, and pointed at Bryan on the TV. Rod turned and looked, then quickly turned his attention back to finishing off the twink he had been pounding.

Rocket looked at Rod Long's face, and then it hit him. He looked like Bryan. Or more accurately, he looked like how Bryan might look when he reached his late forties or early fifties. He figured the other guy told Rod that Bryan looked like a younger version of him.

Rocket flashed back to that time at the end of his junior year in high school, when the guys on the track team had a party at Trevor Zimmerman's house and they watched porn.

Trevor said, "Man. Where do they find guys who are hung like that?"

Rocket said, "Hey, PK! You should have that schlong of yours in porn. You could make a fortune!"

He was kidding, of course. He teased Bryan all the time, especially about his big dick. He was never serious. It was all just good-natured fun because he actually liked Bryan a lot.

Bryan said, "Ummm… I'll pass."

Rocket said, "C'mon dude, you could get paid to get laid! It don't get any better than that."

Bryan said, "Yeah, but then someday you guys will all be sitting around some TV screen, like you are right now, watching me have sex. No thanks!"

And now here he was, watching Bryan have sex on a TV screen. And he had an erection.

Then Rocket realized that that party was the last time he ever saw Bryan.

He looked down at the action taking place on the air mattress in front of him. One of the guys had a large tribal tattoo on his right arm and a 1/8th-inch-thick horseshoe-shaped shiny metal object dangling from the tip of his penis. Rocket winced. He had seen people with rings like this hanging out of their noses, but having one in your dick? Why the hell would anyone do such a thing?

This was obviously Franklin Pierced, whom Bottom Piggy said was the one who procured the party favors. Franklin Pierced was about to start fucking one of them, but the bottom asked if he would take that thing out of his cock first. Franklin Pierced unscrewed the little ball at the one end of the U-shaped ring and rotated it until it was detached from his cock. He screwed the little ball back onto the unit.

Then he extended his hand upward toward Rocket and said, "Hey man, would you hold this for me?"

Rocket was dumbstruck. The fact that he was at a gay orgy and watching guys having sex was bizarre enough. But never in a million years could he have imagined he would be asked to hold some stranger's … penis jewelry, or whatever it was. What did Bottom Piggy call it? A PA? It was the last thing he wanted to do, but he couldn't bring himself to say no – or to say anything, for that matter. He reached out his hand, and the guy dropped the PA into his palm.

And then, as if the moment wasn't surreal enough, Rocket realized Garlow just heard some guy ask, "Would you hold this for me?" and he hadn't answered. *I'll never hear the end of this.*

This also meant he would have to keep standing there holding Franklin Pierced's PA until he asked for it back – and he had no idea when that would be.

He began to melt down. He was holding something that, moments ago, had been attached to another guy's dick. The stench of poppers was making him ill. He was watching a roomful of tweaked-out guys having unprotected sex – with HIV-positive barely legal male prostitutes in some cases. Some guy tried to grab his dick. He had just discovered that his high school friend, who had mysteriously disappeared, was starring in porn videos. And he got an erection while watching it.

Why did he need to stay here, other than to hold this guy's PA? He had determined who purchased the illicit drugs and many of the people who were using them, who the prostitutes were and who hired them, and the pharmacist who was dispensing controlled substances without a prescription. What else was there to do? His work here was finished.

Rocket walked toward the door. He paused and looked at the DVD player sitting on the desk, connected to the TV via HDMI cable. He spotted the DVD case next to it. He walked over to it, stepping carefully between one of the air mattresses and the bed. He looked at the case. The movie was titled, *The Boys of Breckenridge*. He repeated the title several times in his mind, put the case down, laid Franklin Pierced's PA next to it, and then hurried out to the living room. He grabbed his gym bag and carried it over to one of the chairs, pulled out his clothes, and put them on as quickly as he could.

Some guy in the kitchenette stopped snorting a line of coke long enough to ask, "Leaving so soon?"

Rocket said, "Yeah, I've got to go now. I'm kind of overwhelmed." He hoped Garlow heard that. He was relieved to hear Garlow say, "On our way!"

Rocket finished dressing, stood up, and headed for the door. Garlow said, "We're in position. Whenever you're ready!" Rocket collapsed the three-panel room divider and leaned it against the wall. Then he unchained and unlocked the door, pulled it wide open, and stepped aside while twenty uniformed police officers stormed into the suite.

Bedlam ensued. Men frantically disconnected themselves from their sexual partners and searched for anything within reach to cover themselves. Some found hand towels that had been placed around the room for wiping up, while others used pillows. Some weren't so fortunate and had to stand naked.

The police officers herded the men into the living room.

Garlow shouted, "Everyone sit down." The police officers stationed themselves around the room so they could restrain anyone who made any sudden moves.

Jack Hammer yelled, "Hey, you can't do this. Gay sex has been legal since Lawrence v. Texas in 2003."

When everyone had quieted down, Garlow spoke loudly enough so that everyone in the suite could hear. "You are correct. Gay sex among consenting adults is not illegal. We have no interest in that. We are raiding this party because we have sufficient cause to believe that illegal drugs are being used and prostitution is taking place. Since you have all paid to take part in this event, you have all effectively paid for the illegal drugs and prostitutes. We will first arrest those who have been identified as the leaders of this operation, then we will process the rest of you. This will take a while, so just be patient. Remain seated until you are directed to stand."

One man raised his hand and asked, "Officer, may we get dressed?"

Garlow replied, "In a few minutes. Just be patient." He glanced at a list of names on the clipboard he was carrying, then turned to Rocket and asked, "Which one is Big Pharma?"

Rocket took a few steps in his direction and pointed. "This one."

A nearby officer stepped up to Big Pharma and motioned for him to stand. Then he led him to Sergeant Garlow.

Garlow said, "You are under arrest for dispensing controlled drugs without a prescription. Please find your clothing and get dressed. This officer will take you to another room where you will be read your rights and booked." Big Pharma got dressed. The officer handcuffed him and led him to the meeting room on the first floor where the police had set up their base of operations.

Garlow repeated the process for Black Stallion, who was arrested for purchasing illegal drugs. Franklin Pierced was arrested for securing the prostitutes.

Eventually, it was Rod Long's turn. Garlow recognized him from nine years ago. "Well, if it isn't Rev. Brad Bauer."

Rocket was standing nearby and heard that. *What the fuck??? That's Bryan's father? No wonder he looked like Bryan.*

Brad thought fast. "Who? You must be thinking of someone else."

Garlow said, "Get serious. We're going to check your ID as soon as you get dressed."

Rocket quickly put the pieces together. *That fucking asshole! He's gay, and yet he was going to send Bryan off to some place to try to convert him? Bryan had to run away from home because of him? And he had to do porn to survive?* Rocket was livid. He almost lunged for Rev. Bauer to punch him. Fortunately, he stopped himself. As a police officer, he couldn't do that.

Brad glared at Garlow. "If word about this gets out, I'll sue your ass to hell and back."

Garlow glared back. "Police arrests are public information."

The officer who was escorting him said, "Shut up and get dressed."

Again, the urge to beat the shit out of Rev. Bauer swept over Rocket. This evening had been almost too much for him to handle already – and now this. He decided the best thing for him to do would be to leave. He had done enough. The other officers could handle the rest of this. He needed to go home and decompress. He thought about going to the hotel bar and getting shit-faced, but he knew that would be a bad idea.

A half-hour later, the police were almost finished processing all the orgy attendees. One of the officers emerged from the bedroom on the right and said to Garlow, "We have one more in here. You need to see this."

Garlow followed the officer into the room. He saw a chubby man lying on his back in a portable sling, with his ankles and wrists cuffed to the chains, blindfolded, a ball gag in his mouth, and his bare ass pointed directly at Garlow. Semen had drained out, run down his crack, and formed a puddle on the carpet.

Since the other participants had been herded into the living room and ordered to sit down, no one had untied Bottom Piggy from his sling.

Great, Garlow thought. *I'll never be able to unsee this.* 'Okay, men, untie him, take his blindfold off, and take that thing out of his mouth."

When Bottom Piggy stood up and an officer removed his blindfold and ball gag, Garlow was shocked to see another face he recognized from the missing child case nine years ago: Rev. Dr. Ronald Babcock, the so-called therapist who, at that time, ran a counseling practice that purported to "lead people from the homosexual lifestyle" by "praying the gay away." Babcock had been present in Rev. Bauer's living room when he arrived in response to the 911 call. Rev. Bauer had sent his son to Dr. Babcock for counseling.

Despite his current humiliating situation, Babcock couldn't help but smile when he saw the handsome officer he had ogled nine years ago.

Garlow turned and left the room.

Face to Face

Saturday, September 3, 2016

Ryan Robertson waited outside the door of the Baker's Cousin restaurant in Glendale, Arizona, for Chris, his best friend-turned-boyfriend from high school. Chris was the first person Ryan ever fell in love with, and the first person he ever made love with.

Ryan's emotions were pulling him in every direction. Mostly, he was excited about seeing Chris in person for the first time in nine years. But still, he wondered, *What if it's awkward? I've changed, and I'm sure he has, too. What if we've grown apart? We both have partners, but what if the sparks fly? Even if everything goes well, he still lives on the other side of the country. What kind of friendship could we have? What am I really hoping for?*

Despite all his worries, Ryan knew he wanted to see Chris. Even if the meeting fell flat, at least he will have tried. And he won't wonder, *what if?*

Chris pulled into the parking lot driving a Honda Accord that belonged to his partner Seth's mother.

Ryan felt his pulse quicken. He flashed back to the moment they met on the first morning of band camp at the beginning of their freshman year. Ryan – who was Bryan back then, since that was before he changed his name – attended a small Christian school through eighth grade. When he arrived at the public high school, he didn't know any of the other kids. Before the first rehearsal started, he stood by himself on the sideline, as nervous as he was right now. Chris trotted over to Bryan and introduced himself. Ryan remembered Chris's friendly smile, his wavy brown hair bouncing in the breeze, and the glow of Chris's extroverted exuberance.

As Chris approached, Ryan admired his more mature features. In the nine years since they last saw each other in person, Chris's face had transitioned from boyish cuteness to young adult handsomeness. His hair was shorter now, but still wavy enough to look naturally tousled. He had put on a few pounds. He was still irresistibly adorable.

Chris looked like he was entertaining many of the same hopeful yet apprehensive feelings. When he was six steps away, he smiled – just like he smiled when he approached Bryan on the first day of band camp. Ryan's heart melted. He smiled back. In that instant, he knew everything was going to be okay.

A wave of happiness washed over Ryan. He held out his hand. "Hi!"

"Hi!" Chris shook his hand for two seconds, then they both threw their arms around each other and hugged tightly. They gently rocked back and forth, neither wanting to let go.

Chris said, "Oh my God! I can't believe this is actually happening!"

"I know!" They released each other and Ryan took a step back. "You look great!"

"You too! Just as handsome and sexy as ever!" *I hope he doesn't notice I'm getting hard right now.*

Ryan said, "Awww... You're the hot one." Chris smiled sheepishly. Ryan said, "C'mon, let's go in and get something to eat." He opened the door and gestured for Chris to enter first. Ryan affectionately put his hand on Chris's shoulder as he passed.

They placed their orders at the counter, filled their drink cups, and found a booth near the back of the restaurant. For a brief moment, they waited to see who would start and what they would talk about first. Finally, Chris said, "Well, it's not quite Slush Fun, but it will do."

Ryan laughed. "Yeah, I guess I've fallen into that adult habit of trying to eat healthier."

"Well, it shows. You look great!" *God, you're hotter than ever.* "As you can see, I've put on a few pounds."

"I still go running a lot. I mean, not as much as when we were in high school. Just two or three times a week when the weather's cooler."

Chris said, "I need to do better about getting exercise. Work takes up most of my time."

"Still, you look good. We all put on a few pounds as we get older. You're a very handsome man." *I'd do you in a heartbeat.*

"Do they even have Slush Fun out here?"

"They do. I've never gone to one out here, though." *It wouldn't be the same without you.*

Slush Fun was a drive-in restaurant chain that specialized in slushies and all things deep-fried. When Bryan and Chris were best friends in high school, they hung out there frequently. In the privacy of their car, they could crack jokes, laugh, and talk about anything – which they did.

Chris asked, "So, how do you like living out here?"

"I love it! I hope I never have to live someplace where it snows again. Scottsdale's really beautiful. How do you like living in DC?"

"I love it. The city has a lot of character. And there are areas of Northern Virginia and Montgomery County that are really nice. We have a condo in Arlington near one of the metro stations. I work on Capitol Hill. I'd prefer to live near there or Logan Circle, where a lot of gay people live. But Seth works in Reston, out near Dulles Airport. So Arlington is a good compromise. I can take the metro into town and he gets to drive against traffic."

Ryan asked, "What does he do?"

"He works for a government contractor – a Beltway Bandit, as we call it. His job title is Business Analyst, but that can mean just about anything. He does whatever the company's current contract calls for. He's writing training manuals now."

"How's your job? You're working for a senator, right?"

"Yeah. I love it. It's fascinating to see how government really works and be part of it. We've made so much progress with Obama in office. Don't Ask, Don't Tell was repealed, and now with Obergefell v. Hodges, we have marriage equality nationwide. There's still work to be done, though. We need to get an equal employment law passed.

Hillary's a shoo-in for 2016, but we've got to get both the House and Senate controlled by Democrats before that's going to happen. But it's looking good, and it's exciting!"

A restaurant employee delivered their food. Ryan said, "Do you want a refill?"

"Sure. Diet Coke, please."

"Oh, you're drinking diet now, huh?"

"Yeah… I need to stop putting on weight."

When Ryan returned with their refills, he asked, "So are you and Seth going to get married?"

Chris's exuberance dimmed. "We've talked about it. I want to. He says he doesn't see why we need to."

"It's been what, eight years?"

"Yeah, it'll be eight years this fall. So, tell me about this Aaron guy you've met."

"He's nice. We met a few months ago when he joined my gay running club."

"You're in a gay running club? No wonder you're in such great shape."

"Yeah. A couple of summers ago, I went on a gay cruise with this guy who was one of my housemates in LA. His name is Ted. I think I told you about him on one of our Skype calls."

"The former Marine, right?"

"Yeah. Anyway, I met a couple named Kent and Justin on that cruise, and it turns out they were from Phoenix. They told me about the running club and I started going. I've made some friends in that group, which was good since I didn't know very many gay people back then. One day in May they brought Aaron along."

"So did you guys hit it off right away?"

Ryan said, "Oh, the sparks were definitely flying. I could tell he was interested in me, but I wanted to take it slow. For one thing, he just recently came out, so I wasn't sure I wanted to deal with that drama. And let me tell you, there's been some drama. First, his parents reacted badly when they found out he was gay. But they've come around and they're cool with it now. Then, back in July, we went to San Diego for their Gay Pride weekend. We went with Kent and Justin. And, well, we had some issues. He wanted to go bar hopping and I didn't, so the three of them hit the clubs and I just went to bed early. Anyway, he ended up going home with someone."

"Ouch. I would have broken up with him over that."

"Yeah, I was really upset about it. Actually, he hooked up with several people. But here's the thing. We hadn't committed to each other yet. Like I said, I wanted to take it slow. So on the one hand, I wouldn't do something like that if I was on a weekend trip with a guy I was seriously interested in. But on the other hand, we hadn't committed yet and I bailed on going out with them, so it wasn't really cheating. I decided it was wrong for me to blame him. Anyway, we talked and worked through it, and now we're committed."

Chris asked, "Does he know you used to do porn?"

"Yeah, that was another thing. I hadn't gotten around to telling him that yet, but he found out from someone else. Some guy from the band gave him one of the videos I'm in. So we had a big blow-up over that, and I thought it was going to be over at that point. Technically, we broke up for three days. But then he realized he shouldn't hold my past against me. It was like, okay, so I did it, and I can't go back and change it. So if he wanted to have a relationship with me he had to accept that. I mean, it's been four years and I'm never going to do it again. Anyway, he got over it, so we're fine."

"Wow… that *has* been a lot of drama. You must really like this guy."

"I do. He has a lot of nice qualities. He kinda reminds me of you in some ways. Like when we were at the pride festival in San Diego, he was running around checking out all the booths like a kid in a candy store, just like you did that time we went to the festival in Kansas City. And since he recently came out, being gay was all new and exciting to him, just like it was with you. So he has a lot of fresh energy, which I kinda need. Oh, and he likes music, including jazz. He plays trombone."

Chris said, "You mentioned a band a minute ago."

"Yeah. We have an LGBT band here. He convinced me to join it. They also have a jazz ensemble, and I'm in that too."

"I'm glad you're still playing your trumpet. You're so talented! I haven't played my alto sax since I got out of college."

"Until Aaron came along, I hadn't played my trumpet since I left UCLA. I'll be forever grateful to him for convincing me to get my horn out of the closet, so to speak."

"I can't believe you quit playing. You always loved being in band."

"Yeah, I know. But I don't like being in larger groups. So I'm kinda stepping out of my comfort zone to do this. But it's something we can do together."

Chris asked, "How many people are in this band? Is it bigger than our band in high school?"

"It's around 50 or so. But uh… Okay, the reason I don't like to get involved in larger groups is… well… chances are, I'll get recognized from my videos. Then things get awkward."

"So you were going to quit playing music for the rest of your life because you used to do porn?"

"It's not about playing music, it's about being in gay groups. There's a gay group at work too, but I haven't joined it. I really don't want people to find out about it at work."

"Sounds like this is going to follow you around for the rest of your life."

"Yeah, I guess. But since we're on this topic, I wanted to talk about this for a minute."

"Okay…"

"First, do you want a refill?"

Chris's cup was still half full, but since Ryan was getting up anyway, he said, "Sure, you can top me off." *Oh, shit… did I really just say that?*

Ryan grabbed their cups and headed to the soda dispenser. *I wonder if he realizes what he just said. God, I wish I could… No, no…*

Ryan returned with their sodas and sat down. Neither of them said anything about Chris's unintentional double entendre. Ryan took a deep breath. *Here goes.* "Okay, so remember when we were having those Skype calls around Christmas and New Year several years ago?"

"Yeah. Geez, that was what? Late 2008, early 2009? Hard to believe it was that long ago."

"Well anyway, it's like everything was going great until you found out I was doing porn. Then suddenly, everything ground to a halt and you didn't want to talk to me again."

"Yeah, I'm sorry. I guess I didn't react to that very well. It's just that, well, it really took me by surprise. It didn't seem like something you would do. It was like, 'Who are you? What have you turned into?'"

"I get that. And on one level, I understand. But on another level, that really hurt. It's like it was wonderful that we were getting back in touch and we talked about seeing each other the next summer and all that, and then poof! It all got taken away."

Chris looked down at his plate. He took another bite of his sandwich to distract himself.

Ryan continued. "Anyway, so here we are. It's great to see you and talk with you again. But what happens next? I know you have Seth and I have Aaron, so we can't be partners. We live on opposite sides of the country, so we can't hang out together like we did in high school. But I still want to have you in my life. At least we can be in touch now and then. I'd love to be friends again, but I don't want to invest the emotional energy and get my hopes up only to have you drop out of sight again. What do you want out of this? And can you accept the fact that I used to do porn, or is that still going to get in our way?"

Chris took a few seconds to think about how he was going to say what he wanted to say. "I want us to be friends again too. And yeah, it's not going to be like it was in high school, but I'd like to stay in touch. Are you on Facebook?"

"No. Everyone keeps telling me I should get on Facebook, but I don't want to. For one thing, I don't want people who have seen me in videos trying to contact me."

"Is that really a problem, since you aren't doing porn anymore?"

Ryan said, "Yeah. For example, even though they made *The Boys of Breckenridge* seven years ago, it's still selling. Now that it's so easy to find porn on the internet, people will keep seeing videos I was in for a long time to come. If I was still in the business and I wanted to cultivate a fan base, I'd create a page for Luke Loadstar, but I'm not. I really want to leave it all behind."

"So why can't you create a page for Ryan Robertson?"

"Because if someone looks for it, they can find out what porn stars' real names are."

"So create a page with a fake name, like Ry Roberts or something. You can tell your friends it's you."

"Yeah, I suppose. But still, it seems like such a waste of time. The other guys in my house in LA had Facebook pages, and it looked like most of what people posted was stupid shit."

"But even with all the stupid shit, you can still keep up with people."

Ryan said, "Well, I'll think about it. But we can send emails and talk on the phone every so often. I liked those Skype calls."

"Yeah, we can do that. I come out to Phoenix with Seth once or twice a year to see his family – at least at Christmas or Thanksgiving. So we can work in time for a visit."

"I'd like that. So you're okay with the porn thing?"

Chris said, "Yeah, I guess. Especially since you're not doing it anymore. And I totally get that you had to do it to pay for college. So yeah, I'm cool with it. Besides, sitting here talking to you now, I can tell you're still the same ol' Ryan I used to know and love."

"Really? I think I've changed a lot."

"Well, I have too. I guess that's to be expected. People change as they get older. But I guess part of loving someone is embracing how they change as they go along."

Ryan smiled. "Thanks. I feel a lot better because you said all that."

"Good. But since we're having this conversation and clearing the air about a few things, I have something I want to get off my chest."

"Okay…"

"You know how you said it hurt when I stopped communicating with you after we had those Skype calls? Well, how do you think I felt when you ran away from home? The first thing I thought was maybe you killed yourself. Or you had been kidnapped. I had no way of knowing whether you were safe or in danger. I was worried sick about you! Now, I totally understand why you did it and why you had to stay invisible until you turned 18, but why didn't you get back in touch with me then? I mean, I appreciate that you sent me a Christmas card. At least that let me know what happened and that you were alive, but you still didn't give me any way to get in touch with you. I would have liked to send you a Christmas card. It's like you didn't even trust me enough to let me know where you were and how to get in touch with you. That really hurt. It still does. Not to mention how much it hurt to have you ripped out of my life."

"You're right. With 20-20 hindsight, yes, I should have gotten back in touch with you sooner."

"The biggest thing was that you didn't trust me. It could have turned out differently. We could have still gone to college together and we'd be a couple right now."

Ryan sighed. "Yeah, you're totally right. I'm sorry. I'm really, really sorry." Ryan paused to let that sink in. "But there's still the question of how I would have supported myself and paid for college. Even if we went to college together, I still needed to earn a lot more money than I could make at a grocery store job. I doubt that you would have been cool with me doing porn while we were in a relationship, would you?"

"No, probably not."

"So what would I have done? And that's the real reason I didn't get back in touch with you sooner. I didn't want to have to tell you I was doing porn, 'cause I wasn't sure how you'd react. And, well... look how you reacted."

Chris sat quietly for a moment to let that sink in. Finally, he said, "Yeah, I guess that would have been a problem. I'm sure we could have worked something out, but… well, I guess I don't know what."

"Doing porn made it very hard for me to date anyone or even have regular friendships. There was one guy who said he was fine with it, but it turned out he just wanted a fuck buddy while he was at college. When he graduated, he went back home and married his high school girlfriend."

"Ouch."

"Tell me about it. Even my relationship with Aaron blew up when he found out. So yeah, that's why I kept to myself."

Chris said, "Okay, so where are we now?"

"At a Baker's Cousin restaurant in Glendale."

Chris facepalmed his forehead and groaned. "Oh, geez… you haven't changed. You know what I mean."

Ryan chuckled, then got serious again. "I really want to be friends again. I want to stay in touch. I want us to be a part of each other's lives, even though we're on opposite sides of the country and we both have partners. Even if we only talk now and then."

"That's what I want too."

Ryan smiled. He pushed his plate aside, reached across the table with both hands, and held Chris's hands for a moment.

Chris glanced at his watch. "Shit. I need to get going. Seth's grandmother's 80th birthday party is this evening, so I need to get back. His mom probably needs to use the car. Anyway…"

"When are you and Seth flying back?"

"Monday morning."

"Is there any time when the four of us could get together, so I can meet Seth and you can meet Aaron?"

Chris thought for a moment. "Maybe for a little while on Sunday evening."

"Okay, then. Why don't you and Seth come over to my place around 7:30 or 8:00? We can have drinks and nibbles, and you can see my place and meet Aaron."

"I think that'll work. Hang on a sec." Chris pulled out his phone and called Seth.

When Seth answered, the first words out of his mouth were, "Hey man, where are you? Mom needs the car to get some things for the party."

"Sorry, I'm leaving now. Tell her I'll be there in 15 minutes. Anyway, do you think we could get away for an hour or two tomorrow evening? Ryan has invited us over to his place for drinks so we can all meet each other."

"Yeah, that should work. Tell him tentatively yes, but you'll let him know if something comes up."

"Okay, thanks. I'll be there soon. I love you."

"Bye."

Chris tapped his phone to end the call and put it face down on the table. "Okay, we should be able to make it. Anyway, I've got to run." Chris and Ryan slid out from their booth seats. They walked out to the parking lot and turned to say goodbye.

Ryan said, "You know how you said that part of loving someone is embracing how they change?"

Chris nodded.

"I love you. And that means embracing the fact that you're with another guy instead of me and being okay with that. I want you to be happy, even if it's not with me. I'll always want the best for you and I'll always be here if you need me. I always want to be friends."

Chris smiled. "Same here. I'm really glad we had this talk. I love you too."

They hugged each other. When they separated, they looked fondly into each other's eyes. Ryan gave Chris a quick kiss. They smiled, turned, and went their separate ways.

Denial

Sunday, September 4, 2016

The front-page headline on the Sunday edition of the Kansas City Daily News screamed in large, bold letters:

> ## Prairie Village Pastors Arrested in Drug-Fueled Gay Orgy!
>
> Sunday, September 4, 2016
>
> Kansas City, MO (AP) – Rev. Bradley Bauer, head pastor at Eternal Savior Christian Church in Prairie Village, Kansas, and Rev. Ronald Babcock, youth pastor at the same church, were among 35 men arrested at an all-male sex party at a local hotel Friday night.
>
> Police raided the event after receiving a tip that illegal drugs were being provided to attendees. An undercover police officer who infiltrated the event witnessed eighteen participants using cocaine and methamphetamine ("crystal meth"). He discovered that four male prostitutes had been hired to provide sexual services to attendees, and a pharmacist was freely dispensing erection-enhancement drugs without a prescription.
>
> Police arrested the event organizers, participants who engaged in purchasing or using illegal substances, the prostitutes and the person who hired them, and the pharmacist. Attendees who only participated in consensual sexual activities were released.

***

The Sunday service at the Eternal Savior Christian Church began as usual, with the praise band and choir belting out a high-energy song. After the opening prayer, Rev. Bauer made the following announcement:

"Brothers and sisters in Christ, I would like to address the unscrupulous, blasphemous accusations that have been perpetrated against me, Rev. Babcock, and our church's name. If you pay attention to the lamestream media, you may have noticed that police in Kansas City raided a sinful, disgusting homosexual orgy in which dozens of godless perverts were spreading AIDS with their unspeakable sex acts, using illegal drugs, and defiling young male prostitutes."

People throughout the congregation gasped with horror.

"My friends, I can assure you, in no uncertain terms, that neither Rev. Babcock nor I took part in any such event. Apparently, two of the wretched low-lifes who were arrested provided fake IDs with our names and photos. This incident is part of a vast conspiracy by homosexual organizations to bring shame and disgrace upon our glorious church and stop us from sharing God's word with the world. They seek to destroy us because we dare to speak the truth about how God abhors the homosexual lifestyle, which is certainly not the message they want to hear. Yet, while they spread lies, hatred, and disease, we will stand firm in our mission to spread love and truth! Can I get an 'Amen?'"

"AMEN!!!" the congregation roared.

Meet My Partner

Sunday, September 4, 2016

At 7:35, Chris and Seth arrived at Ryan's home in Scottsdale. Chris rang the doorbell. Within seconds, Ryan flung open the door and said, "Welcome! Please come in!"

Once they were inside and Ryan closed the door, Ryan gave Chris a big hug – not enough to be a romantic hug, but definitely a very friendly hug. That did little to assuage the nervousness Aaron and Seth were feeling.

Ryan gestured toward Aaron with his right hand and said, "This is my boyfriend, Aaron." He gestured toward Chris with his left hand and said, "This is my best friend from high school, Chris." Chris shook Aaron's hand and gave him a charming, friendly smile. Aaron smiled back and relaxed a little bit.

Chris said, "And this is my partner, Seth." Seth shook Aaron's hand, then Ryan's. He looked at Ryan as if he had seen him somewhere before.

Ryan said, "Why don't we head back to the family room?" He turned and led the way, and the others followed.

Chris and Seth looked around as they walked toward the back of the house, amazed by what they were seeing. When they reached the family room, Ryan gestured toward the seating area, where a matching couch, loveseat, and two single chairs formed three sides of a rectangle. A wooden coffee table sat on an area rug with a southwestern pattern. Seth sat in one of the single chairs. Chris would have preferred to sit next to him on the couch or loveseat, but since that was no longer an option he sat in the other single chair. Aaron sat down on the right side of the couch, closest to Chris and Seth.

A cheese board with several types of sliced cheeses and crackers sat on the coffee table, along with a bowl of pub mix and an assortment of grapes and berries. There was a stack of small plates and a fancy napkin holder.

Ryan said, "What can I get you to drink? Cocktails, beer, wine, soda, water…"

Seth said, "I'll just have a beer. Bud or Mic Light or something like that would be fine."

"All I have is Leinenkugel Summer Shandy and Shock Top Belgian White."

Seth looked confused by his options. "I'll try the Shock Top."

Chris asked, "What kind of cocktails can you make?"

Ryan said, "Just about anything. What do you like?"

Aaron said, "He makes awesome Mai Tais."

Chris said, "Okay, I'll try a Mai Tai."

Aaron said, "You'll love it. I'd like one too, please."

Ryan smiled and said, "Help yourself to some munchies." He pulled a glass beer mug off a shelf and placed it in the freezer. Chris and Seth watched with wonder as Ryan expertly prepared their drinks at the wet bar near their seats. When he finished, he added a cherry garnish and a colorful straw to each cocktail. He retrieved the beer mug from the freezer, pulled a bottle of Shock Top from the refrigerator, and poured the beer into the glass, achieving a perfect foam head at the top. He presented the beer and one of the cocktails to Seth and Chris, then fetched the other two cocktails and handed one to Aaron. He sat down next to him and raised his glass. "To new friends and reunited old friends!" The other three nervously clinked their glasses together and took sips.

Chris turned to Aaron and said, "You were right! This is awesome!"

Aaron smiled back. Ryan said, "Glad you like it."

Chris tried to process the fact that Ryan, the preacher's kid who would never touch an alcoholic beverage back in high school, now owned a home with a wet bar. He said, "This place is amazing! The nice furniture and all the décor – very tasteful!"

"Thanks. Remember me telling you about the guy named Ted who lived with me in that house in LA?"

Chris nodded. *The really hot one.*

"Most of this is stuff he gave me. When he graduated and moved out, he got an apartment and bought all this furniture. But then four years ago, he got transferred to London and he needed to get rid of his stuff. That was the same time I graduated and moved here, so he gave it to me."

Seth's eyes popped open. "For free?"

"Yeah. I offered to pay him for it, but he refused. I paid to move it here, though. And I bought his BMW."

Chris wondered if there were other ways he had compensated Ted for the furniture.

Ryan said, "C'mon, let me show you around."

They stood up, and Ryan led them into the kitchen. It was a large kitchen with upgraded appliances, plenty of cupboards, and an island counter with stools. Chris and Seth were speechless. Ryan led them into the dining room, which had an elegant eight-person table and a modern, multiple-light fixture with electric faux candles hanging above it.

Ryan led his guests and Aaron from the dining room back out to the living room, then toward the bedroom wing. They ducked into each bedroom long enough to see it. One had a guest bed. "That used to be Ted's," Ryan explained. He showed them his music room and his office, with a large desk, two monitors, a keyboard, a printer, a scanner, and other accessories.

Finally, Ryan showed them the master suite, with a large bed and a headboard with all kinds of mirrors and side shelves and drawers. Chris and Seth were stunned.

Chris asked, "Did Ted give you this, too?"

"This actually came from the house in LA where we lived. It belonged to Hal, the owner. Remember, I introduced him to you on that Skype call when I was showing you around. Sadly, he died a couple of months before I graduated, and they had to sell the house. But I got to take this, the desk you saw in the other room, and the dining room table."

Seth asked, "What happened to him?"

Ryan hesitated. "It's kind of a long story, and not very pleasant. Maybe another time."

Ryan led them through a door from the master suite out to the back patio. It was large, with a barbecue island and a glass-topped table with four chairs. Chris and Seth gazed around the backyard in wonder. There was a beehive fireplace, a hot tub, a tiki bar, and a beautiful pool with a rock waterfall and soft purple lighting. The yard was lined with blooming bougainvilleas.

Chris said, "This is amazing!"

"Thanks. Sometimes at night, I come out here to relax. In summer, I float in the pool on a raft and gaze up at the stars. During the winter, I get in the hot tub. It's very peaceful. And now, thanks to Aaron, I have someone to enjoy it with." He reached for Aaron's hand and smiled at him. "When it's cooler, I eat out here a lot. Sometimes I sit in that hanging chair and read. I have speakers out here, too."

Chris said, "It's like you have your own little corner of paradise."

"Yeah. I'm very lucky and thankful. The house in LA had a backyard kind of like this. I really enjoyed it. Having a comfortable, relaxing place to come home to is important to me. It's my shelter from the storm, you know? I value that more than having designer-name clothes or eating out a lot or clubbing or any of that other stuff. Not that there's anything wrong with that, it's just – well, this is what suits me."

Seth said, "It's like they say, a man's home is his castle."

"Yeah, I agree."

What Seth really wanted to say was, *How the hell can you afford all this?*

They returned to the family room and sat down. Seth asked Ryan, "So, what do you do for a living?"

Ryan said, "I'm a software engineer at a company called Technovations. We develop leading-edge technologies, like the Internet of Things, wearable technology, and new applications for RFID. I'm a quality assurance analyst, so I get to test all that stuff."

Chris said, "That sounds exciting."

Seth said, "That must pay pretty well."

Chris shot Seth a critical glance.

Ryan said, "I can't complain. And I'm lucky to live here in Scottsdale. It's so much cheaper than Los Angeles."

Chris said, "I know what you mean. The whole Washington, DC area is out of control. You can't find a house for under a million dollars without going out into the 'burbs. The two of us can barely afford our condo."

Seth said, "That's why I keep telling you we need to move out here. I'd guess this house is worth, what? About half a million?"

Ryan said, "According to Zillow, around 750. It's appreciated a lot since I bought it."

Seth told Chris, "And this is the rich part of town. Glendale's a lot cheaper than Scottsdale." He turned back toward Ryan and Aaron. "But I guess as long as Chris is doing his political work, we're pretty much tied to DC."

Ryan and Aaron could tell this was a sore spot for Chris and Seth.

Ryan said, "I guess it's all about supply and demand. The places where more people want to live are going to have higher prices."

Aaron said, "It's all relative. When I moved from Troy, Ohio to Tempe, Arizona, I thought things were expensive out here."

Chris asked, "So what do you do, Aaron?"

"I'm a pharmacist with HealthPro. But I'm looking for a job at a pharmacy in a grocery store or wholesale club so I can have more reasonable hours."

Ryan said, "Yeah, he has kind of an unusual schedule where he works every other weekend. One week will be five days on and two days off, and the next will be two days on and five days off. And the days he works are really long days."

Aaron said, "And that messes with my social life. Like our band practice is Thursday night. I can always go since Thursday is one of my days off. But I can only go out to the bar with our friends every other week because I work every other weekend. So half the time I have to be at work early the next day. And I can't be in the jazz ensemble with Ryan because it rehearses on Monday evening and that's always a long work day."

Seth said, "So you guys are both musicians. What do you play?"

Ryan said, "I play trumpet and he plays trombone. I know you guys met in the marching band at Maryland. You play sax, right?"

Seth said, "Yeah, tenor. I used to, anyway. I haven't played since I graduated."

Aaron said, "They have an LGBT band in DC. You guys ought to join it!"

Chris said, "I'd love to, but I have no time. I work a lot of twelve-hour days. And I don't get five days off every other week."

Seth frowned. "Yeah, that's another thing..."

Chris cut him off. "But I really love my work. I feel like I'm making a difference."

Ryan said, "We've come a long way in the past eight years. I remember back in 2008 when I was a freshman at UCLA and Prop 8 passed, I thought we'd never get equal marriage rights, but now here we are."

Chris said, "That and the end of Don't Ask, Don't Tell. Now if we can just get the Employment Non-Discrimination Act passed..."

Seth said, "But enough about politics. How did you guys meet? How long have you been together?"

Aaron and Ryan looked at each other to see which one would answer this question. Ryan said, "We met in our local gay running club. I was involved with it for a couple of years, but then one day a couple friends of mine brought Aaron along."

Aaron said, "I had just joined Desert Pride – that's our gay band – and I met these guys named Kent and Justin. Kent's in the band, and Justin is his husband. Anyway, one day I was chatting with Kent on Facebook and he mentioned the running club. I run several times a week, so he invited me to come along. So I went, and I saw this tall, handsome guy who could easily run faster than anyone else there. I did my best to keep up. I couldn't take my eyes off him. So anyway, at the end of the run, I asked him if he'd like to get together to go running again, and he said yes. So I got his phone number and, well, it kind of took off from there."

Chris said, "Cool. I like hearing stories about how couples met, especially the ones where you're just going about your life and Mr. Right shows up when you least expect it."

Seth said, "Yeah. Seems like everyone's hooking up on Grindr these days."

Chris asked, "And how long ago was that?"

Ryan said, "Hmmm... That would have been the middle of May, so about three and a half months."

Aaron said, "Seems like it's been longer than that. We've covered a lot of ground in those three and a half months. But then, I just came out about six months ago, so everything about my life has changed quickly."

Chris said, "Really? You've only been out for six months?"

Aaron said, "Yep. I kinda knew for a long time. I just didn't want to deal with it."

Ryan added, "That, and you didn't want your parents to find out."

"Yeah, there was that. They blew up at first, but we've worked all that out and they're cool with it now. Anyway, you know how you were saying how you can just be going about your life, and then something happens? Well, one day I was eating in this fast-food place near my apartment, and this guy was wearing a T-shirt with a trombone on it. So I asked him about it, and it turned out he was in Desert Pride. He invited me to their concert, which was the next weekend. So I went, even though it's a gay band and I still thought I was straight. But it made me realize I missed playing in a band, so this guy offered to loan me his trombone, 'cause mine was still in Ohio."

Chris said, "Really? A guy you just met offered to loan you his trombone?"

"I know, right? I guess he thought I looked trustworthy. Anyway, after I went to a rehearsal, one of the guys sitting next to me invited me to go out to a bar where some of the band members go after rehearsal. I was really nervous at first, but long story short, after a couple of weeks I realized I was gay and these were my people."

Ryan said, "And I have Aaron to thank for convincing me to get my trumpet out again and join the band."

Chris said, "And you're playing in their jazz ensemble."

"Yep. They're pretty good, too."

"Remember those times we used to get together to practice in your bedroom or mine, and we'd put on those play-along CDs and jam?"

Ryan said, "I sure do. Man, that was so much fun."

Seth said, "I guess that means you two were practicing homosexuals."

Ryan chuckled. "Yeah, although we didn't really know it at the time. Or at least I didn't."

There was a brief lull in the conversation. Seth finished his beer and was starting to feel a bit loose. He turned to Ryan and asked, "So, what was it like to do porn?"

Aaron and Ryan were too surprised and shocked to say anything. Chris smacked the side of Seth's arm with the back of his hand and said, "You asshole! I told you not to say anything about that!" He turned to Ryan and said, "I am so sorry. You don't have to answer that. God, I'm so embarrassed."

Ryan said, "It was a job. That's all. That's in the past, and that's where it's going to stay." He glared at Seth, signaling the end of this topic.

Aaron was desperate to change the subject. "So how was your grandmother's 80th birthday party?"

Seth rolled his eyes. "It was the most fun you can have with your clothes on."

Chris said, "Seth!"

"Seriously. It was a birthday party for an 80-year-old. How exciting would you expect that to be?"

"It's not about excitement. It's about spending time with your family. Your grandmother is a sweet lady." Chris turned and faced Aaron and Ryan. "It was nice. Most of his extended family was there. His sister and her kids, and several aunts, uncles, and cousins. I met some of them for the first time."

The tension between Chris and Seth had become uncomfortable. Ryan tried changing the subject. He asked Chris, "How are your parents? And how's Tyler?"

"Mom and Dad are fine. Dad's hoping he can retire in about five years. Tyler and his girlfriend got married back in 2010. They have a two-year-old girl and another kid on the way."

"So you're an uncle now!"

"Yeah. Or a guncle, as I like to call it."

Aaron looked confused. Chris said, "A gay uncle."

Ryan said, "Every kid should have one."

Chris smiled. "I remember when I came out to my family back at the end of our junior year. Tyler and I were talking later that evening, and he said every parent should hope they have a gay kid because that's the one who's most likely to take care of them when they get older."

Ryan sighed. "Too bad my parents didn't see it that way."

"Yeah. Well, then I said to Tyler, 'Nice. Now you're trying to shove taking care of Mom and Dad off onto me.' But as it turns out, he's the one who's living in Kansas City, so it will probably be him."

"How often do you go back?"

"About once a year, sometimes twice."

"Do you ever see any of our friends from high school?"

"Sometimes. Mostly our friends from band, not the guys on the track team. I'm friends with Trevor Zimmerman on Facebook, though. He manages a hotel in Kansas City."

Chris glanced at Seth, who was making no attempt to hide his lack of interest in this conversation. Then he glanced at his watch. "Well, we'd better be heading back. Thanks for having us over." Everyone stood up and started heading for the door.

Seth said, "Hey, can I use the bathroom before we hit the road?"

Ryan pointed toward the bedroom hallway and said, "Sure. First door on the left."

After Seth had disappeared into the bathroom, Chris said, "Guys, I am so sorry. I don't know what got into him. He's usually not like this. He's been kind of cranky all weekend. He's missing a Kraftwerk concert back home he really wanted to see, but I told him we should come out for the occasion."

Ryan said, "That's okay. Don't worry about it."

Chris added, "I think maybe he was nervous about meeting you, knowing our history. He was kind of uncomfortable about us getting together yesterday too."

Ryan said, "I guess that's understandable. Anyway, I'm glad we got to meet him. And it's been great to see you again."

Chris turned to Aaron. "I really enjoyed meeting you, Aaron. I'm glad you two found each other."

Aaron shook Chris's hand. "Me too. And I'm glad I got to meet you. Ryan's told me a lot about you."

"Oh, God. I promise you, it's not true. Don't believe any of it."

"He's told me only good things."

"Like I said, they're *not true!*"

Everyone laughed. The tension from a few minutes ago had dissipated.

Chris asked Aaron, "Are you on Facebook?"

"Yeah, I'm on it practically every day. Our band communicates a lot of announcements on Facebook."

Ryan said, "And a lot of gossip."

Chris asked, "Would it be okay if I sent you a friend request?"

Aaron said, "Sure! My last name is Bradbury."

Chris looked at Ryan to make sure he didn't have an issue with that.

Ryan said, "Sounds like you want to talk about me behind my back."

Chris said, "To quote Oscar Wilde, 'There is only one thing in the world worse than being talked about – and that is *not* being talked about.'"

Aaron and Ryan chuckled.

Ryan said, "Let us know next time you're going to be in town. Maybe I can have you over for dinner or something."

Aaron said, "He's an amazing cook."

Chris said, "If you're as good a cook as you are a bartender, I believe it. I think this is our year to come here for Christmas. We spend Thanksgiving with one family and Christmas with the other, and then every other year we swap."

Aaron said, "Hmmm... We've talked about going to visit my folks in Ohio for Christmas this year. But it's not firmed up yet."

Ryan said, "Well, in any case, stay in touch. I'm sure there will be times when you come out here and we can get together."

Seth emerged from the bathroom, and they all hugged and said goodbye.

Ryan watched from the front window as Seth and Chris pulled away from the house. Then he turned to Aaron and said, "Well, that was kind of weird."

Aaron replied, "It sure was. It was like he was trying to figure out how much you make and what the house is worth. And I can't believe he asked about you doing porn."

"I know, right? And did you catch that comment about guys hooking up on Grindr?"

"Yeah. What about it?"

Ryan said, "They've been together almost eight years. Why would he be thinking about Grindr?"

Aaron said, "Everybody knows about Grindr. It doesn't mean he's on it. Or maybe they have an open relationship."

"I don't think Chris would agree to that. But anyway, that's none of our business."

"I guess not. But did you catch how Seth wants them to move out here?"

"Yeah, that was pretty hard to miss."

Aaron asked, "How would you feel about that?"

"I don't know. When we talked yesterday, we decided we wanted to stay in touch and be friends again, although it will be long distance. On the one hand, it would be nice to have him in the same city. But if Seth is part of the package, that might make it a little less pleasant." Ryan paused. "How would you feel about it?"

"I don't know. I like Chris. He's nice. I can see how you and he would have made a nice couple. But I guess a lot depends on what they have in mind. You know, if they're in an open relationship."

"Don't worry, that won't be happening. It takes two to tango – or four, as the case may be."

Aaron forced a weak smile, but Ryan could tell he still had concerns. "What else is on your mind?"

Aaron took a moment to choose his words. "I don't know... I guess I still wonder why Chris was so interested in getting back in touch and seeing you again. I mean, you've been out here four years now. They said they come out here at least once a year to visit his family. Why do you suppose he waited until now to make contact?"

"I don't know. Good question. I guess as time passes, people change how they feel about things. If they're thinking about moving out here, maybe that gave him a little push."

"Yeah, I guess."

"We may never know. But I'm glad Chris reached out to me. We had good talk yesterday. We cleared the air about a few things from our past, like why I didn't get in touch with him sooner and how he felt about that."

Aaron nodded but didn't say anything. He turned and started ambling toward the family room. Ryan took a couple of quick steps and put his hand on Aaron's shoulder. "Hey."

Aaron stopped. Ryan stepped in front of him and gently lifted his chin so they could look eye to eye. He placed his hands on Aaron's shoulders. "Are you worried Chris is going to try to take me away from you?"

"Maybe. It crossed my mind."

"No way. I don't think that's what he has in mind. But even if he does, it's not happening. You're my man. I made a commitment to you, and I have every intention of keeping it. A commitment means you stop looking for anyone else. A commitment means you don't dump your partner when someone else comes along. Not even Chris."

They looked into each other's eyes.

Ryan said, "I love you."

Aaron said, "Thanks. I love you too."

They kissed and held each other in a long embrace.

Ryan said, "Okay, so I know you have to leave to go back to your place in about half an hour. Let's make the best use of that time."

Rocket's Revelations

Tuesday, September 6, 2016

Rocket was an emotional wreck after his experience at the orgy on Friday night. During the days that followed, he could think of little else. To make matters worse, there was no one he felt he could talk to. He rarely spoke with his parents, and this was certainly not the sort of thing he would talk with them about anyway. Same with his buddies. They were good guys and fun to hang out and party with, but he wasn't comfortable sharing emotions and feelings that were this personal. Maybe Trevor Zimmerman – at least he already knew what happened on Friday night.

When he was at the police station on Tuesday afternoon, he spotted Michael Harrison, one of his fellow officers. The police station wasn't a particularly welcoming environment for gay people. Harrison wasn't officially out at work, but everyone knew and no one cared. It certainly didn't matter to Rocket.

Rocket approached and said, "Hey, Harrison, how's it going?"

"Okay."

"Did you do anything fun for Labor Day?"

"Yeah, I went to a cookout with a few of my friends. How about you?"

"I had to work. But that was okay. Somebody's gotta do it, and I didn't have any other plans."

Harrison said, "I understand you had a lot of excitement on Friday night."

"Yeah. That's been on my mind a lot ever since."

"That must have been tough for you. But I appreciate that you did it. Guys who do that sort of thing give the whole community a bad name."

"Thanks. Hey, can I ask a favor? After work, can we go grab a beer? I kinda need someone to talk to."

That request caught Harrison off-guard. He and Rocket got along fine as co-workers, but they had never socialized outside of work. "Well, yeah, I guess. Let me call my roommate and tell him I'll be late for dinner."

"Your roommate?" Rocket looked at Harrison as if to say, 'Really???'

Harrison lowered his voice slightly and said, "My husband."

"That's better. Hey, it's totally cool with me."

Harrison smiled.

Rocket said, "We need to change out of our uniforms anyway. Why don't you go home and have dinner, then maybe we can meet somewhere at around 7:00."

"Yeah, that would work better. Where do you want to go?"

"I don't care. You pick. You can even pick one of your bars if you want."

"There aren't any up here. We'd have to go downtown for that. How about the Wild Hare over on Parvin?"

"That'll work. See you at 7. Thanks, man."

***

Rocket arrived at The Wild Hare fifteen minutes early. He ordered a beer and sat down in a booth near the back of the bar where there weren't many people. He sat facing the door so he could see when Harrison arrived.

He thought through all the things he hoped to ask Harrison. He wasn't sure how to go about asking some of the questions that had been swirling in his head since Friday night. He wasn't even sure what was appropriate to ask or how Harrison would react, especially to some of the more personal topics. The more he thought about it, the more nervous he became. He had already consumed half of his beer when

Harrison arrived at 7:00.

Rocket waved him over. He stood up as Harrison approached, then shook his hand. "Hey, man. What are you drinking? It's on me."

Harrison said, "They have good red sangrias here. I wouldn't mind having one of those."

A server made her way back to the table, and Rocket ordered a sangria and another beer. They sat down. Harrison glanced at Rocket's half-empty beer mug but didn't say anything.

Rocket said, "I really appreciate you meeting me here. I just... well, after everything that happened on Friday night, I kinda need someone to talk to."

"Well, okay. But why me? I mean, I'm happy to help, but..."

"I guess... well... I don't really have any gay friends, and some of what I want to talk about kinda revolves around being gay."

"Yeah, I figured. So what's on your mind?"

"Okay, well right up front, I don't even know if I should even ask some of this stuff. I mean, I don't want to offend you or overstep any boundaries..."

"Don't worry about it. If it gets too inappropriate or too personal, I'll let you know."

Rocket took another swig of his beer. "Okay, well, for starters... Is that what you guys do? You know, have orgies like that."

"No. My husband and I are a monogamous couple. I went to a couple of orgies back when I was younger and single. It was kind of hot in some ways, but it's not what I'm into. I'm happy being settled down with just one man." Harrison paused. "And no, there weren't drugs at those orgies."

"What's your husband's name, and how long have you been together?"

"His name is Gerry. We met seven years ago, when I was 25 and he was 27. We got married five years ago, back in 2011."

"I didn't think two guys could get married in 2011."

"Not here. We had to go to Iowa. Iowa was one of the first states in the country to allow same-sex marriage ... if you can believe that."

"Man, it sucks that you couldn't get married in your own state and you had to go somewhere else."

"Yeah, tell me about it. And not many years before that, we couldn't get married anywhere. But thanks for being supportive. Honestly, I wouldn't have guessed that about you."

Rocket was momentarily taken aback, but he decided that Harrison didn't mean to offend him. "Yeah, I guess I can come off as being kind of crude sometimes. But I'm totally okay with it. Really. It's just the way some people are. When I was in high school, there was a guy on the track team I admired a lot, and he was gay. I'm pretty sure he and his best friend were boyfriends."

"So... what else is on your mind?"

"Well, that guy I just told you about that I admired? The summer after our junior year, he suddenly went missing. He just disappeared. Sergeant Garlow was working on the Prairie Village Police Force back then, and he was the one who responded to the call. He said they never found him, but they had to close the case three months later when he turned 18."

Harrison said, "Yeah, I remember that case. I had just started on the force when that happened. We got missing person alerts about him and it was on the news. Wasn't his father the pastor of some big church?"

"Yeah. He's one of the guys we arrested last Friday night at the orgy."

Harrison almost choked on his sangria. "You're shittin' me! His father was gay too?"

"Yeah. He was fucking some young guy in the ass. One of the male prostitutes they hired. I looked at him, and I thought he looked familiar. Later I realized he looked like an older version of my friend Bryan."

"Wow. So the pastor of that huge church is a closet case."

"Sure looks like it."

"Sadly, I'm not surprised. A lot of times, the biggest homophobes are closet cases. It's like they're fighting off their own demons by attacking openly gay people."

Rocket said, "That's sick, man. But that's not the worst of it. While I was there, they were playing this porno that had a gay orgy scene, and my friend – *his son* – was in it."

"NOOOooo!!! Are you sure it was him?"

"Yeah, I'm sure. When we were on the track team together, I saw him in the shower a few times and..." Rocket leaned in and lowered his voice. "That dude was hung like a racehorse. I'll never forget the first time I saw it. I'd never seen a dick that big before in my life – and I only saw it soft! So yeah... that was definitely him in the video."

"At least now you know he's alive – or at least he was at the time they made the video."

"Yeah, I guess there's that."

"I understand a lot of runaway kids end up doing porn or hustling."

"Really? That's sad. Anyway, I always wondered why he ran away and what happened to him. But then I thought back to when we were in high school. I used to tease him about his dick."

"I thought you liked this guy."

"I did. But I was kind of a jerk back then. I guess I teased him to get his attention. There was this one time at the end of our junior year when a bunch of the guys on the track team had a party. One guy's parents were out of town for the weekend so we had it at his house. Anyway, at one point he put on one of his dad's pornos and I turned to PK – that's what I used to call him because he was a Preacher's Kid – and I said, 'Dude, you should have that schlong of yours in porn. You'd make a fortune!' And then nine years later, I see him in a porno."

Harrison said, "So wait. This guy's father is at a gay orgy fucking a male prostitute at the same time they're showing a porno with his son in it?"

"Right. And someone pointed the guy in the video out to him, and he just turned his head away from the screen."

"Wow. That's fucked up."

"Yeah. So all this had been messing with me ever since Friday night. But mostly, seeing my friend. That's stirred up a lot of stuff from the past. And I've been wondering where he is now."

"Have you tried searching for him on Facebook?"

"Yeah. I couldn't find anything."

"How about his best friend? The one you thought was probably his boyfriend."

"I didn't think of that. I'll have to look him up. But anyway, I wanted to ask you a couple of other things."

Just then the server arrived to ask if they wanted another round. They both said no, and she left. Once she was a comfortable distance away, Rocket leaned in and said, "So... okay, this is going to sound weird, but... do gay guys have bigger dicks?"

"Whaaat??? Are you serious? Where are you getting your information?"

"I mean, my friend's dick is huge. And all the guys in that video were hung like horses. And I saw some pretty big ones at the orgy."

Harrison laughed, in an attempt to diffuse the awkwardness. "No, I can assure you that gay men have the same range of penis sizes as men in general. They look for guys with big dicks for porn because it's part of the fantasy – for some guys, anyway."

"Okay. I mean, I thought so, and that makes sense, but based on what I saw..."

"I'm sure what you saw is not a representative sample. So, moving on..."

"Yeah, sorry. I guess that was a dumb question. Maybe this one is dumb too, but... How did you know you're gay?"

"Well, I dunno... I guess it became pretty obvious in high school. All the other guys were interested in girls but I was interested in the other guys. Figuring out that I liked guys was the easy part. Figuring out whether I should keep it a secret and date girls or accept that I'm different was a lot harder. And then I had to figure out if and when I should tell anyone else – especially my parents."

"Why do you think some people turn out gay?"

"No one knows. Scientists and psychologists have been trying to figure that one out for years. But to me, it doesn't matter. Even if they figure it out, would it change anything? Some of us just are. It comes to us as naturally as being attracted to the opposite sex comes to everyone else. There have always been gay people, and there always will be."

The server stopped by their booth. Rocket asked, "Hey, you want another sangria?"

"No, I'm good."

The server nodded and left.

Harrison said, "So... just curious. You're asking me all these questions. Is there anything else you want to talk about?"

Rocket took a moment to summon the courage to say what he wanted to say next. "Yeah, there is. So, when I was there last Friday night, I dunno, it was just so weird. It's like, it doesn't bother me to be around naked guys. I played football in high school and college so I saw naked guys in the locker room and shower all the time. And I know this is gonna sound kinda strange, but... When a bunch of guys are naked together in the shower, there's something kind of cool about it. It's hard to describe. It's like everyone has to let down their barriers a bit. There's ... I dunno ... an honesty and vulnerability about it. I know for some guys it's awkward at first, but after a few minutes, nobody cares anymore. It's like okay, we've all seen what everyone else looks like, so now it's no big deal."

Harrison said, "It's sort of a male bonding experience."

"Yeah! That's it. That was the phrase I was looking for. It's a male bonding experience. Anyway, on Friday night, the vibe was totally different."

"Well, of course. The guys weren't naked together just to take a shower or change clothes, they were there for sex."

"Yeah. And like, even *that* didn't bother me on one level. I mean, everyone wants to get laid. It was kind of interesting to see what guys do with each other. But it seemed... I don't know... kinda raw. Animalistic. Not romantic, just physical. It even seemed kind of predatory. Like when Bryan's dad was fucking that young guy, one of the prostitutes – he couldn't have been more than 20 – he was really rough with him, like he was trying to dominate him. He was practically attacking him. And I'm thinking, is this how gay guys do it?"

Harrison said, "No, it's not. At least not most of us. I guess that's one of the dynamics of an orgy that's different from when two guys make love. Even the orgies I went to a long time ago weren't like what you just described. Maybe the drugs had something to do with it. Anyway, when Gerry and I make love, it's beautiful. It's intimate. It's romantic. Of course, it's fun too, and it feels great. I mean, yeah, we both want to get off. But really, when two men or two women make love, it's not much different from when a man and a woman make love. We just substitute body parts where necessary. But the feelings are the same. Those guys last Friday weren't there for a romantic experience. They were there to get their rocks off. They were there to be decadent. And for the closet cases, they probably had a lot of pent-up desire."

Rocket paused for a moment to process that and ponder whether to bring up the other topic on his mind.

Harrison was ready to wrap this up. This conversation was already more than he had bargained for. Obviously, Rocket needed someone to talk to, and he felt honored that Rocket trusted him. But still, it was awkward. They were colleagues who would see each other at work.

Rocket took a deep breath and said, "When I was standing there against the wall, with guys fucking all around me, and I was watching my friend in the porno – I started getting hard."

Harrison froze. He had no idea what to say. Finally, he said, "I think I'll have another sangria." Both he and Rocket started to get up. "Nope, I'll get it. Do you want anything?"

"Another beer. No, wait... that looked pretty good. I'll try a sangria. I've never had one."

Harrison slid out from their booth and started walking toward the front of the bar. He spotted their server and said, "We'd like two red sangrias, please. And they're are on me." She nodded and headed toward the bar.

As Harrison walked back to their booth, he thought about how he was going to handle whatever was coming next.

He slid into the booth seat. Rocket was holding his beer mug tipped above his lips. It was already empty for all intents and purposes, but he was trying to drain the remaining few drops into his mouth. It was more a nervous gesture than anything else. He set the mug down. He looked scared.

Harrison said, "So, all right. There was a lot of sexual activity taking place in front of you, both in the room and onscreen. Even if it wasn't what you'd prefer to be doing, it was still stimulating. We're guys. Sex is a turn-on. And there was the curiosity factor. So I wouldn't read too much into it."

Rocket shook his head slightly. "It was Bryan. I didn't get hard until I started watching Bryan fuck some guy in the video."

Neither of them said anything for a moment.

The server delivered the sangrias. Harrison was glad she didn't arrive while they were talking. They each took a few sips.

Rocket said, "Hey, that's pretty good."

Harrison said, "Okay. So basically, it sounds like you're wondering whether you might be gay."

"Yeah. Kinda. I mean, I've never thought I was, but now I'm wondering. I haven't had much luck dating girls. So I dunno... Maybe deep down that's not really what I want."

Harrison took another sip of his sangria. *How the hell did I end up here? And what's the best possible thing I could say right now?* He thought for a moment longer. "Okay, I'm going to try my best here. Humans are complex beings. Sexuality is complex. And while some people may be entirely straight or entirely gay, there are a lot of people who are somewhere in between. It's a spectrum. And you might be almost entirely straight, but then one guy comes along who just gets to you in *that* way. And sometimes it works the other way, too. We have a friend who's as gay as he can be, but he's married to a woman. They both know he's gay, and she's totally cool with it. He'll come right out and say he's gay, not bi or bi-curious or anything else – gay. But somehow, he's attracted to her and they love each other. I can't imagine myself ever doing that, but it works for them.”

“Interesting. But have you ever heard of a straight guy who marries a gay guy, just because he loves that one particular guy?”

“No, I haven’t. But I know some straight guys occasionally get turned on by another guy. Anyway, try not to think of it like it’s a bad thing. It’s neither good nor bad, it just is. It’s how you felt at that moment. It’s part of the broad spectrum of human sexual response.”

“Yeah, I guess. But it made me wonder.”

“Okay, well even if you are gay, remember – it’s not a bad thing. It’s neither good nor bad. It’s just who you are – if that *is* who you are. Earlier in our conversation, you said a couple of times that you’re totally cool with gay people. Are you really? If you’re gay, even just a little bit, shouldn’t you be totally cool with yourself?”

Rocket looked down and sucked the last few drops of his sangria through the straw. He continued to look down at the table, and when he spoke he was barely audible. “I’ve never been cool with myself.”

Harrison looked across the table at his fellow police officer who, until an hour ago, he hardly knew. Rocket always came across as gregarious, confident, and even a little cocky. Harrison felt like he was looking at a completely different person now. They had very little in common aside from their occupation, and he wasn’t sure there was any basis for an ongoing friendship. But he cared about him. And he was concerned for him.

“You’ve been through a lot the past few days. What you experienced on Friday night was traumatic, and I think it’s thrown you for a loop. Your emotions are pulling you all over the place. And that’s totally understandable. Hell, if it was me, I’d have trouble dealing with it.”

He paused. Rocket looked at him with brokenness in his eyes.

Harrison continued. “We have good counseling benefits. In our line of work, sometimes we experience trauma, like when we visit the scene of a shooting or the aftermath of a car crash. It’s part of the job. There’s an employee helpline you can call. They have a list of therapists who are trained to deal with these things. You’ve just been through a lot of stuff that's pretty upsetting. And it sounds like maybe you have some long-term issues deep inside you need to deal with. So make an appointment. Get help. There's nothing to be ashamed of. It will help you a lot."

"Yeah, you're probably right."

"I feel like I'm in over my head. I think we need to let the pros help you at this point."

Rocket tried to pull himself together. "Yeah. But hey, thanks, man. You've been a big help."

"Thanks. I'm glad I could be here for you."

They slid out from their booth. They flagged down their server and asked for their checks. Rocket said, "Seriously, dude. Let me pay for all of it. I owe you big time."

"Nope. I insist."

Rocket didn't press further. "Thanks, man."

They walked out to their cars. When they got to Rocket's car, he turned to Harrison. "Hey, can I ask you one more thing?"

"Sure."

"Are you happy?"

Well, that was a strange thing to ask. "Well, yeah, I guess. I have a wonderful husband and we have a nice home and good jobs. We have good friends. We're healthy. I get annoyed when I get stuck in traffic. I hate cleaning toilets. I wish I didn't still feel like a second-class citizen, especially in this red state. And I'm scared to even think about what's going to happen to our rights if Trump wins. But overall... yeah, I'm happy."

"But are you happy with *you*?"

"Yes, I am. I really am. Being gay can be a challenge sometimes, but in other ways it's great. But in any case, it's who I am. And I wouldn't want it any other way. Happiness is being able to live your life the way you want – not how anyone else thinks you should."

Rocket nodded. "Thanks for everything, man." He held out his hand and Harrison stepped forward and shook it. Instead of releasing his hand, Rocket pulled Harrison toward him and they hugged.

As they separated, Harrison placed his hands on Rocket's shoulders. He looked him in the eyes and said, "I want you to be happy too."

Standing Up for the Truth

Wednesday, September 7, 2016

When Rocket arrived at the police station, he swung by Harrison's desk. "Hey, man, thanks again for spending time with me last night. It really helped."

"You're welcome. I appreciate the trust you placed in me."

"And uh... I called the helpline. I've got an appointment with a counselor scheduled for next Tuesday."

"Good. I'm really glad. Oh, and hey! Did you hear the latest about the pastor of that big church that got arrested last Friday night?"

"No. What happened?"

"Get this. The story made the front page of the Sunday paper. So he stood up in front of his congregation on Sunday morning and insisted that it wasn't him and the youth pastor at the event. He claimed that people were using fake IDs with their names, to try to get them in trouble."

Rocket became livid. "Are you shittin' me?"

"I shit you not. They always record their services and post them on YouTube. See for yourself. I'll send you the link."

Rocket sat down at his desk and turned on his computer. He opened his email, put on his headphones, and clicked the link Harrison sent. He fast-forwarded to 6:30, where Harrison said the announcement started. He pounded his fist on his desk and shouted, "That lying asshole!"

Everyone else in the room turned and looked at Rocket, wondering what was going on.

Rocket stormed into Sergeant Garlow's office and shut the door. After telling him what happened, Garlow was livid too. He said, "It's infuriating. But there's nothing we can do about it."

"There isn't? Couldn't we go to the paper? Couldn't we get on the local TV news shows?"

"That's not the sort of thing we usually do. Besides, that will all get sorted out when his case goes to trial. I think you just need to let it go."

Rocket stood for a moment, trying to make himself calm down without success. "No. I can't just let it go. This is personal for me. My buddy in high school had to run away because that shithead couldn't accept that he was gay. He had to run away so he wouldn't get sent to someplace that was going to try to convert him. And I didn't tell you this, but I saw my friend in one of the porn videos that was playing at the orgy. Yeah, that's right. He had to do porn to get by. And now this asswipe is gay himself? Sorry, man, that's too fucked up. I can't just let this go. And besides, he was up there claiming we couldn't spot a fake ID when we saw one. It's an affront to our police work."

"Well, you've got a point there. Okay, so there's a Public Affairs department at the main office downtown. They handle all of our interactions with the news media. You can go talk to them and let them handle it as they see fit. But don't you go to the press yourself. Understood?"

"Yes, sir."

Rocket left Garlow's office, walked back to his desk, and looked up the number of the Public Affairs office. He spoke with Olivia Nelson, the department's Chief Public Relations Officer. After listening to his story, she said, "Normally, we wouldn't take any action on a case such as this. But Rev. Bauer has a large public platform, and he is spreading lies and disparaging our police force. Plus, there's a human interest angle with the missing kid. I have connections with all the local TV news producers. Let me see if there's any interest in this story. I'll get back to you."

That afternoon, Officer Nelson called back. "We've got you booked on Channel 3's 'Rise and Shine' show on Friday morning at 8:30. Can you come to my office tomorrow at 10 a.m. so I can brief you on how to do a television appearance? There's a lot you need to know about what to say and not say."

"Yes, ma'am. I'll be there at 10:00 tomorrow."

"After your appearance, we will issue a press release to all the local media on Friday at 9:00 a.m."

"Officer Nelson, I can't thank you enough. This means a lot to me. Thank you!"

"Thank you for bringing the matter to our attention and letting us handle it."

***

After church on Sunday morning, the Board of Elders at the Eternal Savior Christian Church held an emergency meeting. They voted unanimously to place Head Pastor Rev. Bradley Bauer, Youth Pastor Rev. Dr. Ronald Babcock, and Facilities Manager Archibald Kilgore (a.k.a. Black Stallion) on administrative leave pending the outcome of their trials.

A New, Improved Rocket

Tuesday, October 11, 2016

At 4:00 p.m., Rocket Crockett walked out of his fifth and final counseling session. It was a crisp, sunny autumn day, and the turning leaves were at the height of their colorful brilliance. Rocket smiled as he headed toward his car. The counseling sessions had been tremendously helpful, not only in helping him work through the traumatic emotional conflicts he experienced at the gay orgy, but also in helping him come to terms with his difficult childhood and adolescence. He felt like a new person. He couldn't recall when he'd been happier, at least not since his college football days at TCU.

He felt like celebrating. He sat down in his car, pulled out his phone, and called Trevor.

"Hey, Trev. Rocket here. How ya doin'?"

"Good, man. What's up?"

"Lots of stuff. So much has happened these past few weeks. You doin' anything after work today? I'd love to get together for a beer."

"Yeah, I can do that. I get off at six. Is that okay?"

"Sounds good."

"You wanna meet in the bar at my hotel? Who knows, the manager may be able to get us a freebie."

Rocket laughed, knowing that Trevor was the manager. "You got a deal. See you there at six."

Rocket drove home and changed out of his uniform. At six, he walked into the bar just off the lobby of the Helton Grand Hotel & Suites. Trevor was waiting for him. Rocket walked up and gave him a big hug. Since Rocket's usual greeting was a firm, manly handshake, Trevor was somewhat taken aback by the more effusive gesture.

Trevor walked toward the barstools and said, "Well! You're in a good mood today."

Rocket smiled. "It's a beautiful day, man. Hey, can we sit at one of the tables over there, where there are fewer people?"

"Yeah, sure. What do you want?"

"Whatever you have on tap. Doesn't matter."

Trevor ordered two beers from the bartender and led Rocket to the table in the far corner. "So, I guess you heard the news and you feel like celebrating."

Rocket looked puzzled. "No, what news? I've been offline this afternoon."

"They found Bauer and Babcock guilty on all counts. Since they were two of the organizers, they had their hands in collecting money from all the attendees and paying for the hookers and blow."

"That means they'll probably get fired from their church."

Trevor said, "Probably. I guess you could say that Karma ran over their dogma."

Rocket chuckled. "Well, whatever. I'm not going to wish bad things on other people."

The bartender brought the beers and a bowl of popcorn to the table. They each took a swig, and Rocket reached for a handful of popcorn. "Anyway, that's not what I wanted to talk to you about."

Trevor said, "Wait. Let me guess. You're gay."

"Huh? What? Why would you say that?"

"Well, today is October 11th."

"So?"

"It's National Coming Out Day. I thought maybe you wanted to get together to tell me you're gay. Maybe they won you over at the orgy." Trevor grinned. It was always Rocket who teased others. Trevor enjoyed the opportunity to tease Rocket for a change.

That left Rocket completely flustered, especially after what he had worked through during his counseling. "Dude. No. Don't be a dick, man. Besides, how would *you* know about National Coming Out Day?"

"Somebody posted about it on Facebook earlier."

"Yeah, right. But anyway, so what if I was? What's wrong with being gay?"

"Nothing. I didn't have any problem with Bryan and Chris being gay. Back then, I kinda wondered if you were too. So yeah, if you told me you were gay, I wouldn't be surprised. And I wouldn't care."

"Wait a minute. You thought I was gay?"

"Not really. But I wondered about it. Mostly because you always seemed so interested in Bryan. Or at least Bryan's cock."

"Well, yeah. Mostly because I had never seen one that huge. You have to admit, you looked at it too."

"How could I not see it? But yeah, everyone checked out everyone else's dick. But the rest of us didn't say anything about it. You teased him about it constantly. Like it was always on your mind."

Rocket took a long swig of his beer, rolled it around in his mouth, and set his glass down. *Here goes.* "Yeah, well, that kinda brings me to what I wanted to tell you. I was pretty shaken up after seeing what was goin' on at that orgy. And it wasn't just some of the stuff they were doin' to each other." Rocket took another drink of his beer. "I've only told a couple of people about this, but you're my buddy and I can trust you, right?"

"Right. Of course."

"Okay. So while I was in there, they had these gay pornos playing on the TV screens, and..." Rocket paused. "Bryan was in one of them."

Trevor's eyes popped open. "You're kidding me!"

"No, I'm not. And don't tell anyone, okay?"

"Okay. But wow." Trevor hesitated for a few seconds, then said, "So..." He dropped his voice to a whisper. "Did you see it hard?"

Rocket nodded.

"How big is it?"

Rocket held out his hands, almost a foot apart.

"Wow..."

"I know, right? But anyway..." Rocket took another long sip. He decided not to tell Trevor that he got hard. That would be TMI and there was no point. He had worked that out in counseling. "Since then, I haven't stopped thinking about Bryan. You know, trying to figure out what happened. Wondering where he is, and how he's doing. Wondering how he got into doing porn."

"Yeah, well he's certainly qualified. Remember the night we had that party at my house, and you made me put on one of my dad's pornos? And you told Bryan he should have that schlong of his in porn?" Trevor chuckled at the memory, but he quickly stopped when he saw that Rocket wasn't laughing.

"Yeah, I remembered that when I saw him in the video. That made me realize I was a real asshole back then."

Trevor almost said, '...and you aren't now?' but he wisely decided against it.

Rocket continued. "So after that night, I was talking to one of my colleagues, and he suggested that I get counseling. So I did. I just had my last appointment this afternoon. I never in a million years thought I'd be seeing a shrink, but I tell you, it has totally changed my life. We processed through all the stuff I saw that night. But then we worked through some things from my childhood." He finished his beer and said, "Hey, can I get another one? I'll pay for this one."

"Sure, and don't worry about it." Trevor signaled to the bartender, who nodded and started filling two more glasses at the tap.

Rocket continued. "Anyway, looking back on high school, I see now that I acted like a jerk a lot of the time."

"But you were popular in high school. You were the star of the football team and the track team. Everyone looked up to you."

"Everyone admired my ability and status, but I don't think people liked *me* very much. I was good at acting like I was popular and confident and stuff, but it was all an act. I was fakin' it. But the truth is, I had low self-esteem. It came from how I was treated at home, but I don't want to get into that. I guess the reason I pushed myself to be so good at football and track was so people would respect me. It's like if I got good enough, people would like me."

Trevor said, "I liked you. I still do. All the other guys liked you, too. I think you're being way too hard on yourself."

"Well, thanks. I appreciate it. And I appreciate you. And one of the things I wanted to tell you today is that I'm sorry I was an asshole back then. Looking back at that party, it was really immature of me to make you put on your dad's pornos. It never occurred to me that some of the guys might not want to see that, especially Bryan and Chris. Hell, they left the party. I still can't believe I did that. I guess I thought doing that would make me look cool or daring or edgy or... whatever. I don't know. Like I had to tell the funniest jokes, or drink the most booze, or be the one in charge of every situation. But now I see it only made me look like a jerk."

"Again, you're being too hard on yourself. We were high school kids. We were all immature back then. We were all just tryin' to look cool to everyone else. That was then, this is now."

"Yeah. But I guess that's one thing that stood out about Bryan. He wasn't immature. He didn't do any of that shit. It's like he didn't worry about whether people liked him or not, they just did. And I was jealous of him for that. And for the fact that he was tall, handsome, smart, and he had that big dick. Now I understand why I teased him so much. I was trying to get his attention. I liked him and wished we could be better friends."

Trevor said, "So you called him 'PK' and teased him about his dick, hoping that would make him want to be friends with you?"

"Yeah. Pretty fucked up, isn't it? But I was pretty fucked up back then."

Trevor sat silently, feeling empathy for his friend but wondering why he was telling him all this.

Rocket said, "I wish I knew how to get a hold of him. I looked for him on Facebook, but I couldn't find him. I want to apologize for how I treated him back then. And I'd like to know where he is, and what he's doing, and that he's okay. I wonder if he and Chris ever got back together."

Trevor said, "Well, I can answer that. Chris is living in Arlington, Virginia. He's an attorney and he works for some senator. He has a boyfriend he's been with for, like, eight years now."

"How do you know all that?"

"We're friends on Facebook. In fact, he's the one who posted about today being National Coming Out Day."

"I tried finding him on Facebook, but there's like 50 million Chris Robertsons. If I knew he lived in Arlington, that might have helped narrow it down."

"Well, just find him on my Friends list and send him a friend request. He'll probably accept. But I don't know anything about Bryan. I asked Chris once, but he just said, 'I think he's in California somewhere.' I got the impression they weren't in touch. But send him a friend request and ask him."

Rocket finished his second beer. "I will. Anyway, thanks for listening. And thanks for being my friend. From now on I'm going to try to be nicer to everyone. I'm gonna be less crude. And I'm learning to appreciate myself for who I am and stop caring about what other people think. I mean, I can't make other people like me. Either they do or they don't. But I can try to be more likable. And at least now, I like myself."

Trevor looked at his friend as he was saying all this. He almost couldn't believe these words were coming from Rocket. He was watching his friend experience a personal breakthrough, and it was beautiful.

Rocket said, "Well, I guess I'd better let you go so you can go home and have dinner. Thanks for the beers. And thanks for listening."

They both stood up. Trevor said, "I'm really happy for you, man. I think you've turned a corner. You're going to be a lot happier. And for the record, I was your friend then, I'm your friend now, and I hope we'll always be friends."

"Thanks, man." They hugged. "Right back atcha."

"And I'm sorry I teased you earlier about that orgy turning you gay. I admire you for doing that. I don't think I could have done it. And now, justice has been served."

"Yeah, but a lot of lives got ruined."

"Maybe. But it was their choice to do what they did. Think of the people who go to that church. All this time, their pastor has been a hypocrite. A closet case. They deserve to know the truth. I mean, if you're going to be gay, at least live your life openly and honestly."

"I guess so."

"And I'll bet Bryan will appreciate what you did if he ever finds out."

That made Rocket smile. "Well, until next time!"

"Take care man." They gave each other another quick hug, then went on their way.

Catching Up with Chris

Tuesday, October 11, 2016

After dinner, Trevor got on Facebook. He smiled when he saw Chris online. He opened a private message window.

Hey Chris! Happy National Coming Out Day! I saw your post earlier.

Thanks, man. How are things in KC?

Pretty good. Hey, Rocket Crockett might send you a friend request. I hope you'll accept.

Yeah, he did, and I did.

Cool. We had a couple of beers earlier, and your name came up. Also Bryan's. Have you heard from him lately?

Actually, yes. He's in Scottsdale now. My partner and I were in Phoenix over Labor Day weekend, and we got together.

Cool! How is he?

He's doing great. He has a new BF. Seems really nice. He has a good job and a beautiful house. And he's playing his trumpet again. So yeah, he's doing well.

Good! Glad to hear it.

I haven't chatted with Rocket yet. How's he doing?

Good. He's had some interesting things happen over the past couple of months. Long story and I'll let him tell you, but he's doing fine now.

Good. So what's new with you?

Not much. But did you hear the big news about Bryan's father?

No, what happened?

The police busted a gay orgy group back on Labor Day weekend. Not for being gay, but because there were illegal drugs and male prostitutes. And get this... One of the people who was arrested was Bryan's father.

WHAT??? Are you shittin' me?

Nope. You can't make this shit up. Hang on, let me find a news article and send you the link. BRB.

Trevor found one of the articles and pasted the link in the chat window. A few minutes later, Chris replied,

Holy shit!

Literally. Oh, and I manage the hotel where it took place. I'm the one who called the police when I saw some unusual activity on the security cameras.

Wow. Small world, isn't it?

It sure is. Is Bryan on Facebook?

No, but his BF is, and we're friends.

Send the link to him, OK? Bryan might like to know. And tell him I said hi.

Will do!

Hey, gotta run. Nice chatting with you

You too. Thanks for the info!

Anytime. Take care!

News from Kansas

Wednesday, October 12, 2016

At 5:45, Aaron entered his apartment with the sushi and sake he had picked up from Food World. He and Ryan had established a tradition of having sushi for dinner on Wednesday since it was on sale at Food World. Ryan was due to arrive at 6:00, so Aaron took a few moments to catch up on Facebook.

He saw a private message from Chris:

> Hey, Aaron. Hope all's well. Here's some news from Kansas that might be of interest to Ryan. Hugs to you both!

Aaron clicked on the link Chris attached. It was an article on the Prairie Village Post's website.

Revs. Bauer, Babcock Busted in Gay Sex/Drug Orgy

Sunday, September 4, 2016

Kansas City, MO (AP) – Rev. Bradley Bauer, head pastor at Eternal Savior Christian Church, and Rev. Ronald Babcock, youth pastor at the same church, were among 35 men arrested at an all-male sex party at a Kansas City hotel on the night of Friday, September 2.

Police raided the event after receiving a tip that illegal drugs were being provided to attendees. An undercover police officer who infiltrated the event witnessed eighteen participants using cocaine and

> methamphetamine ("crystal meth"). He discovered that four male prostitutes had been hired to provide sexual services to attendees, and a pharmacist was dispensing erection-enhancement drugs without a prescription.
>
> Police arrested the event organizers, participants who engaged in purchasing or using illegal substances, the prostitutes and the person who hired them, and the pharmacist. Attendees who only participated in consensual sexual activities were charged with disorderly conduct and released.

Aaron couldn't wait to tell Ryan all about it and see his reaction.

A few minutes later, Ryan knocked on the door. Aaron got up from his computer and greeted Ryan at the front door. After they hugged and kissed, he said, "Your sushi awaits! But first, have I got news for *you!*"

Ryan wasn't sure what news would make Aaron so excited. "Okay..."

Aaron motioned toward the kitchen table. "I think you should be sitting down for this."

Once they were seated, Aaron said, "I just got a private message from Chris. There's been a huge scandal in Prairie Village!"

Ryan couldn't care less about what happened in Prairie Village. He had no plans ever to go back there again. "So...?"

"So! Back on Friday night of Labor Day weekend, the police busted a gay orgy at a hotel in Kansas City. They were using party drugs and they had prostitutes and everything."

"Again. So...?"

"So! One of the men they arrested was none other than the Rev. Brad Bauer, head paster of the Eternal Savior Christian Church of Prairie Village, Kansas!"

Ryan reached for a piece of sushi. "I really couldn't give a flying rat's ass."

"Seriously??? Your dad just got busted at a gay sex and drugs orgy and you don't care?"

"As far as I'm concerned, he's not my father anymore. We've talked about this before. He's dead to me. He can rot in hell, as far as I'm concerned – that is, if I thought there was a hell."

"For real? Your dad is gay, and you don't give a shit?"

"That's correct, I don't. What do you want me to do? Call him up and welcome him to our team? So now we're both gay and that makes everything okay? Geez, trying to force me into gay conversion therapy was bad enough, but at least I can see why a straight person would do that. But to have him do all that when he's actually gay? That's just... that's totally fucked up. That's fucked up beyond all recognition."

"So what do you think's going to happen to him? Do you think the church will fire him?"

"You aren't getting the message, are you? I don't give two shits about what happens to him. As for the church – you obviously don't know much about fundamentalist churches. Well, let me tell you how it will go down. He'll get up on stage and drop to his knees. He'll confess that he fell to temptation and committed terrible sins, while tears flow from his eyes. He'll blame it all on Satan, who led him into temptation in a moment of weakness. But then he'll claim that, through the grace of the Lord Jesus Christ, he's been forgiven. He's repented and been washed clean of his sins. He's been delivered from his unrighteousness and recommitted his life to the Lord. Now his faith is stronger than ever. And the congregation will swallow that entire load of crap and cheer for his miraculous redemption."

"So he'll get away with it."

"Absolutely. Count on it. It happens every time."

Ryan picked up a piece of sushi, dipped it in his wasabi-infused soy sauce, and popped it in his mouth. Aaron didn't know what to say next, and he could tell Ryan didn't want to hear any more about it.

Aaron didn't say any more about the incident in Kansas City. He tried asking Ryan how things were going at work, but Ryan didn't say much. He tried talking about what was going on with their friends in the band, but Ryan wasn't interested. Finally, Aaron said, "Okay, so are you mad at me because I brought up the business about your father?"

"No, not really."

"Well, I'm sorry I brought it up. I wasn't expecting it to strike a nerve like that."

"It's okay. Don't worry about it."

Aaron wanted to ask, 'Well, then, what are you mad at?' but he decided it would be better to let it drop. Maybe the business with his father bothered him more than he was willing to let on. But whatever it was, he didn't want to talk about it.

The mood for the evening was ruined. Silently, they both agreed it would be better to call it an early night.

After they finished dinner, Ryan stood up and said, "Well, I should probably be on my way."

"Okay. See you at rehearsal tomorrow night."

They shared a quick hug and a passionless kiss.

Ryan said, "Sorry I ruined the evening. I'm not mad at you. It's just that... all that stuff brought back some memories and kinda put me in a bad space. It's not your fault."

Aaron said, "I get it," although he wasn't sure he did. "Drive safely. I love you."

"I love you too." Ryan gave Aaron a quick kiss and headed for the door.

Once Aaron finished cleaning up after dinner, he sat down at his computer. He opened a search window and typed 'Bradley Bauer.' Over a dozen pages of results appeared. Some of them were hits for the Eternal Savior Christian Church's website, but many of them were news articles screaming about the scandal.

Eternal Savior Places Bauer, Babcock on Leave in Wake of Scandal

Local Pastors Caught in Drug-fueled Male Orgy

Male Prostitute: Local Pastors Paid for Sex, Drugs

Rev. Bauer's Sordid Secret Life of Sex and Drugs

Bauer Busted! Male Prostitute Reveals Shocking Details!

Aaron clicked the links and read the stories. Soon, he realized they were mostly repeating the same information. But on the third page of search results, a different story caught his eye.

Aaron clicked the link. A brief story in the Prairie Village Post appeared. It was accompanied by a picture of a tall, handsome, slender young man hoisting a basketball, eyes focused in concentration, an instant before releasing a shot. His hair was darker than Ryan's, but the resemblance was unmistakable.

> ### Local Hoops Star Commits to ASU
> March 23, 2016
>
> Brandon Bauer, the 6'7" center who led the Prairie Village High School basketball team to three conference championships and the state finals, has signed a letter of intent to attend Arizona State University. Bauer was awarded a scholarship to play basketball for the Sun Devils. Bauer, the son of prominent local pastor Rev. Bradley Bauer, was actively recruited by many schools including Kansas State and Wichita State. Bauer chose ASU for its large campus and warmer climate. Said Bauer, "ASU has an excellent degree program and abundant educational resources. And I was impressed by the coaching staff." Bauer plans to major in Communications.

Holy shit! Aaron thought. *Ryan's younger brother, who he hasn't seen in nine years, lives five miles away. What can I do? What should I do?*

I should probably tell Ryan his brother is attending ASU on a basketball scholarship and let him take it from there. But what if he does nothing? And if he reconnects with Brandon, Brandon will probably tell his parents about Ryan, and Ryan doesn't want to have any contact with them.

And what about Brandon? Would he even want to see his brother again? Who knows what his right-wing, ultra-conservative parents have told him about Ryan? Maybe Brandon is a right-wing homophobe. Who knows?

The more Aaron thought about this, the more it gnawed at him. *Maybe neither of them ever wants to see the other again. But maybe this is the chance to reunite these two long-lost brothers, who used to have such a close connection. Maybe this is one wrong that can finally be made right.*

Aaron was determined to find out. He decided to find Brandon and ask him how he felt about being reunited with his brother. But how?

After more searching, Aaron learned that the ASU basketball team practices at the Banktopia arena on campus from 4:00 to 6:00 Monday through Friday. Practices for the upcoming basketball season had started.

Aaron assumed that, as a freshman, Brandon probably lived in a dorm. But there was no way to find out which one. Aaron's only option was to hang out near the entrance to the arena and try to spot Brandon when he left basketball practice.

He found the Prairie Village Post article again and printed the picture, although he assumed there weren't too many 6'7" men who looked like a younger version of Ryan with darker hair.

Finding Brandon

Thursday, October 13, 2016

On Thursday at 5:45, Aaron approached the Banktopia Arena on foot. He felt conspicuous and awkward, like some sort of groupie or stalker. A wave of nervousness swept over him. *What am I going to say? How will he react?* He tried to anticipate each contingency and how he would respond to it. But he had no idea how this was going to go. There was no way to prepare for it. And he was still plagued with doubt over whether he should even be doing this.

He strolled back and forth, trying not to look like a loiterer. Only a few other people passed since it was late in the afternoon. None of them paid any attention to Aaron, but he imagined each of them was wondering who he was and what he was doing there.

After twenty long, drawn-out minutes passed, a side door opened. Tall guys slinging backpacks and gym bags emerged one by one or in small groups. So far, none of them looked like Brandon. Finally, the door opened again and a group of three players exited. One of them was, unquestionably, Brandon.

The three of them walked north toward the main campus. They seemed tired but in good spirits. They talked and laughed among themselves.

Aaron couldn't bring himself to approach them and ask to speak to Brandon individually. That would be too weird since Brandon didn't know him from Adam. He was on the verge of chickening out.

He followed them, trying to keep enough distance to escape attention but staying close enough to not lose sight of them.

When they reached University Avenue, they said goodbye, waved, and headed in separate directions. The other two crossed the street and continued into the main part of the campus, while Brandon turned left and headed toward a cluster of dorms.

Aaron sped up. When he was within a few feet, he called out, "Hey! Brandon?"

Brandon glanced back to see who called him. Aaron waved and Brandon stopped. He looked puzzled.

Aaron thought, *Here goes. It's now or never.*

"Are you Brandon Bauer?"

"Yeah…?"

"You don't know me, but… my name is Aaron. Aaron Bradbury."

Aaron extended his hand. Brandon tentatively shook it.

"Look, I know this is awkward, so I'll get right to the point." Aaron took a deep breath. "I know your brother."

Brandon's puzzled expression turned to bewilderment. He looked like he wanted to say something, but couldn't.

"Your older brother, Bryan."

Brandon's face turned white. "How can that be? He's been missing for, like, nine years."

"Well, I saw him yesterday."

Brandon stared in disbelief. He couldn't decide whether this stranger was serious or if he was pulling some sort of cruel hoax. "How do you know him? How do you know we're brothers?"

"I'm his boyfriend." Aaron figured he might as well get that fact out in the open.

"Is this some sort of bad joke?"

Aaron wasn't sure if that was a reaction to Ryan being gay and having a boyfriend or what. "No. I would never do anything like that."

"Okay, I need to ask you a few questions. What are our parents' names?"

"Brad and Brenda. Your father is the pastor of a big church in Prairie Village, Kansas. And by the way, I'm sorry about recent events. That must be really rough for you."

"Yeah, it is. I'm glad I'm not there to deal with it first-hand. So, let me ask you a couple of other things just so I can be sure. In high school, what was he interested in? Did he play basketball, like me?"

"No, he ran track. He still runs. In fact, that's how I met him – in a running club."

Brandon remained silent for a moment as he took it all in and tried to make sense of what was going on. Then he asked, "What was the other thing he was really interested in?"

"He played the trumpet. He still does."

Brandon stood there stunned. His mistrust and disbelief subsided, and the bewilderment returned. Tears began to form. "I'm sorry…" he started sniffling. "This has totally caught me off guard. I… I… I don't know what…"

Aaron stepped forward and placed his hand on Brandon's shoulder. "I know, this must come as quite a shock. Do you want to sit down somewhere?"

He nodded, and they sat down on a nearby bench.

Brandon said, "I haven't seen him since I was in third grade. Mom and I went to Tulsa to visit my grandmother for the weekend. I remember thinking something was wrong because it came up so suddenly and Bryan wasn't going with us. While we were there, Dad called and said he was missing. He went off to work – he worked in a grocery store – and never came home. The police got involved, but they never found him. So after a while, my dad told me we have to go on with our lives as if he's dead and we'll never see him again."

By now, Brandon was sobbing, so Aaron slid a few inches closer and put his arm around him. "I'm sorry. That must have been incredibly difficult for you to go through."

"It was. And something never seemed right. I couldn't help but wonder whether Mom taking me to visit Grandma was somehow connected with Bryan's disappearance."

"Well, from what little he's told me, it probably was. According to him, he found out your parents were going to send him off to someplace in Alabama where they were going to try to make him straight. I checked it out. It's closed now but it looked pretty awful. And your dad was going to put him on a plane and take him there the next day. He found out the day before – the same day your mom took you to visit your grandmother. So he figured the only way to avoid getting sent to this place was to run away from home. He had to disappear. But that's his story to tell, and he doesn't like to talk about it."

Brandon said, "That all checks out. Bryan left me a letter that said pretty much the same thing. He said that someday when we're grown up, he would find me and we'd be reunited. But I guess that time hasn't come yet. And every year, he sent me a Christmas card from somewhere. It never had a return address, and it would be postmarked from a different place each year. I guess he didn't want my parents to figure out where he was."

Aaron said, "Speaking of your parents, before we continue I need to have you promise me that you will not say anything about this to your parents."

"How come?"

"It's really important. Bryan went to great lengths to make sure they wouldn't find him. He never wants to see or hear from them again. He's adamant about that. He will kill me if he finds out I contacted you and then you told them where he is. And that might make him never want to see you again, either."

"Okay, I promise. I'm not too cool with my father these days, anyway."

"And your mother? You can't tell her, either."

"You're right – I can't. She died two and a half years ago."

Now it was Aaron's turn to be shocked. "Oh my God! ... I am so sorry. You've really been through a lot, haven't you?"

"Yeah, and after that, Dad started acting weird too. I had no idea what was going on inside his head. I mean, we've never been close. We never really talked. But now I know what was going on. It's probably been going on for years. That's why I jumped at the chance to go to college somewhere far away. Dad wanted to me to go to school in Kansas so I would be close by, but I had to get out."

"I don't blame you."

Brandon said, "Man, I can't believe I'm telling all this to a total stranger. I'm sorry. I've said way too much. You probably think I'm a hot mess."

"It's all right. I think maybe you needed to talk to someone. It's hard to talk about deeply personal stuff with people you already know. And no, I don't think you're a hot mess. I think you're dealing with everything pretty well."

"Yeah, I guess so. Thanks. And thanks for listening."

"No problem. But back to Bryan…"

Brandon said, "Yeah. Do you think Bryan will want to see me again? I mean, he's made no attempt to contact me other than sending Christmas cards."

"I know he loves you and misses you. Having to leave you behind is the thing he's most angry at your parents about. But he probably felt he couldn't make contact with you while you were still living at home without your parents finding out."

"Yeah, you're probably right."

"And by the way, he changed his name. That's why they weren't able to find him. It's one of the first things he did when he left home."

"So what's his new name?"

"Okay, please promise me again that you will never say anything about this to your dad. Promise?"

"I promise."

"Okay. His name is now Ryan. Ryan Robertson. Here… you wanna see a picture of him?"

Brandon nodded, and Aaron reached for his phone. He flipped through his pictures and found a selfie they took a couple of months ago and showed it to him.

"Oh my God, it *is* him!" Brandon exclaimed. "He looks good. He looks happy."

"Yeah, that was taken in San Diego a couple of months ago."

"So, what's he like now? What's he doing?"

"He's good. He went to UCLA. He got a scholarship and worked to support himself. Now, he works for a technology research company in Scottsdale. He's very smart and successful. He's strong and self-confident and he works hard."

"Yep, that's Bryan – I mean Ryan. In high school, he was a track star and a really great trumpet player and a straight-A student. Whatever he did, he was the best. He was my hero. I looked up to him for everything. And he was the best big brother you could ever want. He treated me like I was special, and he never minded me hanging around. I could talk to him about anything. He was more of a father to me than my father was, but at the same time, we were like best friends. After he was gone it just tore me up."

"It tore him up, too."

Aaron put his arm around Brandon again and held him for a moment, while another round of tears came and went.

Finally, Brandon asked, "So how did you find me?"

"Actually, I found you because of what happened to your dad. I went looking on the internet for news articles, and I found a story in the Prairie Village Post from last March about you getting a basketball scholarship to attend ASU. Congratulations, by the way."

"Thanks." Brandon paused. "So, does he know that I'm here?"

"No. I wanted to find you first to see whether you would be open to being reunited with him. Since your dad is so conservative and homophobic, I thought it's possible you could be that way too. I didn't know how you would react to finding out your brother is gay."

Brandon nodded. "I already knew. We talked about it back then. I'm totally cool with it. Some of my friends are gay. I know, that sounds lame. And I knew Bryan – er, Ryan – and his best friend in high school were boyfriends."

"That would be Chris."

"You know Chris?"

"Yeah. Chris went to Maryland and he lives in Arlington, Virginia now. Last month, Chris and his partner Seth came out here. Seth's family lives in Glendale. We had them over for a visit, and Chris and I friended each other on Facebook. Chris is the one who told me about what happened to your father. So I went looking for more information and I found the article about you. Then I found out when and where the basketball team practices, and now, here we are."

"Wow. You really put some work into this. Thanks."

"It was a risk. But I thought it was a risk worth taking. And just so you know, he really doesn't like to talk about the past. He avoids it at all costs. He keeps a lot of things to himself. But I know he loves you, and I think it will mean everything to him to see you again."

"So, when do I get to meet him?"

"I've been thinking about that. Tomorrow is his birthday. I can't think of a better present to give him than his long-lost brother."

"You mean I should just pop in and surprise him?"

"Yep. I think that would be awesome!"

Brandon thought about it for a moment. "But what if he flips out?"

"That could be kind of fun. I think his reaction will be priceless."

Brandon thought some more. "Can I get back to you? I mean, this has been a lot to take in. I need a little time to process it all and make sure I'm ready for this."

"Okay, but let me know as soon as you decide one way or the other. I have to make plans for how to pull this off."

Brandon and Aaron exchanged phone numbers. Aaron said, "It would be better for you to text me rather than call, in case Ryan is around."

They stood up and shook hands. Then Brandon gave Aaron a hug. "Thanks, man."

"My pleasure. It was nice to meet you."

Brandon smiled. "You too."

He turned and walked toward his dorm, and Aaron walked back to his car. *That went well. Brandon seems like a nice guy, and he's been through a lot. He could use something good happening in his life.*

Dinner Plans

Thursday, October 13, 2016

Aaron arrived at band rehearsal about two minutes before the downbeat. He assembled his trombone quickly and took his seat in the trombone row, just behind where Ryan was sitting with the trumpets.

Ryan turned around and said, "Where were you? We missed you at dinner."

"Sorry! Something came up. I grabbed a sub and ate it on the way in."

The director called the rehearsal to order and began leading the band in their warm-up scales.

At 8:05, Aaron felt his phone vibrating in his pocket. As soon as the director dismissed the band for their break, Aaron pulled out his phone. It was a text message from Brandon.

> Hey Aaron, I'm in. Let's do this.

> Awesome! Can I call you at 9:30?

> Yes

He slid his phone back into his pocket just as Ryan walked up. Ryan kissed Aaron and said, "How was your day?"

"Really good. And yours?"

"Fine. Nothing special."

Aaron said, "Hey, I was thinking about dinner tomorrow night. You said you wanted to go to a Brazilian steakhouse."

"Yeah. There's one near Scottsdale and Shea that Eddie took me to when I stayed with him during my summer internship. I've always wanted to go back."

"Oh. Well, there's one near me. It's supposed to be really good."

Ryan frowned and said, "It's my birthday. I thought I got to pick the place."

"Well, under normal circumstances, yes. But since I have to be at work at 9:00 on Saturday morning, and since I assume you'll want to celebrate your birthday in other ways..." Aaron winked. "...It would make more sense if we spent the night at my place. I'll make breakfast for us in the morning."

Ryan looked at Aaron suspiciously. "You're planning a surprise party, aren't you?"

"No!"

"Good. 'Cause I hate surprise parties."

"Nope. I promise. No surprise party." *A surprise, yes, but technically not a party.*

"Well, okay. I can tell you really want to go to this place."

"Cool. What time should I make the reservation for? 6:00?"

"Yeah, I should be able to make it to your place by around 5:45. Hey, are you coming out to the bar tonight?"

"I shouldn't. I have to be at work at 8:00 tomorrow morning. Charlie's going to fill in for me from 5:30 until closing so I can take you to dinner."

"That's nice of him."

"Yeah, we help each other out whenever something like this comes up. Well, rehearsal's going to start up again in a couple of minutes, and I need to pee." Aaron kissed Ryan and then headed to the restroom.

After band practice, Aaron waited in his car until he saw Ryan pull out and drive away. Then he pulled his phone out and called Brandon. Brandon answered promptly.

Aaron said, "Okay, so here's what I've come up with. I'm going to be taking Ryan out to dinner for his birthday. Our reservation is for

6:00. We'll be there for at least an hour, so we'll probably get back at around 7:30. I'll text you my address. It's an apartment complex in Tempe, near Guadalupe and McClintock. Do you have transportation?"

"Yeah. Dad let me have Mom's car after she died."

"Okay. There are some parking spaces marked for visitors. Just don't park in a space with a number. I'll leave a key under the doormat. You should show up at around 7:00 and let yourself in. I'll text you when we're getting ready to leave the restaurant. You can hide in the bedroom closer to the front door – the one where my desk is. I'll tell him I have to go in there to get his present, then I'll bring you out. How's that sound?"

"Sounds good. Hey, thanks again for finding me and setting all this up! I can't wait to see Bryan – er, Ryan – again."

"My pleasure. But remember, you can't say a word about this to your dad."

"Don't worry, I won't."

Aaron hung up and drove home.

***

Since it was his birthday eve, Ryan decided to go to the bar for a little while and hang out with his bandmates. At one point, one of the band members walked up to Ryan and said, "May I speak with you for a moment?" He nodded his head to one side, indicating that he wanted to step away from the group for a private conversation. Then he said, "Hi! I'm Paul."

"You play flute, right?"

"That's right. Also, I happen to be a medium. You know, someone who can communicate with spirits."

Ryan looked at him skeptically. "Okay..."

"I know not everybody believes in what I do, and it's okay if you don't."

"Actually, there was a guy I lived with in college who was a medium. There were a couple of times he had messages for other guys

I lived with. So yeah, I'm familiar with what a medium is."

"Okay. Well, there's a spirit who shows up for you at band practice almost every week. Would you like to know more? If you'd rather not, that's fine."

"Sure, why not?"

"It's a woman. She stands right behind you to your right, like she's looking over your shoulder. A couple of times when she's seen me looking at her she'll say something like, 'I love listening to him play.' Or, 'He's so good, isn't he?'"

Ryan asked, "Any idea who it is?"

"I think she's your mother. Has your mother passed away?"

"I don't know."

Paul looked puzzled.

Ryan said, "I'm not in touch with my parents. But she's only in her late 40s. I wouldn't think she'd be dead yet."

Paul said, "Well, maybe it's your grandmother. But she has a strong maternal presence. Anyway, tonight she said something else. She said, 'Would you please ask him to take care of Brandon?'"

Ryan froze. His mouth dropped open and he stared at the wall behind Paul.

Paul asked, "Does that make any sense?"

"I don't know." Ryan paused. Thoughts raced through his head. "Brandon is my younger brother."

For a moment, neither of them said anything. Then Paul said, "Oh, and she asked me to wish you a happy birthday. Is today your birthday?"

"It's tomorrow. Close enough."

"Well, then happy birthday! From me, as well as your mother. Can I buy you a drink?"

"Thanks, but no. I don't think I'll stick around much longer. But please let me know if you hear anything else."

"I will." Paul smiled and rejoined his group of friends.

Ryan turned and walked toward the door without saying goodnight to anyone.

Surprise!

Friday, October 14, 2016

Ryan arrived at Aaron's apartment at 5:45. Aaron was exuberant when he opened the door and exclaimed, "Happy Birthday!" He gave Ryan an enthusiastic hug and kiss.

Ryan said, "Well, you're happy."

"Of course! It's your birthday!"

Ryan looked at Aaron suspiciously, then hesitantly walked into the living room.

Aaron asked, "What's wrong?"

After a moment passed and nobody leaped out from behind the furniture or the bedroom doors and yelled, 'Surprise!', Ryan relaxed. "I guess you didn't plan a surprise party for me."

"No, of course not. I said I didn't. What made you think I planned a party for you?"

"Well, first you changed the location from the Brazilian steakhouse in Scottsdale to a place near here. And then when I got here you were so excited, like something's up."

"Nope! Anyway, shall we be on our way?"

"Sure."

***

At 7:20, they finished their dinner. As they were getting ready to leave the restaurant, Aaron said, "Wait here a moment. I have to pee." Aaron entered the men's room and disappeared into a stall. He pulled out his phone and texted Brandon.

Aaron rejoined Ryan and they drove back to Aaron's apartment. As they were driving through the parking lot, Ryan said, "Wait a minute! I think we just passed my mom's car! Back up."

Aaron said, "Err... it probably just looks like it." He pulled into his reserved parking spot.

Ryan got out and hurried back to the car. "Look! It has a decal on the back window for Eternal Savior Christian Church! And it has a Kansas license plate!"

"Wow. What a coincidence. But it's a Toyota Camry. There are millions of those. It probably belongs to someone else who went there. Maybe they're snowbirds. C'mon, let's go inside."

"No, that's definitely her car."

"Maybe she sold it to someone."

"This is freaky, man. What if they found out where I am? What if they're waiting for us at your apartment?" Ryan paused. "You didn't contact them, did you? Don't tell me you had them come out here to surprise me for my birthday. If you did, you and I are over!"

"No, no, no! No way I would do that. Look, I have no idea why that car is here. C'mon, let's go inside."

Ryan let it drop and followed Aaron to his apartment. He recalled the conversation he had last night with Paul. *If Paul was seeing my mother's spirit, that must mean she's dead. But then why would her car be here? Maybe they did sell it. Still, this is creepy.*

Once inside, Aaron led Ryan to a spot in the living room near the doors to the bedrooms. He put his hands on Ryan's shoulders and said, "Okay, wait right here while I get your present. It's kinda big, so I couldn't wrap it. So, close your eyes and don't open them until I say 'when.'"

Ryan rolled his eyes. "Seriously?"

"Oh, come on, humor me for a minute."

"All right." Ryan sighed and closed his eyes.

"No peeking!"

Aaron pulled out his phone and turned the camera on as he walked toward his office door. He opened it and waved for Brandon to come out. He pointed to a spot in front of Ryan. As soon as Brandon reached that spot, Aaron said, "Okay!"

Ryan opened his eyes and saw a 6' 7" young man standing in front of him. He looked confused. Aaron snapped a picture and said, "It's your brother!"

Ryan stared in disbelief. "Brandon?"

Brandon said, "The one and only."

"OMIGOD! OMIGOD! OMIGOD! OMIGOD!!!" Ryan rushed up and they threw their arms around each other.

The two long-separated brothers hugged each other like they were never going to let go. Tears streamed down their faces. It was the most beautiful thing Aaron had ever seen in his life. He snapped a couple more pictures, but then he let them have their moment.

Finally, Ryan took a step back. "Look at you! All grown up! Looks like you're a little taller than me! I guess I can't call you my little brother anymore."

Brandon smiled. "I will always be your little brother."

They hugged some more. Ryan spoke softly into Brandon's ear. "I love you. God, I've missed you so much."

Brandon whispered back, "I love you too. The last nine years have been really hard."

They released each other and Ryan asked, "Okay, so how did this happen?"

Brandon said, "Aaron found me on campus yesterday, after

basketball practice."

Ryan looked confused.

Aaron said, "I was searching the internet looking for articles about what happened to your dad, and I found an article from last March that said Brandon had signed a letter of intent to play basketball at ASU. And I thought, 'Oh my God, that means he's like five miles from here.' So I did some more searching and found out when and where they practice. So, as Brandon said, I went down to campus and hung out near the door to the arena until I saw him come out."

Brandon said, "At first, I couldn't believe it. I thought it was some sort of bad joke. But he knew too many things about you, so I decided he was for real."

Ryan turned to Aaron and said, "You and your internet detective work!"

Aaron said, "Paid off, though, didn't it? Anyway, I bought a bottle of champagne for the occasion and there's birthday cake."

Ryan said, "I'm still stuffed from that 'carnivorgy' we just came from. I don't think I'll eat again for a week."

Aaron said, "Well, we can have the cake later. But let me pop open the champagne."

Brandon and Ryan followed Aaron into the kitchen. He pulled three champagne flutes from the freezer and a bottle of champagne from the refrigerator. He popped the cork and poured some into each glass. "Cheers! To birthdays and reunions!"

Ryan and Brandon said, "Cheers!" and they all clinked their glasses.

Brandon said, "This is the first time I've had champagne. It's... different."

Ryan said, "You're not 21 yet, but from what I hear, at ASU you're never too far from a drink."

Brandon said, "Oh, I've been drinking since I was a sophomore in high school."

"Seriously? Wow... things must have really changed around the house."

When they finished their champagne, Aaron said, "Why don't you guys sit down in the living room? I know you have a lot to catch up on. Do you want anything else to drink?"

Ryan said, "Just a Dr Pepper for now."

Brandon said, "Me too, please."

Ryan and Brandon walked into the living room and sat down. Aaron served their drinks and said, "I'll leave you guys alone for a little while so you can talk. I'll go catch up on my email and Facebook." When he launched Facebook, he saw that he had received a friend request from Brandon, which he accepted. He opened a message to Chris and typed, 'You won't believe what just happened.'

Ryan said, "You know, I saw Mom's car out in the parking lot as we were driving in. That totally freaked me out. I thought maybe they found me and they came out here to get me or something. But now it makes sense – they let you have it."

Brandon's expression changed to sadness. "Well, I guess we should get this out of the way now."

"What...?"

"Mom died about two and a half years ago. It was in February during my sophomore year. So when I turned 16 a couple of months later, Dad let me have the car."

Ryan scooted closer and put his arm around Brandon's shoulder. "Oh my God! I'm so sorry! What happened?"

"Well... things went downhill quickly after you left. It just ruined Mom. Dad was totally focused on his church and his book deals, and he started getting speaking gigs and all that. So he was away more, and he never seemed too concerned that you were gone. At least he didn't show it. So Mom had to grieve alone. They fought constantly. She was depressed all the time. She went to a psychiatrist who put her on anti-depressants. She was supposed to take them only when she needed them, but she ended up taking them all the time. She started drinking, too."

"Really? Mom drank?"

"Yeah, mostly wine."

"I'm surprised Brad let her get away with that. But then, he had a bottle of bourbon hidden behind the safe in his office."

"She got to the point where she didn't care what he said she could or couldn't do. And he knew he couldn't say anything to stop her."

"That's such a shame. I'm surprised they didn't get a divorce."

"I think she wanted to, but she had to play the role of the good pastor's wife. It would have looked really bad for him, being the big hotshot preacher that he was. So they held it together. I think they stayed together for me."

"Yeah, probably."

"But he knew he couldn't do anything to cross her, or she'd go public. Apparently, there were some things she knew that he didn't want to get out in the open. Anyway, I wish they would have just gone ahead and gotten the divorce. They would have both been happier and who knows? Mom might still be alive today. Anyway, at one point, her doctor changed her meds. Either he neglected to mention that one of the side effects was having suicidal thoughts, or she didn't care. Anyway, a week or so after she started taking it, she walked down to the garage and started the car. She died of carbon monoxide poisoning."

"Oh my God, that's horrible! And that must have been devastating for you."

"Yeah, it was. Throughout it all, she did her best to be a good mother to me – and she was. 'Cause you know, Dad was always off doing his own thing. Anyway, after that, I was on my own a lot, 'cause he'd always be going off to speaking gigs or conventions or rallies or whatever the hell they were. So I kinda got out of control – you know, drinking, smoking pot, having sex – all kinds of stuff. But at least I kept my grades up."

"Wow. Part of me can't believe you did all that stuff. But on the other hand, once I got out on my own, I started drinking and having sex too. I never smoked pot, but I did have a brownie once."

Brandon continued. "And one Friday night each month, Dad would stay out real late, like until two or three in the morning. He said he was at a 'men's night,' and now we know what that was all about."

"So Brad was actually gay. That son of a bitch. I can't believe he did all that stuff to me when he was gay himself."

"Yeah, well, he had to hide it. He was the pastor of Kansas's largest mega-church. He had books and speaking gigs. He couldn't have all that and be gay at the same time – or even have a gay son."

"The hypocrisy is unbelievable."

"Yeah. Oh, and you know that Dr. Babcock they sent you to for counseling? Well, get this. He was arrested at that orgy too. And as it turned out, he and Dad were boyfriends back when they were roommates in college."

"No shit! How did you find that out?"

"Mom told me one time when she was drunk. When Mom and I got back from Tulsa, apparently she found out they had sex in her bed while we were gone."

"Noooo....!"

"Yep."

"God, I hated him enough already, and now this. I swear to God, if I ever see his disgusting face again, I'm gonna beat the shit outta him."

Brandon said, "And get this. Dr. Babcock was the youth pastor at the church."

"Jesus Christ! Talk about leaving the fox to watch the chicken coop. God, that guy was such a creep. And he was queer as a three-dollar bill. It was so obvious."

"His wife divorced him after she found out about those 'men's nights.' She and their three daughters moved back to South Carolina, where her family was from. She also found out I was banging one of her daughters."

"WHAT???"

"Like I said, I was out of control. She was also pretty rebellious. Decent-looking, too. Nice boobs. But enough of that. Tell me about you. What's happened to you over all these years?"

Ryan took a deep breath. "Okay, well, where to start? At the beginning, I guess. So, you remember that day when Mom suddenly took you to Tulsa?"

"How could I ever forget? I knew something wasn't right. That trip came up all of a sudden, and she was acting really strange."

"Yeah. Well, I went to the church to do my usual thing where I got the PowerPoint slides ready for the service the next day. When I got there, I could hear Brad in his office talking to someone on the phone. They were talking about making airplane reservations and going to Montgomery, Alabama. And I remember thinking that was strange because he never said anything about going anywhere. Anyway, after he was off the phone, I knocked on the door, and he seemed like he was caught off-guard by my being there. Then I came home, and Mom was whisking you away, and I could tell something was up. So I logged onto the church's web hosting account and looked in his email box. I saw a bunch of emails back and forth between him and Babcock about going to Montgomery the next day. And the really scary thing was that they bought round-trip tickets for them and a one-way ticket for me! Then I saw some emails about this place they were going to take me. It was called the Youth Restoration Project. It was this remote place where they tried to use some kind of 'gay conversion therapy' to turn kids straight."

Brandon said, "I remember in that letter you left me, you said they were going to send you to someplace really bad."

"Yeah, that was it. Anyway, remember I had that summer job at Price Cutter?" Brandon nodded. "My boss there, Mr. Simonton, was gay. So I rode my bike to the store as fast as I could and showed him all that stuff. He heard about those kinds of places and said there was no way I should let them take me there. Anyway, we decided the only real choice I had was to run away. He used to live in Los Angeles and he still had some friends there, So he made arrangements with them to let me stay there for at least the first couple of weeks. So I rode back home and threw a bunch of stuff in a couple of suitcases, then he came and picked me up. Later that night, he took me to the bus station, and I rode a bus to LA. When I got there on Monday morning, I went to this place called the Los Angeles LGBT Youth Project. Mr. Simonton told me they had volunteer attorneys there who would help me change my name and get emancipated from my parents. So they hooked me up with an attorney named Hal Morris. As it turned out, Hal owned a house a few blocks from UCLA, and he had four bedrooms he rented out to gay college guys. He had an empty room, so he offered it to me."

Brandon said, "Wow... that worked out well."

"Yeah, no kidding. That was such a random coincidence, and I totally lucked into it. I guess somebody was looking out for me. Anyway, I lived there for five years – my senior year of high school and the four years I went to UCLA. And Hal and the other three guys who lived there became my new family. They gave me so much love and support, I don't know what I would have done without them. I mean, think about it. I was a 17-year-old kid from Kansas who had just run away from home. There I was in the big city all by myself, not knowing anybody. It could have turned out so much worse."

"So how did you like UCLA? And Los Angeles, for that matter."

"UCLA was great, although I didn't get to enjoy college the same way most other kids do. It would have been different if I lived in a dorm instead of living off-campus. And I had to work to support myself, so I wasn't able to be in the marching band or do very many other extra-curricular activities."

"Where did you work?"

Ryan took a deep breath. *Might as well tell him the truth now and get it over with.* "Okay, well, I've got something to tell you that you might not believe. I have no idea how you're going to react to this. But it's the truth, and I'm not going to hide it from you. So here goes. I needed to make a lot of money, because I had to support myself and save for college. I got a scholarship that covered some of it, but I still needed to come up with a lot of money. At first, I got a job at a grocery store making $10 an hour, but pretty soon it became obvious that wasn't going to cut it." Ryan paused. "So I did porn."

Ryan stopped talking and waited to see Brandon's reaction.

"So... you mean you..."

"I had sex on camera for adult videos."

"With men or women?"

"Mostly men. I did a few videos with women. But that's not really my thing, obviously."

"So... what was it like?"

"It was a job. I mean, yes, I got to have sex, but it wasn't really fun like it is in real life. It certainly wasn't a loving, emotional experience. But it was like making any other kind of movie, where they do multiple takes and they're always fussing with camera angles or lighting or whatever. There's a lot of waiting around. And the director tells you what to do and what positions to be in and even when he wants you to cum. So you're just acting out a role with someone you may or may not find attractive. Anyway, it paid well and I needed the money, so I did it. I'm not proud of it but I'm not ashamed of it either. It's just ... well ... it's what I had to do."

"I always thought it would be cool to do porn."

"That's what a lot of guys think. Like it's an easy way to get laid and get paid. But again, you're not doing this for pleasure. You're an actor playing a role. You're just doing a job."

Brandon said, "Okay, so... how do I say this?" He grinned. "If you're anything like me, I bet you're well-qualified for the job."

"Yes, having a big dick helped. I was definitely in demand. After I got known in the business, I had all the job offers I wanted."

"Do you still do it?"

"Nope. I quit before I graduated. Never again. I have a good job that pays all the money I need."

"Do you have any of the videos you're in?"

"A few. I never watch them. I don't even know why I still hang onto them. And no, I'm not going to let you watch them. That would be, like, totally weird. Plus, I don't think it's the kind of sex you'd want to watch anyway."

"Oh, I don't know. The idea of two guys doin' it doesn't bother me. I mean, I knew you and Chris were gay, and I figured you guys did stuff with each other. That didn't bother me."

"Well, whatever. That's all in the past. So, I need to ask you something. And be honest with me here. Does it bother you that your older brother, whom you used to look up to so much, has starred in porn videos?"

"No, not at all. I understand why you had to do it. And to be honest, I'm a little bit jealous of you."

"Don't be. Seriously. Anyway, I'm glad you're okay with it. I mean, on the one hand, it's not like I need your approval. But I'm glad it won't stand in the way of us having a good relationship again."

"Oh, not at all!"

"Okay, well, let's move on."

Brandon said, "Okay. So... Speaking of Chris... What happened with you and him?"

"Well, when I ran away that meant I had to leave him behind too. I couldn't let anyone know where I was, 'cause I figured the police would be trying to find me to bring me back home. I sent him a Christmas card every year, too. Anyway, he ended up going to the University of Maryland. We reconnected during our freshman year, but he already had a boyfriend he met there. And when he found out about the porn, he couldn't handle it. I didn't hear from him again for a long time after that. In hindsight, I should have gotten back in touch with him sooner. We had talked about going to UCLA together, and maybe we could have. But on the other hand, I still would have had to do porn to make enough money. I don't think we could have maintained a relationship with me doing that. But anyway, we went our own ways. But a couple of months ago, he and his partner came out here to visit. His partner's family lives in Glendale, and it was his grandmother's 80th birthday, so they came out for that. And Chris and I got together and talked, and we worked a lot of stuff out. Then the four of us got together before they left. That was kinda weird, but at least we all know each other now."

Brandon said, "That's too bad that it didn't work out for you guys. You two were so much in love. I really liked him. I hoped the two of you would spend your lives together and get married and everything."

"Yeah, me too. I was bitter about it for a long time. I'll never forgive Brad for what he did, especially because it meant I was separated from you and Chris. For a long time, I thought I'd never meet another guy like Chris and I'd probably be single for the rest of my life. The fact that I used to do porn was a deal-breaker for some guys." Ryan lowered his voice. "In fact, Aaron and I almost broke up over it back in July. But we worked through that. And he's the first guy since Chris I think I can be happy with for the rest of my life. So I'm hopeful."

"He seems really nice. And he's kind of like Chris in some ways."

"I think so too."

Brandon said, "And of course, he brought us back together!"

"Yeah! I'll never be able to thank him enough for that. And... he got me to start playing my trumpet again."

"You mean you quit?"

"Yeah, for like four years. I couldn't be in the marching band at UCLA because I had to work. But they had a jazz ensemble that rehearsed two afternoons a week, and I could do that. So I played throughout college. But when I moved here to start my job, I got so wrapped up in beginning my career and finding a place to live and getting settled into my new life, I never took the time to find a band I could join. As it turns out, there's an LGBT band here. Well, really two bands – a symphonic band and a jazz ensemble. I started playing in both of them back in July."

"That's great. You were so good! God, I remember those times when you'd practice with those play-along jazz CDs. And sometimes Chris would come over and both of you would play. I loved sitting there and listening to you guys."

"Yeah. You were my number one fan."

"I still am. You can never stop playing your trumpet."

"Well, thanks."

"Do you still have those play-along CDs?"

"Yeah, I do. In fact, I dug them out and started playing with them again last summer when I was getting ready to join the band."

Brandon asked, "What does Aaron play?"

"Trombone. He's pretty good, too."

"Do you and he ever practice together?"

"No, we haven't yet. And he's not in the jazz ensemble. It rehearses on Monday night, and he always has to work. So what about you? I remember that day we were driving home from the concert at the end of my junior year. You said you wanted to play trumpet, and we decided you should take a couple years of piano first. Did you ever do that?"

"Yeah. I took two years of piano from Mrs. Schultz. I started teaching myself to play that trumpet you left for me, using the method books you left. But then Mom told me I couldn't play it anymore. She'd hear it and think of you, and that would set her off on another bout of depression. So when band started in fifth grade, I asked if I could play sax, 'cause that's what Chris played. I started on alto, but the band director moved me to baritone 'cause they already had a bunch of altos and they needed someone to play baritone. And he figured I could handle it easier than the other kids because I was so tall."

"How did you like it?"

"It was pretty good. I liked being in band, but I don't think I'll ever be as good as you are. And when I started playing basketball, that took up a lot of my time."

Ryan asked, "Do you still have it?"

"Yeah. It's back at home. I still have your old trumpet too."

"You should bring your sax with you next time you go home. I'm sure there are bands at ASU you can play in."

"Yeah, but it would be hard to do that and play basketball. Our practices started at the beginning of October, and the season runs at least until March, depending on whether we get into the NCAA tournament and how long we last."

"You're probably right. I didn't think of that."

Brandon said, "But what about your band? Is it only for gay people?"

"No, anyone can join, as long as you're supportive."

"I could do that, at least from March through September."

"Really? You'd do that?"

"Of course! That's something I can do with you and Aaron."

Ryan said, "Well, cool. So hey, on the topic of doing stuff together, what are your Sunday evenings like?"

"I'm usually free. That's one of the few times I don't have classes or practices or games."

"Well, why don't you come up to my house in Scottsdale and have dinner with us every Sunday? That's one thing Hal did back at that house I lived in. He'd fix dinner for everyone on Sunday and we'd all get together and talk about whatever was going on. Then we'd watch a movie or play games or something. It was like a family night. I decided I wanted to carry on that tradition. So every Sunday evening, I cook a nice meal. It's usually nothing fancy, just pizza or burgers or chicken or something. Sometimes I invite a friend or two over and sometimes I just eat by myself. Now that I have Aaron, we do that every week. Now that you're here, well, you're family and it would be great to have you there too."

"That sounds great! There may be a week here or there I'd have to miss, but I should be able to make it most of the time."

"Well, of course. Can you come this Sunday?"

Brandon said, "Yeah, I think so. Oh, and I get two comp tickets to each home game. If you guys ever want to come and see a basketball game..."

"I'd love to! When are they?"

"It varies. In November and December, we have non-conference games. They're all over the place. Once the Pac-12 season gets started in January, there's usually a game on Wednesday or Thursday and another one on Saturday or Sunday. I'll send you the schedule."

Ryan said, "Thursdays are kind of iffy because of band practice. If it's early in the season we can skip band, but if it's close to a concert we probably shouldn't. And Aaron's work schedule might get in the way a few times, but I could do it."

"That's okay. I don't expect you to come to every game."

"Yeah, but I'd like to come to as many as I can."

Brandon said, "Man! This is so great. I am so happy! I mean, I was really looking forward to going to college and, to be honest, getting away from Kansas. But I had no idea coming here meant I'd be reunited with you!"

"I know! I still can't believe it. It's gonna be so great! You know, I've lived through a lot of shit over the past nine years. There's been some good times and good people, but a lot of things didn't turn out the way I wish they could have. And since I moved to Scottsdale and started my job, well, that's been good. I really like my job and I really like living here and my house and everything, but... well, like I said, I assumed I'd probably spend my life being single. But this year, I met Aaron, I started playing my trumpet again, I reconnected with Chris, and now we're back together! Suddenly, everything's going great!"

"Yeah, I know what you mean. It hasn't been easy for me either. It wasn't how I thought things would go. First, you left. Then Mom and Dad's marriage fell apart, Mom started battling depression, then she died. And now this mess with Dad."

Ryan said, "Yeah, none of that made for a very happy childhood, did it?"

"Nope. I did the best I could, though."

"Okay, so here's something else we need to talk about. Now that you're out here, and given what just happened back in Kansas, how much contact do you plan to have with Brad?"

"I don't know. We were never close. He never paid much attention to me even after Mom died. Now with the mess he got himself into, and now that I'm reminded of everything he did to you, I kinda don't want to have anything to do with him. But even though I got a scholarship, he's still helping me pay for college. So I can't just shut him off completely."

"I wouldn't expect you to. But honestly, I don't ever want to see his face or hear from him again. He's dead to me."

"I noticed you've been calling him Brad, not Dad."

"As far as I'm concerned, he stopped being my father when he was going to send me away to the Youth Restoration Project. I mean, who would do that to their own son?"

"I get it. I really do. I'm no fan of his, either."

Ryan said, "So anyway, please don't say anything to him about me. Nothing. Not that I live here, or that we're together again, or anything else."

"Okay, I won't."

"I'm sorry. I know that's going to be awkward. It puts you in the middle. I have no right to tell you not to have contact with him, or how much or what kind of contact you can have with him. That's all up to you."

"I get it."

Ryan said, "Well, hey, it's getting late, and there's birthday cake. I'm sure Aaron would like to come out of his office and rejoin us."

They got up and walked toward the kitchen. Ryan swung by Aaron's office door and knocked.

"Yeah?"

Ryan opened the door. "Hey! I think we're ready for some birthday cake now!"

Aaron stood up and walked toward the door. "Chris says hi, by the way. I told him what happened. He's happy for you."

"Cool. Tell him hi for me next time you see him online."

"And he says happy birthday."

They entered the kitchen and Ryan and Brandon sat down at the table. Aaron brought out a cake with two candles shaped like the numbers 2 and 7. He found his barbeque grill lighter in a drawer and lit the candles. "Make a wish!"

Ryan thought for a moment. "I don't know. Seriously, I don't know. I have you, I'm reunited with my brother, Chris and I are friends again... I don't know what else I could wish for."

Aaron said, "Well, think of something before wax starts dripping onto the cake."

Ryan thought a moment longer. "Okay, I've got it." He easily blew out the two candles.

Brandon said, "I can't believe you're 27. Last time I saw you, you were 17."

"I know, right? And last time I saw you, you were 9. And you were about five feet tall. I still can't believe I can look you straight in the eye now."

As the three men sat around the table eating cake, they talked about what classes Brandon was taking, how he liked ASU, and how Aaron and Ryan met.

There was a brief pause. Ryan glanced at Aaron and smiled. Aaron smiled back and winked. Brandon noticed their silent exchange and said, "Well, I should get back. I've got a full day tomorrow, and something tells me you want to ... keep celebrating."

Ryan and Aaron chuckled. Ryan said, "You could say that. But on the other hand, I hate to have this visit come to an end."

Brandon said, "Don't worry. I'll see you on Sunday. And we'll have lots of other times to catch up some more."

"Yeah, you're right. I know you're going to be busy with classes and basketball and all your college friends, but I hope we can find time to spend together. I don't want to not have you in my life ever again."

"Me neither." Brandon turned to Aaron. "And I want to get to know you better, too. I'm really glad you two found each other. And thank you so much for what you did to bring us back together!"

Ryan said, "Seriously. This has been the happiest day of my life!"

Ryan and Brandon hugged each other tightly for at least ten seconds. Ryan whispered, "I love you."

Brandon whispered back, "I love you too."

Then Brandon turned and hugged Aaron. "Thanks again."

Aaron replied, "You're welcome."

Ryan said, "I'll text you my address. See you Sunday at around 6:00."

"I can't wait!"

Aaron opened the door. Brandon walked out, turned around and waved, then continued toward his car. Aaron closed the door and turned to face Ryan.

Ryan said, "You're incredible. I don't know how I can ever

thank you enough for what you have given me today."

Aaron said, "Well, let's see... You could spend the rest of your life with me. That would be one way."

Ryan smiled and said, "How did you know that was what I wished for?"

Aaron said, "And there's another way you can thank me right now." He took Ryan's hand and led him into his bedroom.

Encore!

Saturday, October 15, 2016

At 7:15, Ryan was gently awakened by the sunlight peeking around the edges of the curtains in Aaron's bedroom. They were spooning on their right sides, Aaron in front of Ryan. Ryan's arm lay across Aaron's waist and rested against his stomach. His morning wood pressed against Aaron's back. As he gazed fondly at Aaron's left shoulder and the back of his head, he reflected on the surprise reunion with Brandon that Aaron had made possible. He leaned forward and lightly kissed Aaron on the neck.

Aaron stirred. He turned his head to the left enough to see Ryan out of the corner of his eye. "Well, hello! Fancy meeting you here."

"There's no place I'd rather be." As Ryan leaned forward to kiss Aaron's cheek, Aaron felt Ryan's erection pressing against him.

"Good God! The day's just getting started and you're horny already?"

"How can you blame me? I have the most wonderful man in the world right here in my arms."

"You mean last night wasn't enough for you?"

"That was then, this is now. Let's not live in the past." Ryan wiggled forward to press himself more tightly against Aaron. He stroked Aaron's chest with his left hand and brushed against his nipples. "What time do you have to be at work?"

"9:00."

"Oh, good. We have at least an hour."

Aaron rolled onto his back so he could kiss Ryan more easily. Ryan worked his right arm under his neck.

After a few kisses, Ryan whispered, "Thanks again for

everything you did yesterday. I had the best birthday ever!"

Aaron smiled. "I'm glad I could make you happy."

Ryan lowered his left hand to Aaron's crotch and started gently fondling his hardening cock. "Now what can I possibly do to thank you?"

"Oh, like it's only about me."

Ryan gave Aaron's cock a gentle squeeze. "Your hap-penis is my number one concern."

Aaron rolled his eyes. "You're a giver, that's your crime."

"Who says there can't be something in it for me?"

Aaron propped himself up on his left elbow. "There's going to be something in, all right. Let's start with you on your stomach."

***

An hour later, as they lay in each other's arms with their afterglow gradually receding, Aaron said, "Crap! It's 8:15. We have to get up now."

"Yeah, I could probably get it up now."

Aaron jumped out of bed. "You know what I mean. Jesus, you're insatiable."

"And that's a problem?"

"Right now it is. C'mon, get up. Would you fix breakfast while I grab a quick shower? You can take your shower after I leave."

"You mean we can't take one together?"

"No. 'Cause in your current state we'd be in there for half an hour. Could you fix some scrambled eggs?"

"Sure. I'm starving."

"Starving? Last night you were complaining that you were stuffed. We ate so much food at that place."

"Oh, I never complain about being stuffed."

"Shut! Up! Do you want bacon or sausage?"

"MMMmmm... Well, if you're offering sausage..."

Aaron rolled his eyes. "Oh, geez. I can't even with you."

Ryan walked up to Aaron and kissed him. "I'm sorry. I'll behave. But I love you! And I'm happier than I've been in years."

"Good. I love you too. Bacon or sausage?"

"Bacon."

"Okay. You know where everything is. I'll be out in fifteen minutes."

***

Aaron ate quickly. In between bites, he asked, "So what have you got going today?"

Ryan replied, "I've got a bunch of errands I need to run, laundry to do, and I want to practice my trumpet. Would you like to come up to my house for dinner after you get off work? Then we can spend the night."

"Sure."

Ryan said, "Okay, sounds like a plan."

Aaron shoveled a few more bites into his mouth, then chugged the rest of his orange juice. "I've gotta run. If you can just put the plates and stuff in the dishwasher, I'll wash the skillet when I get home. I love you." He gave Ryan a quick kiss on the lips.

Ryan said, "I love you too. Have a good day and I'll see you at around 6:30."

Aaron hurried out the door.

Ryan finished eating, loaded the dishwasher, and washed the skillet.

Sadness

Saturday, October 15, 2016

During the drive home, Ryan replayed everything that had happened in the last 15 hours. He still couldn't believe he and Brandon were reunited and living in the same city. He was still trying to wrap his head around the fact that Brandon was grown up now. For the past nine years, whenever Ryan thought of Brandon he held onto the mental image of a nine-year-old boy, with an unchanged voice to match. Now Brandon was an inch taller than Ryan, with a rich, deep voice much like his. After hearing about Brandon's high school years, he knew Brandon had lost most of his nine-year-old innocence. But Ryan certainly had his share of experiences, too, and could lay no claim to innocence.

He thought of all the ways his life had just changed because Brandon was back in it. Now there would be basketball games to attend. Brandon would be part of family night, at least some of the time. And he'd finally be able to spend holidays with him again – at least when Brandon wasn't spending them with his dad.

Then Ryan started thinking about his mother and her passing. He tried to imagine how her life must have been after he left. What must it have been like for his mother to suddenly lose one of her sons? No wonder she was miserable.

The more he thought about his mother, the sadder he became.

***

When Aaron arrived at Ryan's house shortly after 6:30, Ryan seemed subdued. Aaron asked, "What's wrong? After how things went this morning, I expected to be pounced on the moment I walked in the door."

"I have a lot on my mind. Let's talk about it after we eat. I don't feel like cooking. Can we just get a pizza delivered?"

"Yeah, sure."

"I'd like to get in the hot tub later. Is that okay?"

"Of course."

Ryan phoned in a pizza order, then walked outside and raised the thermostat on the hot tub.

As they were eating, Ryan said, "So I invited Brandon to dinner tomorrow night. I hope that's okay."

"Of course. I mean, it's your dinner at your house."

"I know, but you're part of it too. We're a couple. But I figured it's family night and he's family, so I'm hoping he can come for dinner on Sunday night whenever his schedule allows."

"Sure. After being apart for so many years, it makes sense that you want to spend a lot of time with him now. You have a lot of catching up to do."

"Good. I just want to make sure I'm still spending enough quality time with you."

"I appreciate that. But it's okay. You need to spend time with him, too. And I like him. I want us to get to know each other, too."

Ryan said, "Okay, good. So, I've been thinking. How are we going to spend Thanksgiving and Christmas? We've talked about going to see your parents in Ohio. But now that Brandon's in the picture..."

"Won't he be going back to Kansas to see his father?"

"I don't know. It might depend on when he has basketball games. Oh, by the way... He can get two comp tickets to every home game. He said we can go see him play whenever we want. We don't have to go to every game, but I'd like to go to at least some of them."

"Yeah, that would be fun. I enjoyed going to basketball games at Ohio State. What nights are they?"

"He sent me the schedule. I'll forward it to you. But he said after the first of the year there is usually a game on Wednesday or Thursday evening, and another one on Saturday or Sunday."

Aaron said, "Well, I don't want to miss band practices very often, and I'll have to work every other weekend until I can get a new job. But I'm sure we can find some nights that work. Speaking of which, I applied at the pharmacy at several Food Worlds here in Scottsdale. I have an interview in the one near here next Thursday."

"Awesome! I know you'll do well."

"I hope so. I want to work more reasonable hours. Anyway, if I don't get that and I'm still working at HealthPro, I'm going to have to work Thanksgiving weekend. We'll be closed on Thanksgiving day, but I'll have to work the rest of the weekend. Charlie will work the days surrounding Christmas so I can have a few days off to go to Ohio."

Ryan said, "Okay, so hopefully we'll be able to have Thanksgiving here with Brandon."

"Yeah, I hope so too."

They ate in silence for a few minutes. There was something else Aaron wanted to discuss, but he could tell Ryan had something serious on his mind, so he wasn't sure if this was the right time. Finally, he decided to go ahead with it. "So, I've been thinking. It's been almost three months since we worked everything out after our trip to San Diego and my trip to Ohio. And, I don't know about you, but I think things are moving along pretty well."

"Yeah. I'm happy with how things are going."

"And, uh, we just talked about our plans for the holidays and how Brandon's going to become part of our lives. And I'm really looking forward to having you meet my parents. I know they can't wait to meet you."

"Yeah..."

"So it seems like, you know, we're blending our lives together. Like both of us are planning on continuing with this relationship. I know I'm happier than I've ever been. And we've been spending a lot of nights together either here or at my place."

Ryan said, "Yeah, right. So quit beating around the bush. Where are you going with this?"

"Well, I was wondering when you think it would be the right

time for us to start, you know... moving in together."

Ryan smiled for the first time in hours. "I thought that was what you were leading up to. Anyway, I don't know. I've never moved in with a guy before. I've never gotten this far into a relationship."

"Me neither. But if I get that job at the Food World near here, they'd probably want me to start in mid to late November."

"It's not lost on me why you applied for jobs in Scottsdale."

"And just by coincidence, the lease on my apartment comes up for renewal at the end of the year..."

"Well, isn't *that* convenient?"

Aaron shrugged and smiled.

Ryan thought for a moment and said, "By mid to late November, we will have been together for four months. On the one hand, that seems kind of soon. But on the other hand, why not? I think we're both pretty sure this thing is going to work out."

Aaron said, "Since you own this house and I'm renting, I figured it makes more sense for me to move in with you."

"Yeah, probably so."

"Of course, I'd pay for half of the utilities and half of the food, and some amount each month to help with the mortgage."

"We can figure all that out later. But yeah. Why don't we plan on you moving in sometime between Thanksgiving and Christmas?"

Aaron got up from the table and hurried around to Ryan's side. He leaned down and kissed Ryan and put his arms around his shoulders. "Thanks, sweetheart!"

"You're welcome."

"I love you."

"I love you too." Ryan smiled again. Aaron walked back around to his chair and sat down. He transferred the last slice of his half of the pizza onto his plate.

"I can bring a few things with me each time I come."

"Yeah. I'll clear out half of the closet in the master bedroom. We can talk about where we'll put the rest of your stuff later."

They finished their pizza and got up from the table. Ryan said,

"Will you please put the plates in the dishwasher? I'll go see if the hot tub is ready." He went out and came back in. "Still a couple of degrees to go, but by the time we get out there, it should be ready. You want some wine?"

"Yeah, sure."

Ryan selected a Pinot Grigio and poured some into two clear plastic wine glasses. They removed their clothes and carried their wine glasses out to the hot tub. Ryan didn't seem interested in sex – a dramatic shift from his behavior that morning.

After they were settled in, Aaron said, "Okay. So what's on your mind?"

Ryan took a sip and swirled the wine in his mouth a little longer than usual. He took a deep breath, then began. "After the excitement of last night started to wear off, I got to thinking about my mom. Brandon said she started getting depressed after I left. She and my father started fighting, which they never did before – at least not in front of Brandon and me. She started drinking, which I can't believe she would do. The psychologist she was seeing prescribed antidepressants for her. According to Brandon, as time went on she took more and more of them. It's like she was depressed all the time and drank and took drugs to keep herself numb. Then her doctor switched her to a different med, and that one caused her to have suicidal thoughts. One day, she went down to the garage and started the car and sat there until she died of carbon monoxide poisoning."

"Brandon mentioned that when we first met. That's so awful!"

"Yeah. That happened right before Brandon turned 16." Ryan started sniffling. "I can't help thinking that if I hadn't run away, or if I had gotten back in touch with them at some point, then maybe none of that would have happened. She would probably still be alive today."

Aaron said, "Maybe. But it's not your fault. You didn't have any way of knowing all that stuff was happening. You didn't make her take those drugs. It's tragic, but you can't blame yourself."

"Yes, I can. I was so hard-headed about never seeing them again. If I had gotten back in touch with them at some point, this probably wouldn't have happened."

"I understand. Looking back on it, I realize I made a mistake by shutting my parents off. When my mom got cancer, they couldn't get in touch with me to let me know because I had blocked their calls. Thank God my aunt was able to get through."

"Yeah, but at least your parents came around and accepted that you're gay. I don't think my parents were ever going to do that. At least not Brad."

Aaron asked, "Do you think your mom knew your dad was gay?"

"Yeah. Right after I left, she found out he slept with that creepy 'pray the gay away' dude they sent me to for counseling. In their bed, no less."

"You're shitting me!"

"I wish I was. It just goes to show you, the biggest homophobes are usually the biggest closet cases. He and my dad knew each other in college, and it turns out they were roommates and boyfriends for three years."

"Don't you think she would be depressed after she found out her husband was gay?"

"Yeah, probably. That makes sense. I mean, I never sensed they were that close romantically, if you know what I mean. That became obvious after I started hanging out at Chris's house. His parents were totally in love with each other. They went out for date nights a couple of times a month. You could sense there was magic between them, and there was none of that magic with my parents. They just kind of went through the motions. Of course, they always put on the right appearances at church, but it was just an act."

Aaron said, "So she was probably unhappy with her marriage already, then she found out her husband was gay. So your disappearance wasn't the entire reason she was depressed."

"Maybe it wasn't the whole reason, but it was a big part of it. At least she had Brandon and me to live for. She was a really good mother. She had to be both a mom and a dad, 'cause he was always off doing stuff for the church."

"Do you think she would have been more accepting of you being gay?"

"She wasn't at the time. But I think if it came down to a choice between having to accept that I'm gay and not having me in her life, she'd choose to accept me."

"Okay, well let me ask you a difficult question. So now you're depressed because your mom died and you'll never get to see her again. And now you wish you had gotten back in touch with them, or at least her, because that might have prevented her from taking her life. But what if she hadn't died? What if she was alive and well today? Would you get back in touch with them?"

Ryan sat silently for a moment. Then he muttered, "I don't know."

"Up until now, you've been adamant about having no contact with them."

"Yeah, but I never imagined it would have such a brutal impact on her."

"But you did everything you could to make sure they couldn't find you. If they had changed their thinking, there was no way they could contact you to let you know."

"I guess it was kind of a no-win situation, huh?"

"That's a good way to put it. Nobody is winning here. You missed out on having Brandon in your life for nine years. Thankfully, that's over now, but that's nine years you'll never get back. You'll never see your mother again, and your disappearance is part of the reason. There's no way you can win that one now. That leaves your dad. What if you found out he had cancer or something, and he only had a short time to live?"

Ryan said, "I really don't give a shit about him. None of this would have happened if he wasn't going to force me to go to that gay conversion therapy camp. None of this would have happened if he had accepted that I'm gay. Yes, my mom's depression might have been partially my fault, but none of that would have happened if it wasn't for

Brad. It still boils down to being his fault."

"Even if it's all his fault, does that make you feel any better?"

"No."

"So then, does assigning fault and placing blame result in anything good?"

"No, I guess not."

"Okay, then, I'm going to suggest something radical. Forgive him."

"What? Forgive him? No way. No. Fucking. Way! Especially not now. Not after what he did to me, and knowing that what he did ultimately resulted in my mother's death. Plus, now I know he was cheating on her with other guys! He made her life miserable for years."

"But why don't you forgive him anyway?"

"That son of a bitch doesn't deserve forgiveness. I don't even consider him my father."

"Maybe he doesn't deserve forgiveness. But you wouldn't be forgiving him for him. You'd be forgiving him for you."

"What do you mean?"

"You'd be forgiving him so you can put this behind you once and for all. You've carried all this anger for years. That's not harming him, it's harming you. You can blame him all you want, but you're the one who's still carrying all this resentment."

"So you're saying I should call him up and say, 'Hey, Dad, remember me? It's Bryan, your son whom you never paid attention to. You know, the gay one you tried to have cured, even though you're a cocksucker yourself? Yeah, it's me. I'm just calling to say I forgive you. So now you're totally off the hook. Everything's just peachy keen again.'"

"You don't have to tell him you've forgiven him. Remember, you're doing this for you, not him. Although it would be a noble thing for you to do."

"I don't know..."

"Maybe you could be the bigger man here. Maybe you could do something for him that he could never do for you."

"What did I do that he needs to forgive me for? Are you saying I need to be forgiven for being gay?"

"No, of course not. I didn't mean him forgiving you. I meant he could never accept that you're gay."

"Fine, but I guess I don't see that it changes anything. All that stuff still happened either way. I still don't want to have any contact with him. So what difference will it make?"

"Maybe you'll be happier. Maybe you'll have one less burden to carry; one less thing to be angry about."

"I'm not angry."

"Yeah, actually, you are. Or at least resentful."

They sat in silence for a few minutes. Ryan finished his wine and said, "You want some more?"

"Yeah, sure."

Ryan climbed out of the hot tub, walked into the house, and returned with the bottle. He poured more into their glasses, then got back in. "So here's something I haven't told you yet. Thursday night after band, I went to the bar for a little while. You know that guy Paul who plays the flute?"

"Yeah..."

"He pulled me aside for a few minutes. He said he's a medium."

"Yeah, I remember him saying that the first night I went to band. That was his first night too. One of the guys sitting next to me joked that he had seen him in the restroom and that he was a large."

"Funny."

"So anyway, is that some kind of psychic or fortune teller or something?"

"Not quite. A medium is someone who can communicate with the spirits of people who have passed on."

Aaron laughed. "You don't really believe that bullshit, do you?"

"Actually, I do. I used to be skeptical too, and Brad used to always preach against that stuff. Of course, now I know he was wrong about everything else, so he's probably wrong about this too. But anyway, there was a guy who lived in my house in LA the last year I lived there. His name was Mykel. He was a medium. One time at Thanksgiving, Ted was there, and Mykel got a message from his former boyfriend who was killed in Afghanistan. And he was able to get in touch with Hal's former partner, who died of AIDS back in the 80s."

"How do you know he wasn't making stuff up?"

"In Ted's case, he knew his boyfriend's name. Neither Ted nor anyone else had ever told him that, and it's not like he could find it on the internet. Same thing with Hal's late partner. He gave Hal that reading on the same day he met Hal, so he knew nothing about him before that day."

Aaron said, "Well, okay. So what did Paul tell you?"

"He said a woman comes to rehearsal each week and stands behind me while I play. She says she enjoys listening to me play and talks about how beautiful it sounds."

"Okay, so?"

"He says it's my mother."

"How do you know it's really her? How do you know there's even someone there? Maybe he's just imagining things."

"I don't know. I didn't know whether to believe him at first. Remember, on Thursday night I didn't know she had died. Then yesterday, I found out she had. But on Thursday night, she said, 'Would you please ask him to take care of Brandon?' Remember, at that time, I had no idea I was going to meet him the next day. And then she asked Paul to wish me a happy birthday. I never told Paul it was my birthday. Did you?"

"No."

"Okay, so all that's a pretty good indication it was really my mother he was communicating with."

Aaron said, "All right, let's say it is, just for the sake of argument. So, how does that change anything?"

Ryan thought about that for a moment. "It lets me know she wants to be around me. It means she's not mad at me. But I wonder what she meant when she asked me to take care of Brandon. He's a grown man now, he can take care of himself."

"Do you suppose Paul could ask her?"

"Yeah, maybe. I guess I could ask Paul if he can do that."

"Watch out! He'll probably want to charge you for it."

"I'd be fine with that. We pay people to do things for us all the time. I'd pay someone to give me trumpet lessons or clean my house or whatever."

"Well, call him and set up a time, if it means that much to you."

"I think I will. Do you have his number?"

"I don't think I have it on my phone, but we're friends on Facebook. He may have his number listed on his profile. If not, I can send him a message and ask him."

"Would you? I'd really appreciate it."

"Remind me when we go back in."

They sat in silence for a few more minutes. Aaron reached over and put his hand on Ryan's leg. Ryan held his hand and gave it a gentle squeeze.

Ryan said, "Sorry I haven't been in a better mood this evening."

"That's okay."

"Thank you for being here."

"There's no place I'd rather be."

"Really? Even when I'm in a shitty mood and I'm being all angry and resentful?"

"Really. We have to be here for each other all the time, not just when we're happy and everything's going well."

Ryan leaned over and kissed Aaron. "Thanks. That means a lot to me."

A moment later, Aaron said, "Plethora."

"Huh? What?"

"Plethora. That means a lot to me."

Ryan groaned. "That's awful. What a way to ruin a tender moment."

Aaron laughed. "Oh, come on. I think we needed a moment of levity. And that's just the sort of joke you would make."

"Yeah, you're probably right."

Aaron asked, "So... Is there anything else you want to talk about?"

"Actually, there is. I've been thinking about Brandon. He'll be here for dinner tomorrow night. And I'm really happy about that, and I'm happy we're going to be part of each other's lives again and everything, but... I wonder what we'll talk about? I mean, what can we talk about that isn't negative? I don't want to keep talking about all the shit that happened. That's going to get depressing fast."

Aaron thought about that for a moment. "Remember how, whenever I asked you something about your past, you'd say, 'I don't want to talk about my past. I'm only interested in today and tomorrow.'"

"Yeah."

"Well, doesn't that apply here?"

Ryan said, "Maybe, but when I avoided talking about uncomfortable things from the past, that didn't work out so well, did it? You had trouble trusting me because there was all that stuff I wouldn't talk about. Remember?"

"Yeah."

"I want to get our new relationship started on the right foot."

Aaron thought for a moment. "I think you just hit the nail right on the head."

"What do you mean?"

"You're starting a new relationship. You're different people now. He's not a little kid anymore, he's a grown man. You're not the same as you were in high school. From what you've told me, you were pretty innocent and naïve in high school, and you certainly aren't anymore. You had to learn how to live on your own and provide for yourself. You used to do porn. You've been through all kinds of things. And you said he's done a bunch of wild and crazy stuff in high school. So you're both different today than you were then. You shouldn't assume things are going to pick up where they left off. On one level, you know you love each other. But on another level, it's like you're totally different people now. You're now a 27-year-old software engineer who happens to be gay, and he's now an 18-year-old college freshman and basketball player. You need to approach this like you're getting to know each other all over again. You're brothers, biologically, but you're now two adults who are beginning a new journey together."

Ryan sat silently while he let that sink in. "Yeah, you're right. And I guess I shouldn't assume we're automatically going to be best friends. We may find out we don't have that much in common anymore."

"Yeah. And what if you find out he's a Republican and he's going to vote for Trump?"

"Oh God. I hadn't thought of that! I mean, our parents were Republicans. So was just about everyone in Kansas. So yeah, it's quite possible he is. At least I know he doesn't have an issue with me being gay."

"Here's another thing. Back then, he was still a little kid and you were almost grown up. He looked up to you almost like you were a father figure. But now you're both grown up. You've got a successful career going and he's just starting college, but still..."

"I get what you're saying. We're on more equal footing now."

"Yeah."

Ryan said, "So I wonder how we should go about starting this new relationship."

"I don't know. Maybe approach this the same way you approached getting to know your new friends in the band. Just talk about stuff going on in your lives and see where that leads. You'll probably find some common ground. And if you don't, you'll figure that out."

"I get what you're saying, and that all sounds great in theory. But I don't think we can totally ignore the past. Sooner or later, we're still going to have to deal with what happened. We can't avoid talking about it forever."

"Okay, so then talk about it and get it over with. Maybe that will happen tomorrow night, or maybe it will happen sometime in the future. I guess you'll both know when the right time is."

"Yeah, I guess."

"Maybe it will help you get closure on certain things."

"There's that."

Ryan scooted next to Aaron and put his arms around him. "You're wonderful."

"So are you. And he'll see that. I'm sure everything will work out fine."

"Thanks for listening and for all the good advice. Thanks for saying what needed to be said."

"You're welcome. I know you'd do the same for me."

They kissed and held each other for a few minutes. When the jets shut off at the end of the cycle, they went back inside.

Brandon's First Family Night

Sunday, October 16, 2016

Brandon arrived at Ryan's house at around 5:30. Ryan greeted him at the door and Brandon gave him a brotherly hug.

Ryan asked, "How was your weekend?"

"Pretty good. Went to a party last night. Got some studying done today. How about you?"

"It's been kind of weird. A lot of ups and downs. I'll tell you about it in a little bit. But first, let me show you around."

Ryan took Brandon on a tour of the house. Brandon was impressed, but when they got out to the backyard with the pool, hot tub, and barbecue island, he exclaimed, "Wow, man, this is awesome!"

"Thanks. The house where I lived in LA had a pool and a hot tub, and I really enjoyed them. So when I moved here, I decided I wanted to have those things too."

"That's amazing. So, how often do you get in the pool?"

"During the summer, two or three times a week. Now that it's the middle of October, the water's too cold. So we've shifted to sitting in the hot tub."

"Cool. So where's Aaron?"

"He'll be here at around 6:30. He has to work every other weekend, and this is his weekend to work. He gets off at 6:00, then he'll get up here as soon as he can. So I hope you don't mind waiting for dinner."

"Nah, that's okay."

Ryan could tell Brandon was hungry and it probably wasn't okay. "You want something to munch on before dinner?"

"Yeah, sure, that would be good."

Ryan said, "Why don't you have a seat there at the kitchen island?" He got out some chips and dip. "You want a beer or anything?"

"What are we having for dinner?"

"I'm making spaghetti and meatballs, so I figured we'd have red wine with that."

"Okay, then just a soda for now."

Ryan got them both a soda and sat down next to Brandon. Brandon said, "That was your favorite meal when you were a kid, right?"

"Yeah. I don't make it much anymore, but I felt like making it tonight."

"That just brought back a memory. Mom made spaghetti and meatballs for dinner on your 18th birthday. I think she meant to do it in honor of you, but it kinda backfired. She got more and more depressed 'cause you weren't there. Dad was totally oblivious. He asked her what was wrong, and she said, 'Don't you even know what day this is?' Then when she told him it was your birthday, he said, 'Well, it's not like he's here to celebrate it with us. He's the one who chose to run away.' Then she threw her plate of spaghetti at him. Hit him right in the face. Then she ran up to her room and locked the door."

Ryan said, "Wow. I can't imagine Mom doing something like that."

"Well, things changed a lot after you left. After she found out Dad slept with Dr. Babcock, she made him sleep on the hide-a-bed in his office. Not long after that, he ended up sleeping in your room. Their marriage was pretty much over at that point."

"That's so sad. But that brings me to something I wanted to talk about. I've been thinking. How are we going to move on from the past? I don't want us to keep talking about all the stuff that happened back in Kansas. I know there's stuff we need to talk about and deal with, but I don't want to get fixated on that. I'm more interested in today and tomorrow."

"Yeah, that's one of the reasons I wanted to go to college outside of Kansas. I wanted to get away from all that."

Ryan chuckled. "That's exactly what Chris and I wanted to do back when we were in high school and we were talking about college. Anyway, I am so happy we're back in each other's lives again."

"Yeah, me too."

"But we're different people now. I mean, back then you were a 9-year-old kid who had just finished third grade. Now, you're an adult and a college freshman. I've been out of your life for as long as I was in it. And I've been through a lot since I left home. I'm not a naïve, innocent high school kid anymore, I'm 27 now. We can't really pick up where we left off, because so much has changed. It's like we need to build a whole new relationship now."

Brandon said, "Yeah, I see what you're saying. It's like we need to get to know each other all over again."

"Exactly. And our relationship isn't big brother-little brother anymore. We'll always be brothers, but we're both men now."

"Okay, so how do we go about that?"

"I guess we do what we're doing now. Spend time together. Talk. Get to know each other for who we are today."

"Cool. I'm down for that."

"Good. But I need to ask you something. And this is going to be a difficult question, but I want you to be honest with me."

"Okay..."

"Are you mad at me?"

"No! Why would I be mad at you?"

Ryan said, "Well, okay, maybe mad is too strong a word. Do you harbor any resentment toward me? After all, I ran away and abandoned you without saying goodbye. And then yesterday, I got to thinking about Mom. And I kept getting sadder and sadder. I kept thinking that maybe if I hadn't run away, or at least if I had gotten back in touch sooner, her depression might not have been as bad and... well, she might still be here today."

"It wasn't your fault. You had no other choice but to run away. And that letter you left for me... that meant so much. I understood why you did what you did. I knew you loved me. And I knew it wasn't about me."

"Well, good. But do you blame me, in any way, shape, or form, for Mom's death?"

"No. Absolutely not."

"You're sure?"

"I'm sure. How is it your fault?"

Ryan said, "It isn't so much about fault. But if I had done things differently, maybe things would have turned out differently."

"We all have 20-20 hindsight."

"I suppose. Well, thanks. I'm relieved to hear that."

Brandon stepped down off his tall swivel chair and said, "Stand up."

Ryan stood up, unsure why Brandon was asking him to do this.

Brandon gave Ryan a big hug. "Stop worrying so much. We're fine. I'm not holding anything against you."

They held each other for a moment, then Brandon let go. "I'll always think the world of you."

"Even though I had to do porn to pay my way through college?"

"That doesn't bother me a bit."

"Okay, good." Ryan and Brandon sat down again. "So moving on, there's something else I wanted to ask you. How are things with you and your father?"

Brandon was about to correct Ryan and say, '*Our* father,' but then he realized why Ryan worded it like that and let it drop. "Okay, I guess. We've never been close. Even after Mom died, he didn't make any effort to step up and become more of a parent. He just assumed I would take over things like grocery shopping and fixing dinner and cleaning the house and all that stuff. Then one day, I said, 'Hey, I'm not your wife. I have plenty of things going on in my life, too.' So he hired a housekeeper who came in once a week and cleaned everything. But he was completely absorbed in his world like he always was, and that didn't change. I mean, I still acknowledge that he's my father. I haven't disowned him like you have. I guess you could say I tolerate him."

Ryan said, "I get it. So, have recent events changed anything?"

"No. Not yet, anyway. He hasn't even told me. He probably thinks I don't know. I found out about it from one of my high school buddies."

Ryan shook his head. "Why am I not surprised? But then, I guess it would be kind of difficult to call your son and say, 'Hey, I just wanted to you know that your old man got busted in a gay sex and drugs orgy.'"

"Somehow I need to let him know that I know, but I haven't figured out how I'm going to do that. He's probably expecting me to go back to Kansas over the holidays and every summer. I'm not looking forward to that, especially after what happened. I want to get away from that place."

"Well, why don't you stay here with me when school's not in session? I have a guest bedroom."

"Could I? Really? Man, that would be great."

"Seriously! You can live here between semesters. By the way, Aaron and I were talking yesterday, and he's going to be moving in during December."

"That's great, man. Congratulations!" Brandon thought for a moment. "But if you two are living here together, won't I be in the way?"

"No, of course not. He really likes you, and he's happy that we're back in each other's lives. He knows it's important for me to spend time with you."

"Cool. I really like him, too. But what will I tell Dad?"

"I don't know... Just tell him you have a friend from school who's offered to let you stay with him. You can even tell him your friend's name is Ryan Robertson. He won't know that's me."

"He'll probably be relieved."

"Yeah, probably. Who knows? Anyway, one more thing about your father. I realize I'm asking a lot of you to not say anything about me to him. I know that means you'll have to be a bit evasive at times or fib a little bit, especially when you live here."

"That's okay. I can deal with it."

"But I don't want to stand in the way of you having whatever kind of relationship you end up having with him. I have no right to say, 'Either him or me.'"

"I get it. And that's okay. I think keeping some distance will be good."

At that point, they heard the garage door open. Ryan said, "Aaron's here."

They got down from their chairs. Ryan hugged Brandon and said, "Thanks for the talk."

"Anytime."

Aaron entered the kitchen from the garage. Everyone hugged. Ryan said, "Okay, I'll get started on dinner now. And while I'm thinking about it, Brandon, if you're not doing anything next Saturday night, my jazz band is playing a concert. You can come if you want. If you have other plans, no problem."

"Seriously? I wouldn't miss that for anything! I remember going to your concerts back when you were in high school. Man, you were so good!"

"Well, just to manage expectations, I only started playing again in July. But most of it has come back. And this band is at least as good as our high school band – probably better."

"Just let me know when and where."

"Next Saturday, starting at 7:00. It's at this hotel near Central Avenue a few miles north of downtown that has a deck up on the roof. It's pretty cool."

Aaron said, "I can pick you up and we can sit together."

Brandon said, "Cool! I can't wait! Man, I'm so happy you're playing your trumpet again. I remember how much you loved it."

Brenda Comes Through

Tuesday, October 18, 2016

Ryan was a nervous wreck as he waited for Paul to arrive at 7:00. *What will Mom have to say? Will she be mad at me? Will she show up at all? Will I be able to see or hear her? How does talking to the dead work, anyway?*

Paul arrived right on time.

Ryan opened the door and ushered Paul into the family room. "Thank you so much for coming. I hope traffic wasn't too bad."

Paul replied, "No, it was pretty good. It's usually pretty well cleared up by 7:00. Wow! This is a nice place you have here!"

"Thanks. May I offer you anything to drink? Water? Soda? Wine? A cocktail?"

"Water would be fine."

Ryan asked, "Would you mind if I have a glass of wine? I'm pretty anxious about all this, and I need to calm down a little."

"No problem. Whatever will make you feel comfortable." Paul paused. "You know what? I'm going to change my mind if that's okay. Alcohol tends to open me up a little bit and make me more receptive."

"Sure. White or red?"

"White, please."

Ryan poured their wines and they sat down. "How has your day gone so far?"

"Pretty good. And you?"

"Work was okay – when I could keep my mind on it. I haven't been able to think about much else besides this. I'm glad you were able to come over so soon. I want to deal with this as soon as possible. So, how does this work?"

Paul said, "Well, first of all, I can't guarantee that your mother will come through. But she's been visiting me all day, and she shows up at rehearsal almost every week, so chances are very good. I think she wants to talk to you as much as you want to hear from her. Other people may show up too. I never know until we get going. One other thing – you might want to get a pad of paper in case you want to write stuff down during the reading. Many of my clients refer back to the notes they've taken for months after their readings."

"Would you mind if I recorded it?"

"Not at all."

Ryan got out his phone and started recording. "Will I hear her, or just you?"

Paul smiled. "Just me. I suppose if you could hear her, you wouldn't need to have this reading with me."

"I guess not."

"Okay, well, your mother is here. And first of all, she says she loves you."

"Tell her I love her too." Ryan was already starting to tear up.

"By the way, she can hear you. So you can talk directly to her. You don't need to go through me."

Ryan said, "I don't get it. If she no longer has a physical body, she has no eyes or ears. How can she see and hear me?"

"I don't know, but spirits can. Anyway, she also wants to tell you she's sorry."

"Sorry? Sorry for what? I'm the one who should be saying 'I'm sorry' to her."

"She's sorry she didn't stand up to your father for you." Paul paused while he tried to understand everything she was telling him. He stared into space like he could see Ryan's mother standing in the room behind him. "She says your father was going to send you away to someplace. She didn't think that was a good idea and she didn't want you to go, but she couldn't convince your father not to do it." He listened some more. "She's sorry she agreed to take Brandon to Tulsa. Does that make any sense?"

"Oh, yeah, totally. See, my father was the pastor of this huge church in Kansas, where I'm from. And he couldn't handle me being gay. So he and this other guy were going to force to me go to some facility in Alabama where they thought they could turn people straight. Brandon is my younger brother. Mom took him to Tulsa to visit our grandmother so he wouldn't be there when they tried to take me away. Mom wasn't happy about me being gay, either."

"Yeah. She says she's sorry about that, too. Now she realizes that's who you were meant to be and she should have accepted that."

"Better late than never, I guess."

Paul stared into space while he listened to Brenda some more. "She says she always knew, but she didn't want to accept it. She believed it was a sin. You were never interested in girls. But she says you were always so happy whenever you were with Chris."

"He was my best friend in high school. We finally figured out we were both gay a few weeks before I got outed to my parents. I was so scared they would find out 'cause I knew they'd flip out – which they did."

"She says she knows now that you and Chris were meant to be together. She's sorry she couldn't accept that at the time." Paul paused. "She says even if she accepted it back when she was still alive, she wouldn't have been able to convince your father that it was okay."

"Yeah, she's got that right. He preached against homosexuality all the time at his church."

"She says he's a big old hypocrite."

"He sure is. But I want to go back to something she just said – that Chris and I were meant to be together. Does that mean we'll get back together again someday?"

Paul listened for her answer, although he looked like he already knew what it would be. "She doesn't know. Spirits can't predict the future. They can see multiple possible outcomes, but they can't tell which one will come to pass. See, we humans have free will. We make choices in our lives all the time. So what happens in the future depends on the choices we make. And it's not only our choices. Other people have free will and can make choices too, and often those choices impact us. So there's no way she can know for sure. Even if she could, she probably wouldn't tell you. Spirits aren't supposed to interfere with the trajectory of our lives."

Ryan paused to let all that sink in. "Wow. That's pretty heavy stuff."

"Yeah."

"So, what does she think of Aaron?"

"She says he's nice. And she says you'll like his parents. She says they're just common folks, but they're good people. She wishes she and your father could have been more like them."

"Tell her I'm really sorry I ran away from home."

"Remember, you can say it like you're talking to her. She can hear you."

"Yeah, okay. It just seems sort of weird. It's like I can see you but I can't see her, so it seems like I should be talking to you."

"Well, she can hear you either way, so whatever works."

"Okay, I'll try. Mom, I'm really sorry I ran away from home. I had no idea it would have such a terrible impact on you. I guess I was only thinking of myself. I didn't really think about how it might have impacted you until Brandon told me you died. Of course, back then I thought you wanted to send me away, too. It's like on the one hand, I know you loved me, but on the other hand, it seemed like you felt the same way as Dad."

Paul listened to Brenda for a moment. "And that's one of the biggest regrets she has. She didn't feel like she had any say in the matter. She believed she had to be subservient to her husband. So your dad made all the decisions and she had to go along with them. She felt powerless. She thought that was how God said it should be. But now, she realizes that was nonsense."

Ryan started crying. "Hang on a second." He stood up and walked into the bathroom, then returned with a box of tissues. Once he had regained his composure, he said, "I don't know whether I should ask this or not, but... Did you intend to commit suicide?"

Paul listened a little longer than usual. A couple of times, he shook his head like he didn't fully understand what she was trying to tell him. Finally, he said, "No, she didn't really mean to take her life. Her doctor had put her on some new drug, and it made her feel numb. She couldn't feel any emotions. In that moment, she didn't care whether she lived or died. And she was so miserable she thought, why not? I'll be over this and no one will really care."

Tears were streaming down Ryan's face. "Now I feel really awful. Like if I hadn't left, none of this would have happened. Or at least if I had gotten back in touch with them."

Paul listened to Brenda some more. "It's more the latter. After all, at the time she died, you would have been out living on your own anyway. But she says the moment she realized she had died and her spirit had crossed over, she regretted doing it. That's usually the way it is. When spirits look back on their life from the vantage point of being on the other side, a lot of things become more clear. For example, they realize that all religions are man-made. A lot of things they believed while they were on Earth, like rules and rituals they're supposed to follow, are all things organized religions created to try to control their followers. There's no basis for them in the greater universe. There's no deity in the universe that wants people to gather in ornate buildings with stained glass windows, sing hymns, and recite unison prayers or any of that stuff."

Ryan asked, "So what about homosexuality? Does the higher power, whatever it is, care about that?"

"Nope. See, spirits don't have bodies. Spirits don't have gender. To spirits, there's only love. There's no such thing as homophobia in the spirit world. Your mother realized everything they did was a huge mistake. But anyway, your mother says she forgives you. She understands why you did what you did. You had no choice. She knows she and your father were wrong, and they put you in that situation."

"Okay, that makes me feel a little bit better, but I still feel like her killing herself was partly my fault."

Paul listened for a moment. "She says she was miserable

anyway. After she found out your father was a closet case, she realized he only married her because he thought he was supposed to marry a woman. He believed it was what God wanted. He knew that to have a successful career as a pastor, he needed to marry a woman and have a couple of kids. She realized she was just an accessory; a prop. She realized there wasn't much love there."

"Oh my god, that's so awful. No wonder she was miserable."

"She says being a mother to you and Brandon made her life more worthwhile. You guys gave her a sense of purpose; something to live for. You were people she could love and be loved by in return."

"So when I left, that removed half of her reason for living."

"Yeah, but she has forgiven you for it. She says it was karma. It's the consequence of her not accepting that you're gay and her not standing up to your father and stopping him from sending you away. And she realizes that when the time came for Brandon to move out, she'd be in the same predicament."

"My father is the one who should be experiencing karma. He's to blame for this a lot more than my mother."

Paul said, "She says he's experiencing his karma right now. His world is crashing down on him as we speak."

"Wow. That's a lot to take in."

Yeah. Pretty heavy stuff, isn't it?"

"I have one other question for her. Is it okay if I ask her questions?"

"You can ask. She has the right to answer or not."

"Okay. So the other day, you said she asked me to take care of Brandon. What does that mean?"

Paul waited to hear the answer from Brenda. "Okay. This gets back to the karma thing we talked about a minute ago. Your dad has been fired from his church. That means he may have to move someplace else if he hopes to still be a pastor, which means he'll have to sell the house. Or he may have to figure out something else to do. Anyway, that means he won't have income for a while, and he may not be able to support Brandon while he's in college."

Ryan said, "That's okay. He's going to stay with me between semesters. And I can help him financially if he needs it."

Paul listened for a moment, then smiled. "She knew she could count on you. She's thrilled that you and Brandon are back together again. He suffered a lot because you were gone, and that wasn't his fault. She says she and your father are to blame for what happened, but he did nothing wrong. But you're back together now, and that's what counts."

Ryan said, "Yeah. I'll always feel bad about that. And I suffered for it because I didn't have my brother in my life for nine years."

"Well, I think your mom has said all she has to say for this visit. She says she loves you and she's very proud of you. You've turned out well."

"Tell her... no wait, I can tell her. I love you, Mom. I'm so sorry for everything I did wrong. I'm sorry I didn't get back in touch with you. But thanks for everything you've told me today."

"She says you're welcome. And she wants you to keep playing your trumpet."

"I will. I can't believe I quit for four years. It's brought so much joy to my life. Anyway, last week you told me that she's usually there at band practice listening to me."

"That's right."

"Does that mean she's following me around all the time?"

"Not all the time. She checks in on Brandon, too."

"So how can I know when she's present?"

"You can't know for sure unless you start developing your ability to sense spirits. Sometimes you might get a feeling that she's around, or you might catch a glimpse of her out of the corner of your eye. Or sometimes you might catch a whiff of her perfume. Do you ever dream that you're seeing and talking to your mother?"

"I have, once or twice."

"That might have been her. Sometimes we're more receptive in our sleep."

"Interesting. Paul, I can't tell you how much this has meant to me. Thank you so much."

"You're welcome. Sometimes doing this can be incredibly rewarding. But before we wrap up, there's someone else here to see you. He's been standing off to the side, patiently waiting for you to finish with your mother."

"Oh? Who is it?"

"He says his name is... sounds like Al. Did you know anyone named Al?"

"Hmmm... Oh! Hal! Is it Hal?"

Paul smiled, "Yes, that's it. Hal's here. He just wants to say hi and tell you he's doing fine."

"Oh my God... Hal! He's the guy who owned the house I lived in for five years in LA before I came here. He was the greatest guy. I met him the day I arrived in LA after I ran away from home. Hal truly came to my rescue. I don't know how I would have made it if it weren't for Hal."

"He says he's glad everything's working out so well for you. He thinks very highly of you." Paul listened some more. "He says regrets what happened that night. He says he should have listened to you when you offered to fix dinner and told him he needed to stop drinking."

"God, I feel so bad about that night. I wish I had checked in on him. I saw him out in the hot tub at around 10:00, and I should have gone out and checked on him. I could have gotten him out of the hot tub before he drowned. And I should have taken away his bourbon bottle instead of just telling him he shouldn't have any more to drink."

"Hal says none of that was your fault. It was totally his fault."

"Yeah, but it's not about fault. If I had done those things, he'd probably still be alive today."

"Still, he says you shouldn't beat yourself up for it."

"And there's one other thing. Are you mad at me because I sold the house after you died?"

After a moment, Paul said, "He says no, that doesn't bother him at all. It was an earthly thing, and earthly things don't matter once you cross over. He says it wasn't fair of him to assume that you'd continue to live there and rent rooms out to others, as he did. Your life needed to move on in the direction it did." Paul listened some more. "He's glad you got some benefit from it. He really likes this house."

"Oh, thanks. I wanted to have a home that was a lot like yours. Hal, you have no idea what a role model you were for me. You were my hero. I really appreciate everything you did for me and the other guys. I probably didn't tell you that often enough."

"He says he knows. And wait, he has one more thing he wants to say." Paul listened intently. He frowned like he didn't understand the meaning of what he was hearing. "Okay, I think what he's saying is that if you want to show your appreciation for what he did, you can pay it forward."

"Okay... Can you tell me more?"

"He says there are kids in Phoenix who need services like they had in Los Angeles. There's a gay youth support group, but so much more needs to be done."

"Ah... I get it."

"Okay. Well, Hal says so long for now."

"Bye."

Ryan ended the recording on his phone and they stood up. Ryan gave Paul a big hug. "Thank you! Thank you! Thank you! This has been so good for me. I heard so many things I needed to hear."

"Glad I could be of service."

"How much do I owe you? And how would you like to be paid?"

"$150. And whatever works for you. Cash, check, credit card, PayPal, Zelle, Venmo..."

"How about Zelle? What's your email address?"

Paul gave Ryan his email address, and Ryan sent him $200. Then Ryan showed Paul to the door, gave him another hug, and sat down to process everything he had just heard.

Brandon's Second Family Night

Sunday, October 23, 2016

Aaron spent Saturday night at Ryan's house, and in the morning, they went running with their gay running club. As they were driving to the grocery store parking lot where the group met, Aaron said, "I'm trying to think of how long it's been since we've done this."

Ryan said, "Yeah, it's been at least six weeks. I used to go every week." He turned to Aaron and smiled. "But I seem to have more going on in my life these days."

"Well, I'm sorry I'm keeping from your physical fitness regimen."

Ryan put his hand on Aaron's leg. "I'm not."

Aaron said, "I need to start running more, though. With all the dinners we've been having lately, I've put on five pounds. I don't know if I'll be able to keep up with you today."

"I don't know if I'll be able to keep up, either. We'll just do our best. It's not a race."

They pulled into the parking lot. Kent and Justin were there, along with ten other guys. After they all hugged each other, Justin said to Ryan, "Dude! We met your brother at the jazz concert last night. You never told us you had a younger brother!"

Kent added, "Or that he was a basketball player at ASU."

Ryan replied, "We've been separated for over nine years. My wonderful boyfriend was able to get us back together again. He surprised me on my birthday last weekend."

Kent said, "He's adorable! Is that what you looked like nine years ago?"

"So what you're saying is, now I'm old. Hell, I just turned 27.

That's still younger than you guys if I'm not mistaken."

Justin said, "He's a hottie! Is he gay, too?"

Ryan said, "Nope. He had girlfriends in high school. But he's totally cool with me being gay, so it's all good."

Kent said, "You two look so much alike. Does he have a huge dick too?"

"Dude! Seriously? How am I supposed to know? We've only been back in touch for a week, and you think I'm going to ask him how big his dick is? Like I even care. Geez, you guys are such pervs."

Justin said, "You know what I think? I think it's time for Luke Loadstar to come out of retirement. And I do mean 'cum.' Brother porn is really hot. With a little makeup, you could pass as twins. You guys would make a fortune!"

Ryan scowled. "Shut! Up! C'mon, let's start running."

Once they got separated into smaller groups, Ryan turned to Aaron and said, "Maybe it's not such a good idea for Brandon to join the band after basketball season ends."

"Oh, they're just being trashy. It's what they do. The novelty will wear off soon enough. Most people in the band are pretty decent."

***

Later that afternoon, Ryan and Aaron took a few minutes to catch up on their email and, in Aaron's case, Facebook. Since he had spent the night, Aaron brought his laptop with him.

When Aaron launched Facebook, he saw a message waiting for him from Chris.

> Hey, how's it going?

> Great. I'm spending the day with Ryan. We're just hanging out until Brandon gets here for dinner.

How did he take the news about his dad?

He doesn't care. As far as he's concerned, he's not his father anymore. He doesn't want to hear anything about him. And he's told Brandon not to say a word about them being back together.

That's too bad, but I guess I can't blame him. Anyway, I have some more news. A couple of weeks ago, I got a friend request from a guy we went to high school with. As it turns out, he's the police officer they sent undercover to infiltrate that orgy Ryan's dad got busted at.

No shit! Is he gay?

I don't think so, but I always kind of wondered. Anyway, when the news came out about the bust, his dad got up in front of his congregation and told them it wasn't him. He said it was someone else with a fake ID.

Seriously?

Yep. So then the cop went on TV to call him on it.

You mean the guy Ryan went to high school with?

Yeah. It's still on the TV channel's video archives. I'll send you the link.

Okay, but he won't want to watch it.

Tell him it's not about his dad, it's about his friend. Trust me, he needs to watch it. When you watch it, you'll see why.

Okay. What is this guy's name?

Rocket Crockett.

Seriously? That's his real name?

Well, his first name is Clayton. But everybody called him Rocket back in high school. He'll know who I'm talking about.

Okay, I'll go talk to him and try to get him to watch it.

Cool. Oh, and Rocket asked me to find out if Ryan would be willing to talk with him sometime. He really wants to get back in touch. He asked if Ryan is on Facebook, but I told him no.

Okay, I'll ask him after he watches the video.

Aaron played the video clip. As soon as he reached the end, he carried his laptop into Ryan's office.

"Hey honey, I was just chatting with Chris."

"How is he?"

"Fine. And he had some news. Do you remember a guy from high school named Rocket Crockett?"

"Yeah. He was on the track team. He was kind of an asshole. He used to call me 'PK,' for Preacher's Kid, and he teased me about my dick."

"Lovely. Anyway, according to Chris, he's a police officer in Kansas City now. And get this! He was the guy who went undercover to the orgy your dad got busted at."

Ryan burst out laughing. "What? They sent him to a gay orgy?"

"That's what Chris said."

"Oh my God! That's hysterical! I wonder if he got any."

Aaron chuckled. "We'll probably never know. Anyway, after the news came out, your dad told his congregation it wasn't really him, it was someone else with a fake ID."

"Figures. That's exactly what he'd do."

"But when Rocket Crockett found out about it, he went on one of the local TV shows. You need to see this."

"Look, I've already told you a hundred times. He's not my father anymore and I really couldn't give two shits about him."

"This isn't about your dad, it's about your friend. I'm serious. You need to watch this."

Aaron set his laptop down on Ryan's desk in front of him. He clicked on the right-pointing triangle to begin playing the clip.

The segment began with a close-up of a beautiful, perky young lady with a flattering red dress, perfect make-up, and blown-out blonde hair. "Welcome back to 'Rise and Shine, Kansas City!' I'm Heather

Spitzer." The scene switched to a different camera showing the host and a handsome police officer in his late 20s, sitting on a semi-circular couch facing each other. The officer sat on the edge of the couch with perfect posture.

Ryan reached for the screen and pressed Pause. "You know, if Heather Spitzer married a man whose last name is Swallows and she hyphenated her name, she'd be Heather Spitzer-Swallows."

Aaron laughed. "You and your name jokes."

"It's what I do."

"And for what it's worth, your friend is kinda hot."

"You think so? Or do you have a uniform fetish?"

"I wouldn't say that, but he does look good in his uniform."

Ryan pressed Play.

"Our next guest is Officer Clayton Crockett, from the Kansas City Police Force. Good morning, Officer Crockett."

"Good morning, Heather. Thanks for having me on the show."

"Officer Crockett, I understand you were involved with the recent incident in which 35 men were arrested for taking part in a gay orgy. Is that true?"

"Yes, ma'am, but to be perfectly clear, they were not arrested because it was a gay event. They were arrested because illegal drug use and prostitution were taking place."

"Understood. And what was your role in this operation?"

"I attended the event undercover to determine whether the alleged activity was taking place. Up until that point, we were just operating on a tip."

Ryan chuckled and said, "*Just* the tip." The very thought of Rocket at a gay orgy amused him.

Heather asked, "So you attended the event pretending to be a participant like everyone else."

"That's correct."

"Can you describe what you witnessed while you attended the event?"

Rocket, who had remained remarkably poised up to this point, suddenly looked uncomfortable. "Much of what I witnessed would not be appropriate to discuss on TV. But I did see the drug use taking place and I was able to confirm that they hired male prostitutes. And for the record, I didn't actually do anything."

Ryan said, "Too bad. He might have enjoyed it."

Heather smiled. "Some of those arrested include prominent members of our community. One participant, in particular, has publicly denied participating in this event. He claims another person presented a fake ID with his name."

"That's correct. Rev. Brad Bauer, head pastor of the Eternal Savior Christian Church in Prairie Village, was present at the event and subsequently made that claim to his congregation."

"Officer Crockett, you were there. Did you observe Rev. Bauer at the event?"

"Yes, I did. I observed him using crystal meth, as well as... um... *interacting* with one of the prostitutes."

"Can you be absolutely certain it was him?"

"Yes, ma'am. I also observed the church's Youth Pastor, Rev. Dr. Ronald Babcock, at the event. I gained a lot of information from speaking with him when I first arrived. Rev. Bauer made the fake ID claim on behalf of Rev. Babcock, too."

Heather turned to the camera and said, "The Police Department has provided us with the mug shots of Rev. Bauer and Rev. Babcock, taken on the night of their arrest. We have also obtained pictures of these two men from the church's website. Benny, would you display those pictures side-by-side, please?"

The mug shot and website photos of Rev. Bauer appeared side-by-side on the screen. Heather said, "Officer Crockett, who is the gentleman pictured in these photos?"

"That's Rev. Bauer. Definitely."

The director switched the photos. "And who is this gentleman?"

"That's Rev. Babcock."

Heather said, "I think we can all agree that the men in each pair of pictures look sufficiently alike to refute Rev. Bauer's fake ID claim."

Rocket said, "Absolutely. I appreciate you having me on your show to debunk their claim. First, because their claim implies shoddy police work, as if we can't spot a fake ID when we see one. Second, as law enforcement officers, we have a duty to ensure that we are not falsely charging innocent people with crimes."

"Officer Clayton Crockett, I want to thank you for taking time out of your busy day to–"

"Heather, may I say something else? I'll keep it short." Heather looked surprised by this interruption, but she didn't stop him. "For me, this is personal. Some of you may know that nine years ago, Rev. Bauer's son Bryan went missing. He had to leave home because his father was going to send him someplace to try to 'cure' him of being gay." Rocket made the air-quote gesture when he said 'cure.' "Bryan was my classmate. He was my friend. And for Rev. Bauer to do that to his own son when he's a homosexual himself?" He shook his head. "I can't even."

Then Rocket looked directly into the camera that was pointed at him. "Bryan? If you're out there somewhere and you see this, I hope you're okay." Rocket paused for a second to maintain his composure. "I miss you, buddy. So do all your friends." He turned back to Heather. "Thank you."

"Thank you, Officer Crockett." She looked into the camera. "Stay tuned. We'll be right back after these messages with a 110-year-old lady who claims that the key to her amazing longevity is daily vibrator use."

Aaron laughed and started singing "Good Vibrations."

Ryan paused the video and moved the slider back 20 seconds to when Rocket was looking at the camera. He replayed the part where Rocket was speaking to him, then pressed Pause. He stared at the screen and didn't move.

Aaron decided to wait until later to ask Ryan about talking with Rocket.

***

A half-hour later, Brandon arrived for dinner. After they had eaten a few bites, Brandon said, "So I talked to Dad on Thursday."

Ryan said, "Not that it matters, but did you call him or did he call you?"

"I called him. Anyway, he told me that, as he put it, he left the church for bigger and better things."

"Did he describe what any of those bigger and better things might be?"

"Of course not. He said he's still evaluating his options. I said, 'You mean you just quit your job not knowing what you'll be doing next?' And he said, 'It was time for me to move on. I have faith that the Lord will provide. He will lead me where He wants me to go next.'"

Aaron said, "Sounds like he omitted the inconvenient little detail that it was the church that decided it was time for him to move on, not him."

"Of course."

Ryan said, "Did you tell him you know?"

"No. I thought about it, but then I was like, why? It's not going to make anything better. It would only make it more awkward for us to deal with each other."

"Yeah, I guess it's better that you took the high road."

"But anyway, then he said his next calling would probably be somewhere other than Prairie Village, so he's going to sell the house. He assumed I would be coming home for Thanksgiving. So he said while I'm there I should pack up any stuff I want to keep and have it shipped here."

Ryan said, "And when he said 'here,' he meant..."

"Not here, specifically. Don't worry, he doesn't know about you. I guess he assumed I'd put everything in my dorm room or rent a storage room or something. I don't think he's thought this through very well yet."

"Well, of course, you can send it here. If he sees where you're sending it, you can say Ryan Robertson is one of your friends or one of your friend's parents."

"Thanks! I really appreciate it."

Ryan thought for a moment. "But I guess that means you won't be spending Thanksgiving with us, as I hoped."

"I guess not. But there's always Christmas."

"Yeah, but we're going to Ohio to spend Christmas with Aaron's parents."

"Shit. Well, we'll figure something out."

Aaron excused himself from the table and headed toward the hall as if he were going to the bathroom. He walked into the master suite at the far end of the house and closed the door. He pulled his phone out of his pocket and called his parents.

Martha answered. "Hi, Honey! How are you?"

"I'm fine, Mom. How are you and Dad?"

"Oh, we're gettin' along fine. It's gettin' colder here and the leaves are turning color. It's really pretty."

"I bet. How's your recovery going?"

"I'm pretty much back to normal. I guess I've reached the point where I can't expect your father to wait on me hand and foot anymore."

Aaron laughed. "Well, milk it for all you can. Anyway, you know how I'm going to be bringing Ryan with me for Christmas this year?"

"Yes! We can hardly wait to meet him!"

"Yeah, well, there's been a development. First, you remember how I told you he's not in touch with his family 'cause they had trouble accepting that he's gay?"

"Yes..."

"Well, it's kind of long and complicated, but the bottom line is, I found out his younger brother is now a freshman at Arizona State! He plays on their basketball team. That means he lives about five miles from my apartment. So I figured out how to get in touch with him. And get this! Ryan's birthday was a week ago Friday, so I arranged for him to be reunited with his brother on his birthday! It was a complete surprise!"

"Oh, my word! I bet that *was* quite a surprise!"

"Yeah. It's been nine years since they've seen each other, so now they're catching up and getting to know each other again. It's going really well. In fact, we're all at Ryan's house having dinner right now. I just stepped away for a moment, so I need to make this quick. Anyway, here's the reason I called. It's been ten years since they spent Christmas together, so it would be nice if they could be together this Christmas. Plus, his brother's situation is such that he can't go home for Christmas. Like I said, it's complicated. So I was wondering if maybe Ryan and I could move our trip a few days later, like maybe go there for New Years..."

Martha interjected, "Bring him along too! We can all have Christmas together!"

"Seriously, Mom? You don't mind having two people you've never met in your house for Christmas?"

"Of course not! It will be fun! That way everyone wins! Ryan and his brother get to spend Christmas together, you get to spend Christmas with us and them, and we get to meet him and his brother! Seems like a no-brainer to me. I don't know where everyone will sleep, but we'll figure something out. Maybe I'll get a couple of air mattresses."

"We can get a hotel room. We'll spend all day with you guys and just go there to sleep."

"Oh, honey, I don't want you spending all that money on a hotel room."

"Don't worry, we can afford it. Besides, that way, Grandma can sleep in my bed and we won't have to take her back and forth between your house and her place in Piqua every day."

"Well, alrighty then. Sounds like a plan. Just let us know what time your flight arrives and how long you'll be staying."

"Okay. Thanks, Mom! I really appreciate you doing this for us."

"I'm glad you'll all be comin'!"

"Okay, well, I'd better get back to dinner. They're probably wondering what happened to me. I love you!"

"I love you too!"

"Bye!"

Aaron practically ran back into the kitchen. Ryan and Brandon looked at him quizzically.

Ryan said, "We thought maybe you fell in."

Brandon said, "Either that or you were having way too much fun in there."

Aaron said, "Neither. Guys, I have some great news! I just called my mom, and you're both invited to come to Ohio for Christmas!"

Ryan said, "What? We can't impose on them like that."

"Oh, yes we can! She's thrilled! She is absolutely tickled pink. She insisted."

"Is their house big enough?"

"I told her we'd get a hotel room nearby. There are a couple of places at the freeway interchange. That way, my Grandma can stay in my bedroom and we won't have to keep driving her back and forth to her place. And we can take them out for dinner once or twice so Mom doesn't have to cook for six all the time. So it's a win all around. You guys get to spend Christmas together, we get to spend Christmas together, I get to see my family, and they get to meet you."

Ryan and Brandon looked at each other. Ryan asked, "Is this okay with you?"

"Yeah, sure. Why not? Sure beats staying here by myself or going back to Kansas."

"Well, okay, then. But we'd better move fast so we can get Brandon on the same flight as us. And hotel rooms are going to fill up quickly, if they haven't already."

Aaron said, "I'll get on it right away."

They ate in silence for a few minutes, each of them waiting for someone else to introduce the next topic. Ryan decided that now was as good a time as any to tell Brandon and Aaron about his reading with Paul. "Okay, well, here's something interesting that happened this past Tuesday. Actually, it started on Thursday the week before that. Brandon, let me catch you up. I went out to the bar with the band guys after rehearsal. There's a guy in the flute section named Paul. He came up to me at the bar and told me he's a medium."

Brandon said, "You don't really believe that stuff, do you?"

"I didn't used to, but I do now."

"Dad always said those psychics and mediums were satanic."

"Yeah, well, how many other things was he wrong about?"

"Fair point."

"Anyway, he said he sees a woman standing next to me at rehearsal every week. Apparently, she enjoys listening to me play my trumpet. Most of the time, if she says anything at all, she just talks about how beautiful it sounds and how much she enjoys it. But that night, she told Paul to tell me that she wants me to take care of Brandon."

Brandon looked stunned. "You mean it's Mom?"

"Yes. And then she wished me a happy birthday."

Brandon said, "Oh, come on. He probably heard about what happened from someone else in the band."

"No! Remember, that was the day before my birthday, so I didn't know you were in town or that she was dead. There's no way he could have known I have a brother named Brandon."

Aaron said, "Well, okay, but so what?"

"So you remember last weekend when I was so depressed about what happened to her? I couldn't help thinking that if I hadn't run away, she might still be alive today. None of this would have happened."

Aaron said, "You didn't really have any choice."

"Maybe, but I still felt guilty about it. Anyway, so I contacted Paul and he came over this past Tuesday and gave me a reading."

Brandon asked, "Was he able to talk to her?"

"Yes. And it was so cathartic. It really cleared a lot of stuff up for me."

"What did she say?"

"A lot of things, but she said she was sorry for not standing up for me and for going along with what Brad wanted to do. She's sorry she participated in the scheme by taking you to Tulsa that weekend."

Brandon said, "She seemed really awkward and uncomfortable the whole time."

"But at the time she felt like she didn't have any say in the matter, like she always had to be subservient to him. And she said she's sorry that she couldn't accept that I was gay. She said she always knew, but she didn't want to accept it. She knew about me and Chris and she knew I was never interested in girls. Anyway, I told her I was sorry for running away from home. I didn't realize at the time how much negative impact it would have on her. I had no idea it would drive her to suicide. I thought she wanted me either cured or gone, too. But I was wrong about all that. Anyway, she said she was miserable anyway. See, at the time, I had no idea how empty their marriage was. I mean, when we were growing up, we just accepted things the way they were. We didn't know any better. But anyway, once she found out he was gay, she realized he only married her because he felt he was supposed to marry a woman. She was just a prop so everyone would think he was straight."

Aaron said, "Okay, so I'm still not convinced any of this is real and he wasn't just making shit up. But in any case, even if it's true, how does it change anything?"

Ryan said, "He told me too many things he had no way of knowing about. But to answer your question, I feel better about the whole thing now. I mean, yes, I wish none of this had ever happened and I wish she was still alive. But I feel like Mom and I have reconciled. She said she was sorry for things she did, and I said I was sorry for things I did, and we forgave each other. I have a better understanding of what she was going through. We have closure. And if we meet again in a future life, or if our spirits meet in the spirit world, things will be fine between us."

Aaron said, "So is she okay with you being gay now?"

"Totally. She realizes now that this is the way I was meant to be. And Paul said something useful. He said on the other side, souls don't have bodies, so there's no such thing as gender. There isn't same-sex or opposite-sex anything. There's no sex. It's just love."

Brandon said, "Wow. Sounds like you had quite an experience."

"Yeah. The more I process it, the more life-changing it is. And it's comforting to know that she comes and listens to me play. She checks in on me. I assume she'll keep doing that, but I guess I'll have to rely on Paul to tell me he saw her."

Brandon said, "Maybe she was at your concert last night."

"I wouldn't be surprised."

Aaron said, "So how much did Paul charge you for this magical mystical fantasy trip?"

"A hundred fifty dollars."

"Are you shittin' me???"

"And I tipped him $50. It was worth every penny. Oh, and Hal came through. It was great to hear from him, too. Anyway, that got me to thinking. He used to have parties at his house on election night. I thought maybe it would be fun if we did that this year."

Aaron said, "But it's a Tuesday night."

"So? Who says you can't have a party on a Tuesday? It doesn't have to go late. And people don't have to get shit-faced."

Brandon said, "If Trump wins, they might."

Aaron asked Brandon, "Just curious. It's none of my business, but who are you voting for? You *are* voting, aren't you?"

"Clinton! I'm not a big fan, but she's a hell of a lot better than him. And yes, I'm still registered in Kansas, so I'm voting absentee."

Aaron said, "Okay, good. I mean, you are from Kansas and your parents are conservative."

"Oh, I get it. But no, I'm a Democrat. They're much better on gay issues, among other things."

Aaron said, "Cool. But getting back to the party, you can have it if you want – it's your house – but that's a work night for me. That is, unless I get that job offer from Food World."

Ryan said, "Sorry, I forgot about that."

"No, seriously. Don't let me stop you. Who were you thinking of inviting?"

"Well, you two, obviously. And maybe a few people from the band and the running club. And a few gay people I know at work, including Eddie, the guy I stayed with while I was an intern. Probably just ten or twelve people, total."

Aaron turned to Brandon. "That means you'll be the only non-gay person there, and probably the youngest by at least eight years."

Ryan said, "You don't have to come if you think you'd feel out of place. I know it's a school night and you'll have homework and stuff. But you're more than welcome."

Brandon said, "Why would being around a bunch of gay people be an issue? I mean, hello! I'm hanging around with gay people right now. And I went to your concert last night. I'd probably be sitting around in the dorm watching the election anyway, so why not?"

Aaron said, "Well, go ahead and set it up. Hopefully, I'll get good news about the job." Then Aaron remembered the message exchange with Chris about Rocket. "Oh, hey, I just thought of something else. You know that video you watched earlier this afternoon?"

"Yeah..."

Aaron took a moment to tell Brandon what that was all about. Then he said to Ryan, "Rocket asked if he could call you sometime. Chris said he really wants to talk to you."

Ryan sighed. "I dunno. He was kind of a jerk. He teased me a lot. Let's just say he wasn't one of my favorite people."

Aaron said, "But look what he did for you."

"He didn't really do that for me. He did it because he was given that assignment. He couldn't have known that he'd catch Brad in there."

"True, but that made it possible for you two to get back together. And think about what he said at the end of the video. Chris said he's a lot more mature and grown up now."

"Well, I sure hope so, for his sake."

"Come on, talk to him. Just once. What's the harm? Especially after what he did and what he said on the air."

"Yeah, I guess you're right."

"I'll let Chris know. Chris was waiting for your permission before he gave Rocket your email address and phone number."

Ryan sighed. "Okay."

True Confessions

Sunday, October 30, 2016

Ryan wasn't looking forward to seeing or talking to Rocket since he had been such an annoyance while they were in high school. But wanting to talk and catch up was a reasonable request and Ryan didn't have a good reason to decline. And after Rocket's emotional message on TV and everything he put himself through to bust the gay orgy group, Ryan felt he owed him a favor.

A few minutes before 2:00, Ryan launched Skype. A moment later, Rocket joined. He was brimming with excitement. Ryan tried to look like he was at least moderately interested in reconnecting with his old classmate.

"Bryan! Dude! Oh, man, it's so great to see you! How the hell are you?"

Ryan smiled. "I'm doing well, thanks. Life is good. Nice to see you too."

"Chris said you're in Scottsdale, Arizona now. What's that like?"

"I really like it. I came here for an internship between my junior and senior year of college and thought, 'I could see myself living here.' And the company I work for is really great, so when they offered me a job, I jumped on it. I didn't even interview anywhere else."

"What do you do?"

"I'm a Software Engineer for a company called Technovations. They develop and test new technologies involving computers, small devices, and medical equipment."

"Wow. Sounds impressive. But you were always real smart."

"So what about you? I hear you went to TCU and played

football, and now you're a police officer."

"Yeah, that about sums it up."

"Are you married or seeing anybody?"

"No, still single. Chris tells me you have a new boyfriend."

"Yeah. His name is Aaron. We met a few months ago. It was kind of rocky at first, but we worked through all that, and now we're getting along really well. He's going to move in next month. I think he might be the one."

"Good for you! It's funny how life turns out. I always thought you and Chris would spend your lives together."

"Yeah, me too, but it didn't work out that way." Ryan paused. "Thanks to my dad."

Rocket decided he should change the subject. "Isn't it really hot out there?"

"Yeah, during the summer it's pretty intense. But for the rest of the year, it's beautiful. I don't ever want to live where it snows and gets freezing cold again. But even in the summer, the humidity is much lower, so it doesn't feel any more uncomfortable than the summers we had in Kansas where it's hot *and* humid. And I have a pool, so that helps a lot."

"Yeah. Chris was telling me you've got a super nice place. I'm really happy for you." Rocket paused. "So, uh... Do you ever go skinny-dipping in your pool?"

Ryan rolled his eyes. Apparently, Rocket hadn't changed that much. "Actually, yes. I have a private backyard. No two-story houses around. None of the neighbors can see my pool." Ryan decided to turn the tables and tease Rocket. "Sounds like you miss seeing my dick in the locker room."

Rocket forced a chuckle. "Yeah, well, you have to admit, it was something to look at." His demeanor turned serious. "So, uh, I guess that kinda leads into something I wanted to say to you. I know I teased you about that back when we were in high school. And I called you 'PK' and all that. Anyway, looking back on it now, I realize I acted like an asshole back then. I shouldn't have teased you about that stuff. So, I wanted to tell you I'm sorry about all that."

"That's okay. I knew you were only trying to have fun and you didn't mean to be hurtful."

"Yeah, but that doesn't make it right. And that time on the bus after the track meet, when you dropped the baton in the relay, and I said, 'Too much lube on your hands?' Man, I totally regret I ever said that."

"You apologized for that a couple of days later, remember? I let it go after that."

"Yeah, but still. And just for the record, I never had any problem with you and Chris being gay. Like, that was totally cool with me. I mean, some guys are gay. That's just how it is."

Ryan said, "Cool. And I don't think you ever teased me or Chris about being gay, other than the lube comment. And about you calling me PK... well, at the time I thought that wasn't really an insult because that's what I was – a preacher's kid. But it was more like I wanted to be identified as me, not as my father's son. Everywhere I went, especially at our church, I wasn't Bryan, I was Rev. Bauer's son. Just like I wanted to be identified as me, not as the guy with the big dick."

"Yeah, I get it. So anyway... Did Chris tell you I was the undercover cop who went to that orgy?"

There were all sorts of things Ryan wanted to say at that moment, but he knew this was not a moment for teasing or levity. "Yeah, he mentioned it. I bet that was awkward. You must have felt uncomfortable and out of place. But I'm grateful you did it."

"It was eye-opening, that's for sure. And, I don't know... I saw a bunch of things that kinda messed with my head. So I went and got counseling. As it turns out, it was really helpful. Not only because I was able to work through what I experienced at the event, but because we got into some things from my childhood. Now I understand why I acted the way I did when we were in high school."

Rocket paused for a moment to gather the strength for what he was about to say. He wondered if he should even say it. But yes – he had to. He reached for the bottle of beer that was sitting off-camera and took a swig. Then he began.

"I never told anybody this, but my family was pretty dysfunctional. My mom and dad fought all the time. I'd go hide in my room, but I could still hear them yelling at each other. When I was 12, my mom got sent to prison for embezzling money from the place where she worked. That left my dad to raise me and my older brother by himself. He was a raging alcoholic. He had trouble keeping a job because he was drunk most of the time. My brother was 16 when my mom got sent to prison, so Dad made him get a job so we'd have money for food. As soon as he turned 18, he ran off and joined the Army. Anyway, my dad wasn't very nice to me and my brother. He'd criticize us for every little thing, like nothing we did was ever good enough. I remember him saying we'd never amount to anything. On the plus side, I guess that's how I got to be so good at football. I kept thinking that if I got good enough, he'd like me. I needed to prove to him and everyone else that I wasn't worthless. I guess most of all, I needed to prove to myself that I wasn't worthless. And that's why I acted the way I did, teasing people and cracking jokes and all that stuff. I needed to be the center of attention. I needed to have people notice me and like me, 'cause my dad never paid any attention to me at home – well, except to yell at me."

Rocket avoided looking directly at the screen while he was saying that. But when he paused, he glanced at the screen and his eyes met Ryan's. Ryan looked genuinely empathetic. "Wow. I'm really sorry. I had no idea."

"Yeah, well there's no way I would have said anything about that at school."

"You probably felt like you had no one to talk to."

"That's right. But anyway, when you joined the track team during our sophomore year, well, I guess I felt all kinds of things I didn't know how to handle. I finally worked through all that stuff in counseling. First, I was jealous of you. You were tall and good-looking and smart, and after you were on the team awhile, you could run faster than me." *And of course, that huge dick.* "And you had Chris. At first, I couldn't figure out whether you guys were gay or not, but either way –

you were best friends. I never had a best friend. Hell, I didn't have that many friends. And even though I was jealous of you for all that stuff, I really liked you. I mean, what's not to like? You were so nice to everyone all the time. I guess deep down, I wished you and I could have been better friends."

"So you teased me about my dick and called me PK because you wanted to be friends?"

"I know. That sounds totally fucked up, and it is. But I was totally fucked up."

"That sounds like your dad talking. Sounds like after hearing that message at home for so long, you started believing it. Anyway, no one else thought you were fucked up. I mean, you were the most popular guy around! The star of the football team! All the guys wanted to hang around you. It's like you would walk into the room and take command of it. Chris and I talked about that a couple of times. We wondered how you were so charismatic that everyone else wanted to hang around with you."

"Everyone except you and Chris. And you were the guys I wanted to hang out with the most. Anyway, it was all an act. People admired me because I was good at football and track. They wanted to hang with the football star, 'cause they thought that would make them look cool too. But I don't think anyone wanted to hang around me because they liked me."

"Chris and I never felt like we fit in on the track team. It's like we weren't really jocks. It's hard to describe, but the social interaction between a bunch of guys on a sports team is a lot different than the social interaction we had with our friends in band. We really belonged with the band kids."

"And I probably had a lot to do with that."

Ryan wasn't going to say anything, but that was the truth.

Rocket said, "Anyway, back in high school, I thought you had everything. So yeah, I was jealous. But when you disappeared, well, I didn't know what to make of it. But I wondered if maybe things were going on in your home you had to get away from. Anyway, I was really concerned about you. I've never been religious, but I prayed that you were okay and you'd get home safely."

"Thanks. That means a lot to me. When I got back in touch with Chris, he said you seemed concerned and you asked about me a lot."

"Anyway, not too long ago I found out what happened. I realized that maybe things weren't great for you at home either. I guess you had stuff to deal with too. And of course, I didn't know any of that at the time."

"Well, like you, that's not something I talked about with anyone except Chris."

"Yeah. See, my boss, Sergeant Garlow, worked for the Prairie Village Police Force before he switched to Kansas City. He was the one who responded when your dad called to report that you were missing. When he went to your house to take a report, that Rev. Babcock guy was there too. During the investigation, they discovered that he ran some sort of counseling practice where they tried to convert gay people to be straight."

"Yeah, that's where they sent me when they first found out. That guy was so creepy! It was obvious to me that he was still gay, even though he had a wife and three daughters and he claimed he was cured."

"Yeah, my boss said that when he went to your house, it seemed like that Babcock guy was gazing at him like he was interested in him. So get this. When I showed up at the orgy, he's the one who showed me around and explained what was going on. Everybody there had a fake name, and his was Bottom Piggy."

Ryan shook his head. "Oh, good Lord..."

"Yeah. He was like totally swishy and flamboyant, and he made it clear that he wanted me to fuck him. Anyway, later on, he was in this thing they call a sling. He was blindfolded and his wrists and ankles were tied up, and guys were waiting in line to take their turn."

Ryan couldn't resist. "Did you get in line?"

"Oh, hell no! Dude, I promise you, I didn't do anything. But anyway, when the bust happened and all the cops rushed into the room, there was Bottom Piggy tied up in his sling. And when my boss walked into that room, the first thing he saw was Bottom Piggy's drippy ass staring up at him."

Ryan laughed, "Oh my God. That is both disgusting and funny at the same time."

"I know, right?"

"No wonder you needed therapy. Sounds like you got quite an eyeful that night."

Rocket became more uncomfortable. "Yeah, that was something I'll never forget, for all kinds of reasons. I mean, on one level, it doesn't bother me to see guys naked. Hell, I saw that all the time in the locker room showers when I was in high school and college. I see it when I go to the gym. So seeing naked guys is no big deal. And it wasn't so much that guys were sucking and fucking. I mean, that's what I assume gay guys do."

"Just like what straight people do."

"Yeah, but... I don't know, it seemed so impersonal. It was actually kind of shocking. It was like sex overload. But enough of that. What happened to you after you left home?"

Ryan said, "Well, it's a long story and I don't want to go into a lot of detail. But I took a bus to LA. I bought one of those Explore America passes so they wouldn't be able to tell where I went. Anyway, when I got there, I went to this place called the Los Angeles LGBT Youth Project. They have resources to help kids who are out on their own. A lot of times, they're homeless, which I guess I was at that time. I asked them if I could see an attorney about changing my name and getting legally emancipated from my parents. So they hooked me up with this guy named Hal Morris. Hal owned a house near UCLA and had four bedrooms he rented to gay college students. Technically, I wasn't a college student yet – I was going to be a senior in high school. But he had a room available, so he rented it to me. And that's where I lived for the next five years until I graduated from UCLA. Anyway, that was really great. Hal became like a father to me and the other three guys who lived there were like my brothers. They cared for me and helped me get adjusted to living on my own."

Rocket said, "It's like you had a new family."

"Exactly. And in a lot of ways, they were more of a family than my biological one."

"So you changed your name?"

"Yeah. I changed it to Ryan. But I know you're used to calling me Bryan. It's okay."

"I'll do my best. So how did you get by? Did you have to get a job?"

"Yeah. I got a job in a grocery store, like I had back in Prairie Village."

"How did you survive on that?"

"Well, that didn't pay very well. So I did some other things too."

There was an awkward silence. Ryan didn't want to tell Rocket he did porn. Rocket wasn't sure whether to tell Ryan he already knew. *What the hell... we've been sharing so much already.* "So you did porn."

Ryan looked shocked. "Okay, how did you find out? Did Chris tell you?"

"No. At the orgy, they had pornos playing on all the TVs. And uh..."

"Oh. My. God." Ryan buried his head in his hands. "You saw me in a video. You saw me... having sex." *Why the hell did I agree to this call?*

"Dude, it's okay. Seriously. It doesn't matter. I'm cool with it. I figured you only did it 'cause you needed the money."

"Yeah, that's exactly it. I never would have done it otherwise."

"I hafta admit, I was really surprised to see you doin' that, just because you were always so... you know, clean cut."

"The Preacher's Kid."

"Exactly. Oh, God. Do you remember the time at that party when I said–"

Ryan finished his sentence. "–that I should have this schlong of mine in porn. Yeah, I'll never forget that."

"That's another thing I feel bad about now. I should never have said that. Hell, I can't believe I even had Trevor put on his father's pornos. I mean, what was I thinking?"

"That turned out to be prophetic, didn't it?"

"Yeah."

"And you were right. I made a fortune. I paid for my college education and saved up a bunch of money for the down payment on this house. So I guess there's that."

Rocket lowered his filters a bit more. "And I gotta tell ya, man, like, I'm no expert on gay porn, but that was actually kinda hot. Dude, you were gettin' it done!" *And I got hard. But there's no way I'm saying that.*

"Well, uh... Thanks. I guess. Do you have any idea which video it was?"

"Yeah, it was *The Boys of Breckenridge*. I saw the box."

"Look, I'd appreciate it if you wouldn't say anything about that to anyone else. I know you're in touch with some of our friends from high school. It's like I'm not ashamed of it, but I don't go bragging about it either. I did it because I had to. But that's in my past, and I want to leave it there. Whenever people find out I did porn, it always changes how they relate to me – and never in a good way. So please don't spread it around, okay?"

"Okay. Does Chris know?"

"Yeah. That's kind of a sore spot. We got back in touch around Christmas of our freshman year. We had a few Skype calls. The first two went really well, and I started to think maybe we could find a way to get back together again. But when he found out I was doing porn, well, that put an end to that."

"Aw, man, I'm sorry."

"Yeah. That made it difficult to date other guys too. Remember when I said Aaron and I had some stuff to work through when we first got together? Well, it was mostly that. We actually broke up for a few days, but he decided he could overlook that and we got back together."

They both looked at each other.

Ryan said, "Well, we've covered a lot of ground today, haven't we?"

"Yeah, we sure have. It's too bad we don't live in the same place. I'd love to hang out. Maybe we could finally be friends after all."

"We've both changed a lot, and we're growing into the people we're meant to be."

"Well, I'm still workin' on it, but I hear what you're saying. Anyway, if you ever make it back to Kansas City, let's get together, okay?"

"Yeah, sure. I have no idea when that might happen, though."

"I get it."

It felt like the call was coming to an end, but Ryan had one more thing he wanted to say. "Hey, Rocket, I really appreciate what you did. That must have been pretty far out of your comfort zone."

"You have no idea."

"Yeah, I bet. But you know, even though I was in a few orgy scenes while I was doing porn, that's not something I have any desire to do in real life."

"When I got the assignment, I had no idea your father was going to be in there. But after it turned out that he was, I'm glad I did it. I mean, on the one hand, I don't care if he's gay. But he was being a hypocrite, standing up there in front of his church pretending to be straight and preaching against gays. And then when he lied and said it wasn't him that was in there, man, I just couldn't let that slide. But after I learned what he did to you, I'm glad he finally got what was coming to him. It's like the karma train finally pulled into the station."

"Thanks. But you know, after everything he did, I seriously don't give a shit about him. But you know what else happened because of what you did? I got reunited with my younger brother! We hadn't seen each other for over nine years."

"Huh? How did that happen?"

Ryan said, "When the orgy bust got on the news, Chris told my boyfriend Aaron about it. Then Aaron started looking on the web for news stories about what happened. And while he was looking for that, he found this article about Brandon accepting a scholarship to come to Arizona State to play basketball. Somehow Aaron located Brandon, and he surprised me on my birthday by reuniting me with my brother!"

"Oh, man, that's awesome!"

"Yeah. That happened two weeks ago. He's come up here to the house a couple of times for dinner. And when basketball season starts next month, we'll go to some of his home games. He's staying in the dorm while school is in session, but he's going to come and live with me between semesters. It's been great. I am so happy now that we're back together. And none of that would have happened if you hadn't done what you did at that orgy. So thanks!"

"Awww... Well, I just did what I was assigned to do. I had no idea about any of that at the time. All that happened afterward. But I'm really glad it worked out that way."

"Me too."

There was a lull in the conversation. Ryan said, "Well, it's been great talking with you, Rocket."

"Yeah, man. And it's great seeing you. You've been through a lot of shit, but I'm glad everything has worked out so well for you."

"You too. Thanks for everything you did. And congratulations on getting that football scholarship!"

"Thanks. Lord knows, I probably wouldn't have made it to college without it."

"Well, hey, you take care. And tell Trevor I said hi."

"I sure will. I hope we can stay in touch."

"Yeah."

Rocket asked, "Are you on Facebook?"

"Nope. I know, everyone says I should."

"Seriously. I like keeping up with my buddies from high school."

"Well, I'll think about it. Anyway, you have my email."

"Yeah. Well, you take care man."

"You too."

"Bye."

"Bye."

Ryan grabbed his mouse and clicked the button to end the call.

And the Winner Is...

Tuesday, November 8, 2016

The election night party started on a happy, upbeat note. Everyone was optimistic about how it would turn out. Hillary Clinton's polling lead over Donald Trump had varied throughout the campaign, but heading into election night, her numbers looked good.

Aaron was able to attend and co-host the party. The day after the second family night dinner with Brandon, he received a job offer from Food World, which he promptly accepted. He gave two weeks' notice to HealthPro, and his last day was Tuesday, November 1. His start date at Food World was Monday, November 14, so he had almost two weeks to enjoy some time off and start moving in with Ryan. As an added benefit, he was able to join Ryan in attending Brandon's first two home games on Friday and Sunday – days that would have been work days had he still been at HealthPro.

They invited Kent, Justin, and a couple of other friends from the gay running club. From the band, in addition to Kent, they invited Rob, a couple of others from the trombone and trumpet sections, and Paul, the flutist and medium. Ryan invited Eddie, his host during his summer internship, and a couple of other gay friends from work. And of course, Brandon was there.

At one point, Eddie and Rob happened to be at the food table at the same time. Rob asked Eddie, "So how do you know Ryan or Aaron?"

Eddie replied, "Ryan lived with me during the summer between his junior and senior years of college. He had an internship at Technovations, where I work. I placed a listing on a website that pairs interns looking for housing with people who have rooms available.

That's how we ended up together."

"That was a nice thing for you to do."

"Thanks. As it turns out, it was just what I needed. I had ended a relationship not too long before that, so I was living alone. Having him there brought me out of my funk. We did a lot of things together that summer and had a lot of long talks. So I went into it only expecting a renter for three months, but I ended up with a good friend. We still have lunch together every couple of weeks."

"He seems like a nice young man. Aaron sure has fallen for him."

"Oh, he is. I got to know him really well. He's a wonderful person. And I'm thrilled that he's found someone. For the first few years he lived here, he wasn't having much luck meeting people. So how do you know Aaron?"

Rob smiled. "We met by accident. One day, I went to Tempe to visit a bookstore I like. After that, I ate lunch at a fast-food restaurant across the street called Wok Around the Clok. I was wearing this T-shirt that said, 'If I seem quiet, it's because you haven't seen me with my trombone.' He was having lunch there, and when he got up to get a soda refill he saw my shirt. He smiled and said, 'Nice T-shirt.' I said, 'Do you play trombone?' He said he used to, but he didn't anymore. Anyway, to make a long story short, I invited him to the Desert Pride concert the following weekend. Then I invited him to join the band. Something just told me he needed to start playing his trombone again. Oh, and I should mention that he hadn't come out yet. So he was like, 'But it's a gay band.' I told him you don't have to be gay; allies are welcome. So anyway, that's how he came to be in the band. Next thing you know, he realized he was attracted to the guy sitting next to him."

"Was that Ryan?"

"No, it was a guy named Jeremy. Anyway, one day Aaron and I had lunch, and by the end of the lunch, he came out to me."

Kent wandered up to the food table, so Rob introduced Kent to Eddie.

Eddie asked, "So what happened to Jeremy?"

"He got a job offer in Austin and moved away. That really tore Aaron up. But they hung out together long enough for Aaron to be initiated into the fraternity, so to speak."

Kent said, "It's funny... the first day Aaron showed up to a band rehearsal, the band director asked all the new people to stand up and introduce themselves and to tell us something interesting about themselves. And when it was Aaron's turn, he said he was straight. The guy sitting next to me leaned over and said, 'Oh, I bet he's not.' So he and I bet $20 on it. I may have lost $20 but I gained a friend. I'm the one who invited Aaron to come to our gay running club. That's where he met Ryan."

Eddie said, "Yeah, Ryan loved to run. He was a star on his high school track team. He won first place in their state championship meet one year."

Rob said, "It's hard to believe they met just a few months ago. Look at them now."

Eddie said, "So really, they're together because of you two." Turning to Rob, he said, "We have you to thank for inviting Aaron to join the band and pulling him out of the closet." Turning to Kent, he said, "And we have you to thank for introducing them."

While Eddie was speaking, Ryan walked up to the food table to see if anything needed to be replenished. "That's right. And Eddie, I have you to thank for me being here in Scottsdale. I had such a great time living with you that summer. You showed me all around the area, and I fell in love with it and decided to move here. You telling me that Technovations was a gay-friendly place to work helped too. And you know what? If it wasn't for you guys putting the pieces in place for us to meet, I wouldn't be reunited with my brother now!"

Rob said, "Well, isn't it wonderful how life works out sometimes?"

Eddie said, "Yeah. You take a bunch of little things that seem inconsequential by themselves and put them together, and lives get changed."

Kent said, "So, when are you boys moving in together?"

Ryan said, "Funny you should ask. Aaron's moving his stuff up here now."

Rob said, "Seriously? That's fantastic!"

There was a lull in the election coverage while the news station took a commercial break. Guys started heading to the kitchen for more food and drink refills. Ryan called out, "Hey, everyone! May I have your attention for a moment?"

People stopped what they were doing and listened. "First, I want to thank you all for being here. So much has happened in the last six months. Many of you are friends I've met in the past six months, including Aaron. Thanks to him, I'm playing my trumpet again and now I know all the rest of you. And thanks to Aaron, I'm now reunited with my brother Brandon! Now, as some of you know, Aaron just received a new job offer. He's going to join the pharmacy department at the Food World store over at Scottsdale and Shea."

Everyone applauded.

Ryan continued, "Anyway, Aaron, you've changed my life. You rock my world. So I just wanted to let you all know we've decided it's time for us to move in together!"

Everyone cheered and applauded.

Justin was standing next to Aaron, "Congratulations, honey!"

"Thanks!"

"It's been, what? About four months?"

"Yep."

"Don't you think that's a little soon?"

"Maybe. But it feels right."

"Oh, I bet it does." Justin's knowing glance made the intended double entendre obvious.

"Shut up. Geez... Why do we keep hanging around with you guys?"

"Maybe because you're eternally grateful to us for introducing you to each other."

"Oh, yeah. There's that." Aaron rolled his eyes. "Besides, according to Ryan, you know how good it feels."

"I vaguely recall."

"Bullshit. Especially since you own one of those dildos they made from his cock back when he did porn. I'm sure you remind yourself of how good it feels at least once a week."

"I don't keep track."

"You've lost count."

"Whatever."

The commercial break ended and guys started paying attention to the election coverage again.

Brandon said, "I dunno, guys. She's lost Florida and Ohio. It's a little too close. I'm starting to get concerned."

Aaron said, "She'll win. She was ahead in all the polls. Five Thirty Eight says she'll win, and they've been incredibly accurate in the past two elections."

Kent said, "Yeah, but they also said the Dems were a slight favorite to take control of the Senate, and that's not happening."

Ryan said, "And I've never seen so many prominent Republicans come out against Trump. A lot of people in his own party won't support him."

Rob said, "Yeah, but they get only one vote on election day, just like everyone else. Pennsylvania and Michigan should have gone for Clinton."

Kent said, "She's winning the popular vote."

Eddie said, "True. But it's the electoral votes that win elections."

The mood in the room turned more somber as the evening progressed. At one point, a network analyst desperately suggested that even though Wisconsin was leaning toward Trump, the counties with remaining votes to be counted were mostly Democratic. Still, panic showed on his face.

At 10:30, Wisconsin was called for Trump. At 10:40, Clinton conceded. What was supposed to be a celebratory event took on the sad solemnity of a funeral. Everyone's hopes for at least four more years of progress toward LGBT equality were shattered.

Justin said, "Looks like Trump just grabbed America by the

pussy."

Kent turned to Ryan and Aaron and said, "If you boys are going to get married, better hurry up and do it soon."

Rob summed it up by saying, "We're fucked. Totally. Completely. Fucked."

The party died quickly. The guests hugged each other, thanked Ryan and Aaron for hosting the party, and shuffled out to their cars. Ryan and Aaron started putting the leftover food away.

Ryan said, "Oh, I just remembered. The 'Please Come In' sign is still on the door. Would you please take it down?"

"Sure." Aaron walked to the front door and opened it long enough to pull down the taped sign. He glanced out toward the street. He closed the door and called into the kitchen, "Hey, Ryan! Come take a look at this!"

Ryan walked into the living room. Aaron pulled the curtain in the picture window aside just enough for them to look out. Across the street, next to Rob's car, Rob and Eddie were talking. A moment later, they hugged and kissed. Then Eddie started walking toward his car. He turned, and Rob and Eddie smiled and waved to each other one more time.

Ryan said, "Awww... Isn't that sweet?"

"I think they'd make a good couple, don't you?"

"Yeah, I do. So maybe some good came out of this evening after all."

Christmas in Ohio

Friday, December 23, 2016

Aaron, Ryan, and Brandon arrived at the airport in Dayton, Ohio, at 4:14 p.m. They had mailed their presents for Aaron's parents and grandmother to their home in advance, so they were able to fit all their clothing into carry-on luggage. Aaron's father was waiting for them at the exit from the secured area.

As Aaron approached, Ralph extended his hand. Aaron ignored that and gave his father a big hug. Ralph was momentarily taken aback, given all the other people passing by, but no one seemed to notice or care. He realized it was okay to hug his son in public.

Then Aaron said, "Dad, I'd like you to meet my partner, Ryan, and his brother, Brandon."

"Ralph Bradbury." He extended his hand and Ryan and Brandon shook it, figuring their first meeting was too soon for hugs. Ralph looked up toward the ceiling. "How's the weather up there?"

It took Ryan and Brandon a moment to realize Ralph was joking about their height.

Ralph turned to Aaron and asked, "How do you kiss him? Do ya hafta get up on a step stool?"

Aaron turned to Ryan and Brandon and said, "Dad has, shall we say, a *unique* sense of humor."

"Oh, hush. I'm just tryin' to be friendly. I hope we can fit you two in the car without having to fold you in half."

Ryan and Brandon chuckled. Ryan said, "I see where you get your sense of humor."

"Shut. UP!"

As corny as he was, Ralph had made an endearing first

impression upon Ryan and Brandon.

They started walking toward the front door. The parking garage was just across the pick-up and drop-off road, and in five minutes they were on their way out of the airport.

Ralph asked, "How was your trip?"

Aaron replied, "Our flights were on time, but oh my God, we're exhausted. We had to get up at 4:00 a.m. so we could be at the airport by 5:30 for our 7:15 flight. Then we had a two-hour layover in Dallas. The airports in Phoenix and Dallas were madhouses."

Ralph said, "Well, you shouldn't have waited until two days before Christmas to come."

"We didn't have much choice. Brandon had a home game last night, and we went to see him."

Brandon added, "I play basketball for Arizona State."

Ralph said, "Well, you ought to, seein' as you're so tall. Didja win?"

"Yes. We beat Central Arkansas 98 to 62."

"Well, good. So I guess I have another team to root for now. Except if you play the University of Dayton or Ohio State. Then you better lose. But I hope you win all your other games."

Brandon chuckled. "Thankfully, they're not on our schedule, unless we play them in the NCAA tournament."

Aaron said, "So we didn't get home from that until around 11:00, so we're operating on only five hours of sleep."

Ryan added, "And I don't know about you guys, but I'm starving."

Ralph said, "Well, Martha's at home right now whipping up a big feast for y'all."

Aaron said, "Dad! We told her we wanted to take everyone out for dinner!"

"Oh, she wasn't havin' that. She didn't want you to spend all that money on dinner when you've already paid for three airfares and three nights in a hotel."

Aaron sighed. He knew it was pointless to argue.

Twenty minutes later, Ralph pulled into their driveway. He said, "I figure you boys can leave your suitcases in the trunk. I'll let you drive my car to your hotel later this evening."

The four men entered through the side door into the kitchen. The tantalizing aroma of home cooking filled the air, making the already hungry young men even hungrier. Martha stopped stirring the mashed potatoes and ran up to Aaron. She flung her arms around him and smothered him with kisses. "Oh, honey! It's so good to have you home!" She took her time letting him go. "Awww... I love you so much."

Finally, she released him, and Aaron introduced Ryan and Brandon to Martha and his grandmother. He gently hugged his grandmother and kissed her on the cheek. "Merry Christmas, Grandma. You look great."

"Thank you, dear. I'm hangin' in there as best as I can."

Martha exclaimed, "Good heavens, you boys are tall!"

Ralph said, "I bet you save a lot of money on haircuts."

Brandon looked puzzled. "What do you mean?"

"All you have to do is stand under a ceiling fan!"

Brandon and Ryan forced a polite chuckle. Aaron rolled his eyes.

Martha said, "Dinner will be ready in about ten minutes. I made meatloaf, mashed potatoes, green bean casserole, and some fresh cornbread. And there's apple pie for dessert, so save some room!"

Brandon said, "That sounds delicious. It smells wonderful, too."

Ryan said, "Wow, Mrs. Bradbury, you really went all out!"

"Oh, honey, just call me Martha. None of that Mrs. Bradbury nonsense. We're all adults. Anyway, I hope you like it. I guess I should have asked if either of you have any food allergies."

Ryan replied, "Nope. We eat pretty much anything."

Martha said, "Aaron, why don't you show them where the bathroom is, in case they want to get washed up."

Aaron led them into the living room, where a six-foot-tall over-decorated Christmas tree rose above a sea of gift-wrapped boxes, including the ones they had mailed earlier in the month. A fire crackled in the fireplace. Ryan and Brandon were surprised to see six stockings hanging from the mantle, including one for each of them. Ryan said, "I can't believe they put stockings out for us!"

Martha heard him from the kitchen and called out, "Well, of course! You came all the way from Arizona to celebrate Christmas with us! We want you to feel like part of the family!"

Aaron led them into the bedroom hallway. "That's the bathroom there on your right. And this was my bedroom." He opened the door and showed them his old room. There were still some memorabilia from his childhood years mounted on the walls, along with a large Ohio State Buckeyes flag.

Soon, everyone was seated around the dining room table. Martha said, "This is so exciting! We haven't had this many people sitting around this table since all of Aaron's grandparents were still alive."

There wasn't much talk while the food was being passed and everyone was taking their first few bites. Then Ryan said, "Martha, this is amazing. Everything is delicious! I can't believe you went to all this trouble."

"Oh, it was no trouble at all. And the mashed potatoes are from a mix. It's not like I spend all afternoon mashing them."

"It tastes excellent. I can't tell the difference."

"Well, thank you, dear. So, what are your parents doing for Christmas?"

Aaron gulped. Apparently, his mother had forgotten his call two months ago, when he asked if he could bring Brandon along for Christmas and he mentioned that Ryan wasn't in touch with his parents.

Ryan thought, *At some point during the visit I'm going to have to tell the Bradburys about my past. But do we have to do that now, during our first dinner together? We just got here and I'm tired.*

Brandon said, "Actually, our mother passed away about two and a half years ago."

Martha set her fork down and clasped her hands in front of her chest. "Oh, honey, I'm so sorry. I didn't know."

"That's okay. I visited my dad over Thanksgiving. I'm not sure what he's doing for Christmas. I'll probably call him at some point. Things are kind of in turmoil now, 'cause he's getting ready to put his house on the market and move somewhere else."

Neither Ralph, Martha, nor Grandma said anything, for fear of saying something unintentionally inappropriate. After a moment of awkward silence, Ryan said, "My father and I aren't on good terms."

Martha said, "Well, I'm sorry, honey. It's too bad when things end up that way, but sometimes I guess it just can't be helped."

Aaron couldn't remember his father ever being quiet for this long.

Martha said, "So Aaron told me this is the first time in several years you two boys have been able to spend Christmas together."

Ryan thought, *Might as well go there now. There's going to be an elephant in the room until this gets talked about.* "That's right. So let me give you the quick version. It's kind of a long story and not a pleasant one. So here goes. Basically, my parents found out I was gay during the summer between my junior and senior years of high school. And Brad – er – my father was the pastor of a huge church where we lived, so he's really religious and conservative. So our parents – well, mostly my dad – couldn't deal with it, so I had to run away. And that meant I had to run away from Brandon, too, which really killed me. But anyway, as long as Brandon was still living at home, there was no way I could get in touch with him without having our parents find out where I was. So fast forward to a couple of months ago. Through... well... let's just say it was a sequence of events, Aaron found out Brandon was attending Arizona State on a basketball scholarship. That was right before October 14, which was my birthday, so he arranged for Brandon to surprise me on my birthday."

Grandma said, "I bet that was quite a surprise!"

Ryan said, "It sure was! It was literally the happiest moment of my life. So for the past two months, we've been getting to know each other again and catching up."

Brandon said, "See, back when that happened, I was in third grade. We're eight years apart. But Ryan was – and is – the best big brother ever. I looked up to him for everything. I still do."

Ryan said, "It's been great. But we figured out pretty quickly that a 9-year-old and a 17-year-old relate to each other a lot differently than an 18-year-old and a 27-year-old. We're both men now. And we've both been through a lot during those nine years we were apart. So in a lot of ways, we're getting to know each other all over again. But the bottom line is, we love each other, and that will never change."

Brandon added, "And we owe it all to Aaron. There's no way we'll ever be able to repay you for what you've given us."

Aaron joked, "But you can keep trying."

Ryan said, "And that's why it means so much to us that you offered to let Brandon come here with us for Christmas."

Martha said, "Honey, we're happy to do it. We're thrilled that you came."

"And I've been looking forward to meeting the people who raised this wonderful man I'm in love with."

Finally, Ralph spoke. "I'm sorry you had all those problems with your parents. Things started out that way for us when we found out Aaron was gay. But thank God we pulled our heads out of our asses and got over ourselves."

Martha was about to chide Ralph for his use of crude language at the dinner table, but she let it go. She knew he was right.

They silently agreed this was enough talk about those matters for the time being. Martha tried to steer the conversation to a lighter topic. "What do you boys have planned for tomorrow?"

Aaron said, "I don't know. We haven't talked about it. We were just focused on getting here and spending time with you."

Ryan said, "Maybe you could show us around Troy."

Ralph said, "That'll take about ten minutes. There's ain't much to see here. I mean, it's a nice place to live, but there's not much goin' on."

Brandon said, "How about Dayton?"

Aaron said, "There's not too much there either."

Grandma said, "You could take them to the Air Force Museum

at Wright-Patterson Air Force Base."

Aaron said, "That's a great idea. And we could have lunch at Skyline Chili." Aaron looked at Ryan and Brandon for approval.

Ryan shrugged and said, "Sure, why not?"

Brandon said, "What's Skyline Chili?"

Aaron said, "It's Cincinnati-style chili. They make it with a special blend of spices, then serve it over spaghetti with a huge mound of shredded cheese on top. It's awesome!"

Martha said, "It's probably southwestern Ohio's only claim to regional cuisine."

Ryan said, "Sounds good to me. Why don't we all go? It'll be something we can do together."

They all looked around the table at each other. Everyone seemed to like the idea.

They finished dinner and Martha got up from the table. "Aaron, would you please help me clear the plates?" Aaron got up, along with Ryan and Brandon. They started carrying plates and serving dishes into the kitchen. Martha said, "Now, I didn't mean to put you two to work. You're our guests."

Brandon smiled and said, "That's okay, we had just gotten up anyway."

Ryan added, "Many hands make light work."

Martha said, "Well, that's mighty nice of you." After she put the plates in the sink, she cut her homemade apple pie into sixths. "Who wants ice cream?"

Grandma said, "Just a small piece for me, and just a taste of ice cream. I'm already full."

After everyone enjoyed dessert, they moved into the living room. Martha picked up the paper and said to no one in particular, "I wonder what's on TV. I think *It's a Wonderful Life* might be on."

Grandma said, "No, I think that was last night. They were showing it in the TV room at my retirement home."

Martha scanned the listings. "Let's see... it's 5:45... *It's a SpongeBob Christmas* started at 5:30."

"Pass!" Ralph exclaimed.

"Or there's *The Year Without a Santa Claus* that started just a few minutes ago, and *A Dream of Christmas* at 6:00 on the Hallmark channel."

Aaron said, "The Hallmark channel? Barf."

Brandon said, "I saw *The Year Without a Santa Claus* a couple of years ago. It's not bad."

Ralph said, "I wonder what bowl games are on." He held his hand out toward Martha, and she reluctantly handed him the paper. "Let's see... the Armed Forces Bowl is goin' on right now – Louisiana Tech versus Navy. Then at 8:00, we have the Dollar General Bowl with Troy versus Ohio U."

Brandon said, "You have a university here in Troy?"

Ralph said, "No, I think it's in Alabama."

Brandon said, "Still, it's funny. We're here in Troy, Ohio, and Troy and Ohio are playing in a bowl game."

Ryan said, "I can't believe there's a Dollar General Bowl. Is that some sort of consolation prize?"

Aaron said, "I read that there are 42 bowl games this year. It's gotten totally out of control. They're even letting some teams with 6-6 and 5-7 records play in bowls, just so they can fill them all up."

Martha took control. "Well, I don't want to sit around watching football – at least not one of the minor games. I say we go with *The Year Without a Santa Claus*." As an afterthought, she turned to Brandon. "That is, if you don't mind seeing it again."

Brandon said, "No, that's fine."

As everyone sat and watched the movie, Ryan caught himself nodding off every few minutes. While he was awake, he looked around the room and noticed that Aaron, Brandon, and Grandma had heavy eyelids too. At one point, Ralph started to snore.

When the movie ended a few minutes before 7:00, Aaron asked, "Would it be okay if we headed over to our hotel now? We've had a long day and we got just five hours of sleep last night, so we're pretty tired."

Martha said, "Well, I suppose so. We have a big day tomorrow! What time are you boys going to be here for breakfast?"

Aaron said, "I think they have breakfast at the hotel."

Martha frowned. That was obviously not the answer she wanted to hear.

Ryan stepped in. "But if that dinner was any indication, I'm sure breakfast here would be so much better. How about 8:00?"

Martha smiled. "That's what I was thinkin'. Certainly no later than that, 'specially if we're going to get in and out of the museum before lunch."

Everyone hugged and said goodnight. Ralph gave Aaron the keys to his car and said, "Now, you drive careful."

Once they were in the car, Aaron said, "Great. I really wanted to sleep in tomorrow."

Ryan said, "Relax. We'll still get nine or ten hours of sleep. We can get up at 6:30 and take turns in the shower."

Brandon said, "You mean you two aren't going to shower together?"

"That would take longer than if we showered separately if you know what I mean."

Brandon said, "Yeah, well better that than doin' it in bed while I'm tryin' to sleep."

Aaron said, "I'm so exhausted, I'm not going to be doing anything except sleeping."

They arrived at their hotel. Fortunately, they got a room with two queen beds, as they had reserved. Half an hour later, they were all asleep.

***

Saturday was a full but exciting day. They spent three hours exploring the Air Force Museum, and Ryan and Brandon enjoyed their first taste of Cincinnati-style chili.

Ryan said, "I'm going to learn how to make this at home. I bet I can find a recipe online."

Martha said, "I think they sell packets of the spice mix in the grocery stores here. We can stop in and check. I need a few things for tomorrow anyway."

After dinner, they watched another Christmas special and then played games. Martha brought out some photo albums and regaled Ryan and Brandon with pictures from Aaron's childhood, much to his embarrassment. "C'mon," Ryan said, "You were a cute kid. Get over yourself." *You're lucky you have photos from your childhood,* he thought.

"I was such a dork."

"You were a cute dork."

Finally, at 10:15, Aaron, Ryan, and Brandon said goodbye and returned to their hotel room.

Five minutes after they returned to their room, Brandon said, "I think I'll go down to the hotel's fitness center and get in a light workout."

Ryan said, "At 10:30 at night? Aren't you tired?"

"Not really. But I'm sure a good workout will tire me out."

"Suit yourself, but we still have to get up at 6:30 tomorrow morning."

Brandon sighed loudly. "Dude... I'm trying to give you guys some time alone. Duh!"

Aaron said, "That's really thoughtful, but–"

Ryan cut him off. "Thanks, bro! I really appreciate it! We'll try to keep it under two hours so you won't have to stay up all night."

Brandon's eyes popped open. "Whaaaaat???"

Ryan laughed. "Just kidding. A half-hour should be plenty. We do need to get some sleep."

Brandon quickly changed into sweatpants and a T-shirt.

Ryan said, "Put the 'Do Not Disturb' sign out. We'll take it in when we're done."

Brandon grabbed a towel and his key card and left the room.

Aaron said, "You're serious, aren't you?"

Ryan gave Aaron a loving kiss on the lips and wrapped his arms around his back. "Are you complaining? Surely you wouldn't say no to me on Christmas Eve."

Aaron smiled, "You know I can't say no to you."

Ryan kissed him again. "And I hope you never will."

A Very Special Gift

Sunday, December 25, 2016

On Christmas morning, Martha had scrambled eggs, bacon, and freshly baked frosted cinnamon rolls ready for the guys when they arrived. Christmas music was playing on the stereo.

As they were eating, Ralph said, "So I went to the ASU basketball website to look at their schedule, and I noticed your name isn't Brandon Robertson, it's Brandon Bauer."

Ryan said, "That's because I changed my name when I turned 18. That was only three months after I left home, and I didn't want my parents to find me. Plus, my father was becoming better known as a pastor. He had just gotten a book deal and he had visions of being a nationally-known televangelist. So I didn't want to have the same name as him."

Ralph asked, "Did you change your first name, too?"

"Yes. My birth name was Bryan Bauer. I chose Ryan because it sounds almost the same, and I figured it would be easier to get used to the sound of my new name."

Martha said, "Bauer... Is your father Brad Bauer, that big-shot pastor from Kansas?"

"The one and only."

"Oh my word... Isn't he the one that got caught at some kind of gay orgy a few months ago?"

"Yep. That was him all right."

Grandma spoke up. "That doesn't surprise me a bit. Those big-name televangelists always get caught doing something naughty sooner or later. Either they get caught with a prostitute, or they're having an affair, or embezzling money, or doin' drugs, or something. They reach a certain point and they think they're better than everyone else. They think the rules don't apply to them anymore. It's like the holier they act, the more you know there's gotta be somethin' they ain't telling you."

Ralph said, "So wait a minute. He got caught at a gay orgy, but he tried to force you to go to gay conversion therapy?"

"That's right."

"Well, ain't that the shit."

Martha said, "We bought a couple of his books back when we were goin' to that fundamentalist church. Our pastor recommended them to everyone in the congregation. They sold them at the little bookstore they have there. So after reading his books and some of the others they sell there, that's why we treated Aaron so badly when we found out he was gay. But after we came to our senses and switched churches, those books went in the trash."

Ralph said, "I can see why you don't want to have the same name as him. So why did you choose Robertson?"

Ryan said, "Well, at the time – and remember, this was when I was in high school – I had a boyfriend named Chris Robertson. We were planning to go to college and spend the rest of our lives together. So I thought if it ever became possible for us to get married, I'd already have the same last name."

Grandma said, "Awww, that's sweet. But what happened to him?"

"Well, once I ran away and went into hiding, that meant I had to leave him behind too, just like with Brandon. He went to college at the University of Maryland and he met a guy there. They're still together."

Martha said, "Everything about what happened to you is so sad. I feel sorry for you. You're such a nice young man. You didn't deserve to get cut off from your family and have all that stuff happen to you."

"Thanks. But it hasn't all been bad. The guys I lived with in Los Angeles were wonderful. They were my chosen family. And of course, now I have Aaron and I'm reunited with Brandon and I've got a good job and a nice place to live. So really, my life turned out pretty well after all."

After breakfast, everyone helped clear the table. People migrated into the living room to open their presents. Ryan made a side trip to use the bathroom. When he came out, Ralph was walking down the hall toward the living room, having just used the bathroom in their master bedroom. Ryan paused to let him pass, but Ralph stopped and said, in a low voice, "Young man, I have a question I need to ask you." He paused and leaned in closer. "What are your intentions for my son?"

Ryan did not see that coming. He stared at Ralph and thought, *What the hell kind of question is that? Are these people stuck in the fifties? How am I going to answer that?*

Then, inspiration struck. Ryan looked Ralph directly in the eyes, with a serious look on his face, and said, "I'm going to use him for my sex slave."

Now it was Ralph's turn to be shocked. The two men stared at each other, neither one batting an eye. After a few tense seconds, Ryan broke out laughing. A second later, Ralph started laughing too. "Good one! You had me there for a second. Young man, you and I are going to get along just fine."

Ryan motioned for Ralph to head back into the living room. He let Ralph go first. When Ryan passed the coat closet he stopped long enough to get something out of his coat pocket.

Aaron donned a Santa hat and passed out everyone's presents like he used to do when he was a kid. Martha had her camera close at hand to take pictures of people as they opened their presents. Ryan took some pictures on his phone too, so Martha would be in some of them.

After the excitement of the gift opening had subsided and the torn gift wrap had been disposed of, everyone settled into their places around the living room. Ralph reached for the remote and said, "I wonder what's on."

Ryan said, "Before we get into watching TV and doing other stuff, there's something I'd like to say."

Everyone turned to Ryan and gave him their attention.

"First, I just want to say this is the best Christmas I've ever had. Seriously. Ever since I left home nine years ago, I've spent most

Christmases alone. And that's okay, I've gotten used to it. I still enjoy the Christmas season, with all the lights, decorations, parties, concerts, and all that stuff. And back when I was growing up, Christmas always meant going to church on Christmas Eve and again on Christmas morning. We had presents and Christmas dinner and stuff, but – I don't know, I can't quite put my finger on it, but – my family was never like this. It's kinda like we just went through the motions. But you folks laugh and have fun and truly enjoy each other. There is so much love in this room! I've never felt anything like it. I mean, you never even met Brandon and me before, but you've made us feel welcome and included and... well, loved. So yeah, this is the best Christmas I've ever had. Thank you!"

Brandon said, "I second that. After Ryan left, Christmases were never the same, especially after Mom died. But even before, it was always focused on church and... well, it was like Ryan said. It was okay, but it didn't have the warmth and love that you've shown us here. The energy is totally different. And I'm not even the one who's dating your son, I'm just your son's boyfriend's brother. But you've opened your home and your hearts to me and made me feel so welcome."

Martha said, "Well, that's so sweet of you to say all that. Having you boys here has been a joy for us. It's the most exciting Christmas we've had around here for quite a few years. I hope you come back next year and every year after that. You're always welcome in our home."

Ralph said, "Yeah. You're like family to us already."

Ryan said, "Well, that leads nicely to the other thing I wanted to say. You've made us feel like part of your family, and it's great to have a family to be part of again. So I'd like to make it official." Ryan took a few steps over to where Aaron was seated and dropped to one knee. He reached into his pocket and pulled out the small box he had retrieved from his coat pocket earlier. "Aaron Bradbury, in the last six months, you have totally changed my life. You convinced me to start playing my trumpet again. You reunited me with my brother. And most of all, you've loved me. Relationships have been difficult for me, for a variety of reasons. I had pretty much resigned myself to being single for the rest of my life. But you came along and changed all of that. Now, I'm filled with hope for everything that lies ahead in the years to come - but only if I can share those experiences with you." He paused and took a deep breath. The anticipation and excitement in the room was palpable. "Aaron, will you marry me?" He opened the box to reveal a ring.

Aaron could barely believe what he had just heard. He was so shocked and overtaken with emotion that he couldn't speak.

After a few tense seconds, Ralph said, "Well, say yes, dummy!"

That jolted Aaron out of his momentary paralysis. "Yes! Yes! Of course! Yes, yes, yes! Oh my God!!!" Aaron leaned forward in his chair, grabbed the sides of Ryan's head, and planted several huge kisses on him. Up to this point, he had been hesitant to kiss Ryan in front of his parents and grandmother or show any other kind of physical affection. But in this moment, he couldn't care less. Everybody, even Ralph, was reveling in this moment. Brandon, whom Ryan had tipped off ahead of time, was capturing the whole event on video with his phone.

When Aaron stopped kissing Ryan, he had tears streaming down his cheeks. He wiped them with his sleeve. Ryan said, "Here, let me put the ring on your finger." Aaron looked confused, so Ryan reached for his left hand. "This one." He slid the ring onto Aaron's ring finger.

Martha clasped her hands in front of her chest and exclaimed, "I can't believe our son is getting married!"

Ralph couldn't resist the temptation to tease Aaron. "Well, since he gave the ring to you, does that make you the bride? Shit. That means I'm gonna hafta pay for the wedding. And does that mean you're gonna be wearin' a wedding dress?"

Aaron wasn't amused. "Dad! Of course not! We're men, and we're going to dress like men. Sheesh."

"Oh, come on now. I was just teasin' you."

Ryan laughed and said, "Don't worry, we can pay for the wedding. And of course, we want you all there. We can pay for your airfare if that would be helpful."

Ralph said, "I think we can swing that, but thanks for the offer."

Grandma said, "I'd love to be there, but I don't know... I may not be up for a long airplane flight."

Martha said, "Maybe we can decide on that closer to the time."

Aaron said, "If you can't make it, we can livestream it on Facebook, so you can watch it live."

Grandma said, "I'm not sure I know how to do that. I'm not on Facebook."

Ryan said, "Maybe Zoom or Skype would be easier."

Aaron said, "Well, we'll get it all figured out and get you set up."

Martha asked, "So, have you picked a date yet?"

Aaron replied, "Mom, I just now found out about it. This was a total surprise!"

Ryan said, "We'll talk about it and let you know as soon as we decide. But I was thinking maybe next fall, like September or October."

Ralph said, "Good. Just don't have it in the middle of summer when it's so blasted hot out there."

Ryan said, "Yeah, that's why I was thinking about the fall. The weather will be perfect then. We'll talk about it and let you know. But one thing I do know... Brandon, I want you to be my best man." Brandon smiled and nodded.

Aaron said, "And Dad? I want you to be my best man."

Ralph looked genuinely surprised. "Really? Are you serious? Usually, guys pick their best friend."

"There's no one I'd rather give this honor to. And Mom, we'll find some special way for you to be part of the ceremony."

Grandma said, "Martha, do you still have that little essay I read at your wedding?"

"Of course I do, Mom."

"Good. Even if you didn't, I still have my copy. But anyway, when Martha and Ralph got married, they asked me to read a short essay at their wedding. It was just a few bits of wisdom and advice for having a happy marriage."

Martha said, "It was really good. I still get it out and read it now and then."

Ryan said, "Well, then, would you please read it at our wedding?"

Aaron added, "Yes! I think that would be a great idea."

Martha said, "Well, okay. I'm not much of a public speaker, but I'll try my best."

Aaron said, "I know you'll do fine."

Martha stood up and said, "Stand up, boys! I wanna hug you."

Everyone stood up and hugged each other. Then Martha said, "And I want to take some pictures! We need some new family photos. And I want to be able to show off my soon-to-be son-in-law to my friends."

Ralph said, "Let me get out the tripod. I can set the timer on the camera so we can all be in the picture."

After they had finished taking dozens of pictures with various combinations of people, Ralph collapsed the tripod and headed toward the master bedroom to put it back in the closet. Aaron headed in that direction at the same time because he wanted to use the hall bathroom. Ralph turned to Aaron and said, "I still can't believe you asked me to be your best man. That means a lot to me."

Aaron smiled. "I really appreciate how supportive you are about this whole thing, and how nice you've been to Ryan and Brandon."

"They're fine young men. And y'know, if you're gonna spend your life with another man, I think you picked a really good one. I mean, it's not like you need my permission or anything, but..."

"I don't, but it's nice to have your support. Thanks, Dad." He paused. "I love you."

"I love you too, son."

"I love you *and* your terrible jokes."

Ralph chuckled. "Well, it's a good thing. They come with the package."

They hugged, then Ralph resumed his trip to the master bedroom. Aaron stepped into the bathroom. While he was seated on the throne, he pulled out his phone and launched Facebook. After scrolling through dozens of 'Merry Christmas' posts from his friends, he realized he had post-worthy news. He turned on the phone's camera, held his hand out with the ring on his finger, and snapped a close-up photo. He posted it with the caption, 'Of course I said yes!'

Then he navigated to his profile and changed his relationship status to 'Engaged.'

Meanwhile, Martha headed into the kitchen to start making their Christmas dinner. Ryan followed her in. "Martha, may I help with anything?"

"Thanks, honey, but I can manage..." Then she realized Ryan wasn't offering just to be polite. This was an opportunity for a bonding experience. She smiled. "You know, on second thought, I'd appreciate a little help."

"I'm a pretty good cook, so just let me know what you'd like me to do."

"Yes, Aaron has raved about your cooking. Can I put you in charge of the salads? There are two heads of lettuce in the refrigerator, a package of cherry tomatoes, and a cucumber you can slice up."

"I'd be glad to."

"And then when the ham comes out of the oven, you can slice it." After a few minutes, she said, "You know, I probably should've done more to teach Aaron how to cook. I just assumed he'd marry a woman someday and she'd do most of the cooking. I guess it never occurred to me that there might be other possibilities."

"Yeah, that's how it works most of the time."

"You know, I was starting to get worried about him. He's 28, and he never mentioned having a girlfriend. In fact, he avoided the topic. Whenever I asked, he'd get flustered and change the subject. Now I know why. But it didn't seem like he had many friends either. No social life. But now, he has you, he's playing his trombone again, which I'm really happy about, and he seems to have a lot of friends now."

"It's funny how much has changed in the last six months – both for him and for me. I have a lot more friends now, too."

"So, did your mother teach you how to cook?"

"A little. Sometimes if she was busy at the church, she'd ask me to make lunch for Brandon and me. Nothing complicated, though. She did almost all the cooking. My parents bought into the stereotypical gender roles, which meant the woman did all the cooking."

"Yeah, we're kinda like that too. But if I go first, heaven forbid, I don't think Ralph would starve. He knows how to use a microwave! Of course, he could stand to lose a little weight."

Ryan chuckled. "When I lived in LA, I rented a room in a house near UCLA. The guy who owned it, Hal, was a really good cook. Every Sunday evening, he'd cook dinner for the four of us who lived there. It was a chance for everyone to be together – sort of a family night. I learned a lot about cooking from Hal." Ryan paused. "I learned a lot about life from Hal. He was more like a father to me than my real father."

"So are you going to call him sometime today and wish him a Merry Christmas and tell him you're engaged?"

Ryan sighed. "Hal passed away suddenly near the end of my senior year."

"Ohhh... I'm so sorry! What happened to him?"

Ryan's eyes moistened. "Well, it's kind of a long story, but the short version is he got depressed and started drinking. Later in the evening, he got in his hot tub. He passed out, slumped down into the water, and drowned."

"Oh, my word! How terrible!"

Ryan sniffled. The tears were starting to flow. "I was the one who found him the next morning."

Martha stopped whipping the mashed sweet potatoes and set the spoon down. She turned to Ryan and hugged him. "Oh, honey, I'm so sorry. I shouldn't have brought it up. I ask too many questions sometimes."

Martha's hug was surprisingly comforting. Ryan pulled himself together and said, "That's okay. You didn't know."

"You've been through a lot, haven't you?"

"You have no idea. But it's made me a stronger person. I've

learned that life's going to throw stuff at you whether you like it or not. It doesn't do you any good to blame others or say, 'I don't deserve this.' You just have to accept responsibility for yourself and deal with it as best as you can. There will always be good times and bad times, and you have to work through the bad until the good comes around again. Really, though, I'm very fortunate. I got a good education, I have a good job, I live in a nice house in a beautiful community, I have bands to play in, I have friends, I'm back together with my brother, and now I'm engaged to a wonderful man who has wonderful parents. I'm truly thankful for everything I have. I'm very well off in all the ways that count. And I'm pretty sure I'm strong enough to deal with whatever comes along in the future."

As Ryan was speaking, Martha gazed up at him in admiration. Then she hugged him again and said, "You're a wonderful man. Aaron is so lucky he found you."

"I'm the lucky one."

They resumed their food preparation. A moment later, Martha said, "You know, back when Ralph and I were engaged and we were making plans for our life together, we always talked about having two or three kids. But when Aaron came along it was a difficult pregnancy, and the doctor said I shouldn't have more kids. We were disappointed at the time, but we got over it and let it go, and we just focused on being thankful for Aaron. But now, I feel like I have a second son after all!"

Ryan smiled.

Martha added, "Three, actually."

"Thanks! You've certainly made us feel like we're part of the family."

"That's 'cause you are. And I hope you'll come and visit us whenever you can."

"That goes for you too. We have a guest bedroom. You and Ralph need to come out and visit us sometime."

"We'll certainly be coming out for your wedding!"

Ryan snickered. "Just think! You now have two more sons and you didn't have to change any diapers or pay for college."

Martha chuckled. "You got that right. And you two are so big, I'm glad I didn't have to try to push you out of my birth canal."

Ryan laughed. "Mom said we were long, slender babies, so it might have been easier. I was 24" long when I was born."

"It's never easy. But oh Lord! Aaron was 17" long and that darn near killed me."

The timer dinged and Martha pulled the ham and the dinner rolls out of the oven. She and Ryan worked together to transfer the ham to the cutting board so Ryan could slice it.

Dinner was delicious and conversation flowed freely. Brandon talked about his first semester at ASU and his experience with being on the basketball team. Aaron talked about his new job at the Food World pharmacy and Desert Pride's holiday concert. Ryan attempted to explain what he did for a living, but due to the technical nature of his job and the intellectual property restrictions he was bound by, he couldn't say too much. But he talked about playing his trumpet, how much he loved jazz, and getting reconnected with his high school boyfriend, Chris.

They talked about Ralph's job and when he planned to retire, and what Martha and Ralph planned to do after he retired. Grandma talked about activities they had at her retirement home.

In the evening, they sat around the table and played games. Ryan recalled the game nights he and his housemates enjoyed during the years he lived in LA. He said to Aaron, "This is so much fun. We should start hosting game nights with some of our friends."

Hours passed and nobody noticed. Finally, Aaron pulled his phone from his pocket and said, "Good lord! It's 11:15 already. We'd better get back to the hotel and get some sleep. We have to get up at 6:00 a.m. Our flight's at 9:15."

Ryan said, "Thanks, everyone, for the best Christmas ever."

Aaron said, "And thank *you* for the best Christmas present ever."

Everyone got up and hugged each other, and then Aaron, Ryan, and Brandon drove back to the hotel.

Once they were in the room, Brandon said, "Am I going to have to go for another workout tonight?"

Ryan said, "Well, as much as I'd love to fuck my new fiancé's brains out right now, we really need to get to sleep."

Brandon feigned disgust and said, "Dude... really?"

Aaron kissed Ryan and said, "Now I understand why you were so... *enthusiastic* last night."

Brandon covered his ears and winced. "Oh, God... TMI! TMI!"

Ryan said, "You should be happy your brother and his fiancé have a robust, satisfying sex life."

Brandon replied, "I *am* happy for you. I just don't want to hear about it!"

Aaron said, "Fiancé. I like the sound of that."

Ryan said, "Well, it'll do for the time being. I think 'husband' sounds even better."

Stalled Out

Monday, December 26, 2016

On their return trip, the guys had a two-hour layover in Dallas. Their flight from Dayton arrived at Gate C4, and their departure gate, C26, was in the same concourse.

As they passed Dick's Pork Pit, Ryan asked, "Are either of you hungry? We have enough time to grab a bite."

Aaron replied, "Nah… I'm still full from all those pancakes Mom stuffed into us at breakfast."

Brandon said, "Me too. I'm good."

Ryan couldn't pass up the chance for a bad joke. "You sure you don't feel like eating any Dick's today?"

Brandon shot him a glance that said '*Really???*' "No thanks. Remember, you are what you eat."

Aaron chuckled. *It's great that Brandon is comfortable enough with his brother being gay that they can tease each other like this.*

"Okay, just thought I'd ask. Let's head to the gate and maybe grab a soda along the way."

As they approached Gate C26, Ryan scanned the seating area to locate three empty chairs together. The area was busy with holiday travelers and the seats for Gate C26 were almost full an hour and a half before the flight. But there were some empty seats in the waiting area for C24. Close enough.

They entered a nearly empty row. Ryan and Aaron sat down next to each other facing C24 and retrieved their Kindles from their carry-ons. Brandon sat across from them, pulled out his earbuds, and paired them with his phone.

After about fifteen minutes passed, Ryan finished a chapter of his book and looked up. The seating area for C24 was filling up with passengers waiting for their flight to Salt Lake City. As he scanned the new arrivals, he noticed a 30ish mom and dad trying to keep two excited, hyperactive kids contained in their small tract of waiting area real estate. The mother was facing Ryan and the father was facing away. The kids looked cute in their Mickey Mouse T-shirts and mouse ears. The boy wanted to explore the concourse, but each time he took a few tentative steps away, his mom called him back.

Ryan smiled as he thought back to the trip his family had taken to Disney World. It was one of the few extravagant vacations his family had ever taken. Ryan was 13 at the time, so Brandon would have been five, about the same age this little boy is now.

Ryan fondly recalled spending much of the day in Fantasyland, either riding the kids' rides with Brandon or watching him with their parents from the sidelines. They all rode Pirates of the Caribbean, the Haunted House, and It's a Small World. The latter was torturous for Ryan, but the cuteness overload and the cloyingly repetitious soundtrack were magical to Brandon.

Ryan, who at age 13 had already reached 6' 2", had a few opportunities to experience the grown-up rides like Space Mountain and Big Thunder Mountain Railway with his father, while his mother gave Brandon the honor of chauffeuring her around in a tiny car on the mini-turnpike. It occurred to Ryan that that was probably the most fun he ever had with his dad. For a few brief days, they laughed, relaxed, and shared a carefree father-son rapport. That never seemed possible at home when his dad was constantly absorbed with his church commitments. It was as if they had taken a vacation from Jesus.

That was the only time Ryan and his family ever visited Walt Disney World. Soon thereafter, his dad discovered that the Disney empire valued their gay employees enough to offer them domestic partner benefits. Disney World and Disneyland even allowed so-called 'Gay Days' to take place once a year. From that moment on, none of the Bauer family's hard-earned dollars would be spent on anything Disney.

A couple of aisles away, the little boy successfully made a break for it. Dad sprang up from his seat and chased after the boy, catching him after about a dozen steps and leading him back to their encampment. Ryan was able to get a better look at the father, whose face stirred a painful memory from his college days at UCLA.

Ryan reached over and tapped Brandon on his knee. Brandon pulled one earbud out. Ryan said, "Hey, swap seats with me, okay?"

Brandon looked puzzled by this sudden request but he got up and changed places with Ryan. As they passed within a few inches of each other, Ryan whispered, "There's someone I would rather not see – or be seen by. I'll tell you more later."

The seat swap distracted Aaron from his book. He closed the lid on his Kindle, spent a few minutes looking around, and then said, "I'm going to go find a restroom. Watch my stuff, okay?"

Ryan glanced behind him, hoping he wouldn't be spotted. It looked like Dad had left the scene, leaving Mom to manage the two kids on her own. They had settled down.

Five minutes later, Aaron returned to the boarding area. He walked up to the gate and spoke briefly with one of the gate agents. After exchanging a few sentences, Aaron returned to his seat and sat down.

Ryan leaned into Aaron and asked in a low voice, "What was that about?"

Aaron sighed. "As I walked past the urinals on my way to an open stall, I passed this guy who was just standing there with his dick in his hand, not peeing or anything. Almost like he was showing it off. He winked at me as I passed. Anyway, I went into a stall and did my business. As I was coming out, I saw that guy and some other guy going into the stall next to me. It was the last one on the row – the handicapped stall.

"Anyway, after I washed my hands, I looked back at that stall and I could see two pairs of feet – one sitting on the toilet and the other facing the toilet. It was pretty obvious what was going on. So I reported it to the gate agent. He said he would call the airport police."

"Maybe you just busted another Republican senator."

Aaron didn't get it. Ryan let it go.

Ryan said, "I've gotta pee, so watch my stuff."

"Stay away from the last stall!"

"Damn. I was hoping to make it a three-way."

Aaron rolled his eyes as Ryan stood up to leave.

Ryan saw three vacant urinals in a row. He pulled up to the middle one, leaving the customary one-urinal gap on each side. He unzipped, pulled it out, and began peeing.

A moment later, the last stall door opened. An embarrassed man emerged and hurried out, trying his best not to make eye contact with anyone.

About ten seconds later, a second figure cautiously emerged from the stall. It was Cody, whom Ryan had dated for a year during college.

Ryan stared at the wall in front of him, angling slightly away with the hope that Cody wouldn't recognize him. No such luck. Cody pulled up to the urinal next to Ryan. He pulled his dick out, and in a soft but excited voice, said, "Well, fancy meeting you here!"

"Don't talk to me." Ryan continued staring at the wall, hoping Cody would get the hint and leave. He didn't.

Cody said, "I still think about you a lot."

Ryan shook the last few drops from his dick, and Cody leaned over to get a better view. He wasn't even trying to be discrete. "I think about *that* a lot too."

Ryan reeled it in as fast as he could and zipped up. He turned and glared at Cody. "Too bad you don't think about what a dishonest, disgusting sack of shit you are." He spoke loud enough that several other men within earshot heard it. He pointed to a gooey glob on Cody's shirt, about six inches below his chin. "Jesus Christ. You can't even swallow it all." Cody glanced down, horrified.

And with that, Ryan turned and walked quickly toward the door. He passed his hands under the motion-activated spigot, barely getting his hands wet. He grabbed a section of paper towel, wiped his hands, and slammed the wadded towel into the trash can – all while hardly missing a step.

When he zigzagged through the privacy switchback at the entrance, he nearly collided with two policemen heading into the restroom. "Are you looking for the guy who was giving head in the last stall?"

They stopped on a dime.

Ryan said, "I saw him and another guy come out of the stall. He tried to come on to me while I was taking a piss. Blond guy, 30ish. He's at the sink trying to clean the cum off his Disney World T-shirt."

The cops snickered. One of them said, "Thanks, man. Would you mind hanging around for a few minutes so we can get a statement from you?"

"Sure."

"Just stand over there and I'll be over in a few minutes. Unless you're in a hurry to catch your plane."

"No, I've got time."

And with that, the cops headed into the restroom.

Ryan waited in the concourse near the entrance to the restroom. A couple more cops arrived and headed inside.

A few minutes later, Cody was led out in handcuffs and escorted down the concourse in a most embarrassing walk of shame. Most other people were in a hurry or were too engrossed in their books or headphones to notice, but some did. Ryan glanced in the direction of Cody's wife and kids. Sadly, they witnessed the whole thing.

The officer who had spoken with Ryan at the restroom entrance approached him. He asked for Ryan's name and contact information, and then asked him to recount what he saw.

"Well, I went into the men's room to take a leak. As I walked toward the urinals, it looked like there were two pairs of feet in that last stall. I heard a few sounds coming from in there, like sighs and moans. Anyway, I was standing there peeing when the door opened and one guy came out. He hurried out of there quickly."

"Can you describe him?"

"I only got a quick glance. About 5'10", dark hair. Looked like he could have been Middle Eastern or something. After eight or ten seconds passed, the door opened again, and the guy you just apprehended came out. He came up to the urinal next to me and said hello. I told him not to talk to me and I just stared straight ahead at the wall. He kept trying to talk to me, and when I was shaking my dick off at the end, he leaned over the partition to look at it."

"You said he came up and said hi to you. Have you met this guy before?"

"We both went to UCLA five or six years ago. He told me he was going to go back to Utah after he graduated and marry his high school sweetheart. I think that's her and their two kids sitting over there by Gate C24. I saw him sitting with them earlier."

"So did you go into the restroom after you saw him walking in there?"

Ryan didn't like what that question insinuated, but he let it pass. "No, I had no idea it was him in the stall until he came out. I just went in to pee."

"Were you the one who reported the two men in the stall?"

"No sir, I did not."

"Okay, thank you very much for your time. Have a safe flight."

The officer hurried off, and Ryan made his way back to his seat.

Brandon asked, "What was that all about?" Aaron looked like he knew.

Ryan leaned toward Brandon. "I'll tell you later when there aren't so many people around."

A couple of minutes later, Cody's wife approached. "Excuse me, sir, I'm sorry to bother you. Could I please speak to you for a moment?"

Ryan glanced at Aaron and Brandon, then got up and followed her to an empty spot along the side of the concourse. He dreaded the conversation that was about to take place and was trying to decide how he would explain what happened.

The woman spoke first. "I saw you talking to the police officer after they took that man away. Do you know what was going on?"

"May I ask why you're interested?"

"That man is my husband."

Ryan was almost certain of that, but it would have been inappropriate to divulge what he knew to a casual bystander.

He took a deep breath. "Your husband was in one of the toilet stalls having oral sex with another man."

She looked incredulous. "That can't be right. There must be some mistake."

"When I went in, I saw two pairs of feet in that stall. Then while I was standing at the urinal peeing, they both came out."

"But you didn't actually see what they were doing in there."

"No, but I heard sounds. And there's really only one reason why two men would go into a bathroom stall together. Besides, he came on to me afterward."

"No. You must have misinterpreted whatever it was he did."

"Look, I know this is difficult for you, but I know when I'm being hit on. It was obvious. I also know when someone is trying to get a look at my private parts. He wasn't subtle about it."

As the truth was setting in, Cody's wife became more flustered – or angry. Ryan wasn't sure which. "There must be some mistake. My husband is NOT gay! I'm his wife and we have two children."

"So do lots of closet cases." Ryan took a deep breath and tried to remain calm. "Jennifer…"

Cody's wife froze. "Wait a minute. How do you know my name?"

Ryan sighed. "Okay, you deserve to know the truth. Cody and I went to UCLA at the same time. And... well... we dated for a year. During our senior year, I took him out to a nice restaurant on Valentine's Day. He chose that evening to tell me he had proposed to you over Christmas break and that he was going to marry you that summer. Up to that point, I thought we were a couple. I thought we were going to have a long-term relationship. I was even willing to take a job in Lehi because he said he wanted to go back to Utah after he graduated. But that all crashed and burned. So, that's how I know your name – and your husband."

Jennifer was too stunned to say anything.

Ryan said, "I don't know whether he's gay or bi or straight or whatever. He would probably say he's straight, he just loves to suck cock and get fucked in the ass – which, by the way, he couldn't get enough of. Anyway, I'm sorry for you. I'm sorry you had to find out about his past and his ... proclivities this way."

Jennifer tried to process this new, unsettling information. "Well, okay. Thank you... I guess. I'm sorry he treated you that way."

"It really hurt at the time. But I guess I was pretty naïve. I should have seen the situation for what it was."

Jennifer looked over at her kids, who were being watched by an elderly couple sitting next to them. "What am I going to do?"

"Well, they're starting to board your flight. I suggest that you and your kids get in line and get on the plane." Jennifer looked shocked at the suggestion. "Give his carry-on to the gate agent. Or leave it. Or take it with you. Whatever. He got himself into this mess, he can get himself out of it."

The gravity of the situation was still setting in. "What am I going to tell my children?"

Ryan couldn't imagine how Jennifer would explain this. *Shoplifting, maybe? Or he got lost in the airport? That would be easier than trying to explain that their father was a cocksucker.* "I don't know. That's going to be very difficult. I guess one option would be to tell them the truth."

The truth will set you free, Ryan thought. *But first, it will piss you off.* He knew he shouldn't say that.

Jennifer turned and headed toward her kids.

Ryan called out, "Good luck. I hope things turn out for the best for you and your kids."

Jennifer turned back and glanced at Ryan. "Thanks."

Planning a Wedding

Sunday, January 22, 2017

Aaron remembered from his early days in the band that Rob officiated weddings. Ryan agreed that Rob would be an excellent choice, so they invited Rob and Eddie to dinner on Sunday. The ASU basketball team had an away game at USC, so Brandon was gone.

They arrived promptly at 5:00. After a round of hugs, Rob asked, "How was your Christmas?"

Aaron said, "Really great. We went to Ohio to visit my parents. Brandon went too." He held out his ring finger. "And I got this!"

Eddie and Rob admired his ring and offered their congratulations. Eddie said, "That's wonderful. Of all the gay couples I know, I'm not aware of anyone who gave their partner an engagement ring."

Rob said, "Me neither. But then, the fact that we can even get married is a recent development. I think it will take a while before we form traditions and norms in our community."

Ryan said, "If they form at all. Since we're non-traditional by definition, I can see where every couple might do whatever they feel like doing."

Rob said, "I think you're right. The gay and lesbian weddings I've officiated so far have been all over the place in terms of what they chose to do."

The oven timer dinged and Ryan pulled two homemade pizzas out of the oven. He sliced them, carried the pizza pans over to the dining room table, and set them down on trivets in the center. Everyone sat down and helped themselves to a slice.

Once they had eaten their first few bites, Ryan asked Rob, "How long have you been officiating weddings?"

"Since October 2014. That's when same-sex marriage became legal in Arizona. Justin and Kent were the first couple I married. They had already been together for eight years, so they wanted something simple at their home with a few of their friends. They didn't want a religious wedding and they wanted someone gay to officiate it. In the time it took me to fill out an online form, I got ordained by the Universal Freedom Church. Two of the other couples they invited wanted to get married too, so they hired me. Back then, since marriage equality had just come to Arizona, hundreds of gay and lesbian couples wanted to get married. I recognized a business opportunity. I threw together a website and bought a listing in the LGBT Chamber of Commerce's business directory. The calls started coming in! Now, two years and three months later, I've officiated almost 200 weddings. I'm getting business from straight couples, too."

Aaron said, "Wow! Almost 200 weddings in just over two years? You've been busy."

"Yeah, it really takes up a lot of my time. Besides performing the wedding itself, I meet with the couple for a consultation, work up several options for wedding scripts, and go back and forth with them about what they want for their wedding. But I enjoy it. Each wedding is special in its own way. I've met some very nice people. And it's a privilege to play a significant role in one of the most special days of a couple's life."

Ryan said, "You mean you don't just say the same thing at each wedding?"

"No, I customize it for each couple."

"And you got your ordination from someplace online in a couple of minutes? Is that even legal?"

"It sure is. One of the beautiful things about the separation of church and state is that the government can't tell churches how they should ordain their clergy. The Universal Freedom Church believes everyone should be able to pursue their own ministry in whatever manner they see fit. They also provide a lot of resources on their website for things like how to officiate a wedding. There's a lot of other information you can find online too."

Aaron asked, "So how's it been going with you guys?"

Eddie said, "We've been seeing each other for two and a half months now, ever since we met at your election night party. We'll always be indebted to you for that. It's way too soon to talk about moving in together, let alone marriage, but it's going really well. How long have you guys been together?"

Ryan said, "We met back in May when he came to the gay running club I belong to. So that would be eight months ago."

Rob said, "Wow. That's kind of fast."

Aaron said, "Maybe so, but it feels right. We're looking at a date in October, so it'll be another nine months until we get married."

Ryan said, "So we have nine months to discover the skeletons in each other's closets."

Aaron asked, "You mean there are *more*?"

Ryan shot back, "No, I just haven't found yours yet."

Everyone laughed.

Rob said, "I have some questions I'll ask you after we finish eating and I can more easily write stuff down. But we can get started with a few things now. Tell me what you have in mind for your wedding."

Ryan said, "I don't even know where to start. I can't remember ever attending a wedding. I know that sounds hard to believe, but my family didn't have any relatives in the area and I didn't stay in touch with any of my straight friends from high school. Even during college, all my friends were gay. So I guess the only weddings I've seen have been on TV shows or movies, and you only see little bits of those."

Aaron said, "I've been to ten or twelve weddings of high school or college friends."

Rob asked, "Were those weddings held in churches or wedding venues or somewhere else?"

"Mostly churches. I went to one that was in the couple's backyard."

Ryan said, "Well, we definitely don't want a church wedding. We don't belong to a church and we aren't religious. I hope that's not a problem for you."

Rob said, "Oh, I'm not religious either. It's funny – I'm an ordained minister, but I'm not religious. But a lot of couples, both gay and straight, don't want a religious wedding, so that's why they hire me. So then, do you want any prayers or any mention of Jesus or God?"

Aaron and Ryan looked at each other and shook their heads. Aaron said, "None of the above. We want something completely secular."

Rob said, "That's fine. Here in Arizona where the weather's nice most of the time, people have a lot more outdoor weddings than in many other parts of the country. And there are some really nice wedding venues all over the valley. Many of them have their ceremony space outdoors and their reception space indoors."

Ryan looked at Aaron. "I hadn't even thought of having it at a venue. What about you?"

"No. Like I said, most of the weddings I've been to have been in churches. They usually go to some kind of reception hall afterward."

Ryan asked, "So, generally speaking, how much do these wedding venues cost?"

Rob said, "I don't know. I never see the bill, but I'd guess they're expensive. A lot of them are pretty swanky. I bet they're anywhere from twenty to fifty thousand dollars, depending on how nice it is and how many people you're feeding. Of course, most of the time those are the straight weddings, where the father of the bride is paying for it with money he's been saving for years."

Ryan turned to Aaron. "Honey, no offense, but... you know I love you, but I can't see spending that kind of money on a wedding."

Aaron said, "Me neither. So what do gay couples usually do?"

"A lot of times, they have something small at home with only a few friends. Or they might find a nice spot at one of the parks in the area. Sometimes, it's only them and they pay me to bring a couple of witnesses along. Personally, I think a lot of gay couples sell themselves short on their weddings. Getting married is a major life event. I believe it should be celebrated. Most of these couples aren't hurting for money. They could spend some money on themselves for their wedding. But that's not my decision to make. I give them the best ceremony I can, no matter how large or small the wedding is."

Eddie says, "Based on what Rob has told me, a lot of these couples have already been together 20, 30, or even 40 years. In some cases, they may have had commitment ceremonies already. They're just doing it to get the marriage license and the legal protection it provides."

"Eddie's right. The fact that these couples had to wait so many years to get married should be all the more reason to celebrate. But that's just me. Anyway, back to you guys. How many people were you thinking of inviting?"

Aaron and Ryan looked at each other. Aaron said, "I don't know. We haven't really talked about it. My parents are going to come out here for the wedding. And of course, there's Brandon. But other than that? I dunno... I was thinking maybe we'd invite everyone from the band and maybe the running club. And Ryan might want to invite some of his colleagues from work. I don't feel the need to invite anyone from my work."

Ryan said, "Everyone in the band and the running club? Once you figure in their partners or spouses, we're talking at least 100 people. I don't want a wedding that big."

Aaron said, "But then how do you decide who gets invited and who doesn't? Where do you draw the line? I don't want to offend anyone."

Rob said, "I've been in the band a few years longer than you guys have. I think most people will be fine either way. I mean, they're adults. Very few of them, if any, would invite the entire band to their wedding. If it were me, I'd only invite the people I'm closest with. In other words, I'd invite my friends, but not my acquaintances."

Ryan said, "I think that's a good way to put it. Friends, yes; acquaintances, no."

Aaron said, "So that would leave us with maybe 15 or 20

people."

Ryan said, "Yeah. Besides Eddie, I might want to invite a few people from work. And I'd like to invite Ted, Darnell, and Ricky, my housemates from LA. I doubt they'd travel in for it, but I want to at least invite them."

Aaron said, "What about the guys in San Diego?"

"Ehhh... Maybe Kevin and Chase. But I can go either way on the other three guys. Let's wait until we draw up a list and see how many people are already on it."

Aaron said, "So now we're talking anywhere from 20 to 30 people."

"That sounds about right to me. I don't need it to be any bigger than that. What do you think?"

"I'm fine with that. Oh, what about Grandma? We talked at one point about livestreaming it for her since she might not be up for traveling."

Ryan turned to Rob. "Do you have any objection if we livestream the wedding?"

"No, not at all. I've had quite a few couples do that. Or sometimes they record it on video."

Ryan turned back to Aaron. "Who do you think we should get to run that for us? I don't want us to have to mess with it during the ceremony."

"I don't know. We'll think of someone."

Eddie said, "I'd be happy to do it. I have a good quality video camera with a shotgun mic and a wind sock. I can hook it up to my laptop and run the livestream."

Ryan said, "That would be great! Thanks! And Ted, Darnell, and Ricky can watch the livestream if they don't come."

Rob said, "So now that you've decided on the size, you can make a better decision about the place."

Aaron said, "You said some people have their weddings in their homes or backyards. We could have our wedding here!"

Ryan thought about it for a moment. "Ehhh... I'm not ruling it out, but that doesn't excite me."

Rob said, "Some couples find a restaurant with a separate dining room people can reserve for private events. That would work well for 20 or 30 people."

Ryan said, "Of everything we've talked about so far, the idea of having it outdoors in a nice park appeals to me the most. What do you think?"

Aaron said, "I could see us doing that. Then we could have dinner afterward."

"You mean for us or for everyone?"

"Everyone. We could find a restaurant with a private dining room."

Rob said, "Do you want to have dancing at your reception? Because you probably couldn't do that in a restaurant."

Ryan said, "That would be fun, but I don't really have to have it. As far as I'm concerned, as long as we have dinner, a wedding cake, a champagne toast, and some mingling, that's enough for me."

Aaron said, "And an open bar."

"Well, yeah. So, Rob, what are some parks you've been to that are nice places for weddings?"

"Hmmm... Well, my favorite is Papago Park. There's Encanto Park, South Mountain, Tumbleweed Park in Gilbert, and Usury Mountain northeast of Mesa. Those are the ones that come to mind. I'm sure I'll think of others later."

Ryan said, "Okay, that gives us a good place to start. We can go look at some of those."

Aaron said, "For dinner, you know that Brazilian Steakhouse where we went for your birthday? They have a separate dining room in the back that would be the right size."

"Yeah, I could see going there. Your dad would be in heaven with all that meat."

They finished eating. Aaron and Ryan cleared the table and sat down again. Rob pulled out a notebook and a pen. "I created this list of questions to ask every couple. That way I don't forget anything and have to go back to them later. This might sound like an interview, but it helps me understand exactly what you want for your wedding."

Ryan looked over at his page full of pre-printed questions. "You're well organized. I like that."

Rob said, "Okay. We've already talked about the religion thing. No prayers or anything else. So now, is someone going to walk either or both of you down the aisle?"

Aaron and Ryan looked at each other and shrugged. Ryan said, "That sounds like a bride thing. What do two guys usually do?"

"It varies. Oh, and I should also ask, how big will your wedding party be?"

Aaron and Ryan looked confused. Aaron said, "Well, 20 or 30, like we said."

Rob smiled. "No, I mean bridesmaids and groomsmen. How many people will be standing up in front with you and me?

Ryan said, "Well, my brother Brandon is going to be my best man and Aaron's father Ralph is going to be his. Do we need to have anyone else up there?"

"That's up to you."

"What would those other people do?"

"Just stand up there and look nice, honestly."

"Well, then, I don't see the point. Do you, honey?"

Aaron shook his head.

Rob said, "Okay, then back to walking down the aisle. At most straight weddings, the groom and the officiant enter first, usually from the side but sometimes down the aisle. Sometimes the groomsmen also enter from the side, but more often, they escort the bridesmaids down the aisle. Then if there's a ringbearer and/or flower girl, they walk down the aisle. Then the bride enters, usually escorted by her father."

Ryan said, "All that sounds nice for straight weddings, but that seems like too much theatrics to me. And we're not going to have bridesmaids and groomsmen, and certainly not a bride."

Aaron said, "Then why don't we both just enter from the sides? My dad and me on one side and you and Brandon on the other. Then maybe at the end, we'll walk up the aisle together."

Ryan said, "Yeah, that sounds nice."

Rob said, "Sounds good to me too. So, are you thinking of having anyone else participate in the ceremony in any way? Usually, the answer is no, but occasionally somebody will want to have a friend sing or read something."

Aaron said, "My mom wants to read something. When she and my dad got married, her mother read this little essay about how to have a successful marriage. We want to have Mom read that at ours."

"Okay, no problem. I'll start with some opening remarks, then I'll invite her to come up and read what she has."

Ryan said, "You know, if Darnell comes to the wedding, I'd love to have him sing. He has an incredible voice and great stage presence."

Aaron said, "Are you thinking he'd do it in drag?"

Eddie said, "Oh, is that the guy who was one of your housemates? The guy who does Whitney Austin?"

Ryan said, "Yeah. But no, I think if he did it in drag that might be a bit much for a wedding."

Rob said, "Wait... you know Whitney Austin?"

"Yeah, I lived with the guy who performs as Whitney for four and a half years. He's a wonderful friend. And he's just as fabulous in real life as he is in character."

"I love Whitney Austin! I saw her once in P-Town, and one time she came to Phoenix to do a benefit for our LGBT youth organization. But anyway, as much as I love Whitney, I agree that it would be a distraction at your wedding. You don't want her to upstage you."

Ryan said, "Actually, that wouldn't bother me. But if we have the wedding in a park there will be no place for her to change into her outfit. But I'll contact him and ask, first of all, if he can come to the wedding, and then if he'll sing – as him. He may just want to be a guest."

Rob asked, "Do you guys want to write your own vows? Some couples do and some don't. For those who don't, I have a bunch of choices you can pick from."

Ryan and Aaron looked at each other. Ryan said, "What are

vows? Is that when you say, 'Do you take this man to be your lawfully wedded husband?' and we say, 'I do?'"

"No, that part comes next, after the vows. The vows are promises you make to each other. Like you promise to support each other and care for each other and be faithful and all that. Some couples also include stuff about how much they mean to each other or what they see in each other that makes them want to get married."

Ryan said, "I'd like to write mine."

Aaron said, "Me too, but I have no idea what I'd write."

Rob said, "No problem. I'll send you all the options I give to couples who don't want to write their own. That will give you some good ideas. You might find a few lines you want to incorporate into yours."

Ryan said, "Is this something we would memorize, or would we read them from a piece of paper?"

Rob said, "Some couples like to read them from a piece of paper or a little booklet. Others prefer to repeat each line after I say it. I've never had a couple say their vows to each other from memory."

Ryan said, "I think doing repeat-after-me would sap all the meaning out of it. I want to try memorizing them. It will seem more like it's coming from the heart. We can read them off paper if we can't memorize them."

Aaron said, "How long are your vows supposed to be?"

Rob said, "They can be as short or as long as you like. If you're going to memorize yours, you might want to go with something shorter. But you should agree on how long you want them to be. It could be awkward if one of you says three sentences and the other talks for three minutes."

Aaron and Ryan nodded.

"Also, agree upon the tone. Do you want to have some humor or do you want it to be serious? How romantic do you want to get? That sort of thing. Then after the vows, I'll ask The Big Question. That's where you say, 'I do.' Then we do the ring exchange. I have a short introduction explaining why rings are significant, as if people don't already know. Then you'll say, 'I give you this ring,' yada yada, and then you slide the rings onto each other's fingers. I'll give you several options for what you say at that point. Now, this is usually a repeat-after-me thing. Is that okay, or would you rather read it or memorize it?"

Ryan thought for a moment. "I'm okay with repeating after you for the rings."

Aaron said, "Me too. So now, do we have the rings in our pockets or do you have them, or what?"

"Since you won't be having a ring bearer, usually the best man has the rings. In your case, since you have two best men, each of them will have one of the rings. I'll say, 'May we have the rings, please?' when it's time for them to give the rings to you."

Aaron and Ryan nodded.

Rob said, "Okay, that's all the questions I have. What questions do you have?"

Aaron said, "My mind's already overloaded with all this new information. I can't think of anything. Of course, I don't even know what I'm supposed to ask."

"Well, if you think of anything, just email me or ask me at band."

Ryan asked, "How would you like to be paid?"

"Well, the next step is, I'll write up a script for your wedding. I'll give you several options for each part of the ceremony. You're free to pick and choose the options you like best, and you can customize them any way you want. That way, you know exactly what I'm going to say at your wedding and it's what you want. There will be no surprises. I never go off-script. So assuming you find things you like among the choices I give you and you decide to have me officiate your wedding, you would send me a 50% deposit at that point. The balance is due on the day of the wedding. You can pay with cash, check, credit or debit card, PayPal, VenMo, or Zelle – whatever you prefer."

Ryan looked at Aaron with an expression that said, 'Well? Yes?'

Aaron nodded.

Ryan said, "We've decided. We want you. Can I pay you the full amount now and be done with it?"

"Well... sure."

"Okay. I'll write you a check before you leave."

Too Much Information

Sunday, May 14, 2017

At 2:30, Ryan checked the temperature of the pool water. Then he hurried into the house to find Aaron.

"Hey, honey! The pool's 84 degrees. Want to get in?"

"That's still kind of chilly, isn't it?"

"A little. But we'll get used to it after a minute. 84 is my threshold for when it's warm enough to get in. And it's a bright sunny day. That'll make it feel warmer."

"Yeah, well, you don't have to worry about shrinkage. Some of us aren't so fortunate."

"Oh, come on. You don't need to worry about shrinkage either. It's not like we're putting on a show for anyone."

Aaron said, "Speaking of which, now that Brandon is living with us for the summer, we probably shouldn't get in naked."

"He works until 5:00 today, so we have two and a half hours. I doubt we'll stay in that long. But yeah, when he's here, we'll need to wear swimsuits."

"Bummer. That limits us for other pool activities, too."

Ryan smiled. "We'll just have to be mindful of his schedule and carpe diem when we can. Like today, for example."

"Okay, you've convinced me. I'll get the silicone lube."

"What do you want to drink?"

Aaron pondered his options. "Our mint plant is going crazy. How about a mojito?"

"Two mojitos coming up. Why don't you select the music and turn it on? And get out a couple of the floaties."

Fifteen minutes later, they eased themselves into the pool, one step at a time.

Aaron said, "Yikes! This water is frigid! Are you sure you read the thermometer right?"

"Yep."

Aaron took another step down, and his genitals entered the water. "Jesus Christ! I think my nuts have disappeared inside my body."

Ryan took the last step into the pool. Then he glided forward until the water was up to his neck. "Oh, stop being a wimp. Just get it over with. I'm already getting used to it. It's refreshing!"

A few minutes later, they were drifting around the pool sipping mojitos, buoyed by their floaties, fully acclimated to the water.

Ryan said, "And so begins another pool season. I love having a pool. It's one of the biggest reasons I love living here. And now that I have someone to share it with, it's even better."

Aaron smiled. As he gazed lovingly at Ryan, he thought, *Just think, it was almost exactly a year ago that I came out. What a year it's been! Now this tall, handsome, sexy man is my fiancé. And this is my home. Man, I sure have lucked out.* He paddled over to the edge of the pool closest to the house and set his glass on the deck. He paddled over to Ryan to kiss him and get things started when he heard, "Hey guys, mind if I join you?"

Aaron and Ryan turned toward the sliding glass door and saw Brandon standing in the doorway. Aaron and Ryan jumped off their floaties and hurried toward the edge of the pool, so Brandon could only see their shoulders and heads.

Ryan said, "Uh... We're naked."

Brandon replied, "No problem!" He pulled his T-shirt up over his head while he stepped out of his sandals. A second later, he pushed his gym shorts down to his ankles and stepped out of them. He briefly considered cannonballing into the pool but thought better of it. Instead, he ran over to the steps and bounded into the pool. The water temperature didn't bother him a bit.

Aaron couldn't help but stare. Then he caught himself and looked away, hoping Brandon hadn't noticed. Clearly, Brandon and

Ryan were products of the same gene pool. Aaron grabbed his floatie and held it in front of him, hoping Brandon wouldn't see the lingering evidence of what he and Ryan were about to do. He *wasn't* suffering from shrinkage.

After an awkward moment, Ryan said, "I thought you had to work until 5:00."

"Nope. 3:00. They changed my schedule on Friday."

"It would have been nice if you told us."

"Sorry. I didn't think it would make any difference."

"From now on, would you please write your hours on the calendar in the kitchen? And remember to update it if they change."

"Yeah, okay."

For a moment, no one said anything. Then Aaron said, "Well, this is awkward."

Brandon said, "Why? We're all guys. Guys have dicks. And you guys like dicks, if I understand this gay thing correctly."

Ryan said, "Yeah, but..."

"But what? So now we've seen each other's dicks. BFD. From this point on, it doesn't matter anymore. Like on my basketball team. After everyone sees everyone else in the shower on the first day, nobody cares."

Neither Aaron nor Ryan could argue with that logic, but still. For another few seconds, nobody said anything.

Then Brandon spotted the lube bottle on the edge of the deck. "Oh. Did I interrupt something?"

Ryan said, "Yeah, you kinda did."

"I'm sorry. If you want, I'll go back inside."

By now, Aaron's dick had gone soft. "No, that's okay. The moment has passed."

Ryan added, "Now you see why it's so important that we know your schedule."

Brandon said, "I get it. Sorry. But... can you really fuck in the pool? I thought lube was water-soluble."

Aaron said, "That's silicone lube. It won't break down in the water. And it's super slick."

"Sounds like you're speaking from experience."

Aaron smiled. "Yeah. Actually, one of the first times I ever had sex with a guy was in a swimming pool."

Ryan cocked his head and looked at Aaron. "Oh, really? And when was this?"

Aaron said, "That was around this time last year. Yeah, it was Memorial Day weekend. Remember me telling you about that guy I dated for a couple of weeks named Jeremy? That was right before I met you. He played trombone in Desert Pride, and he had a house near South Mountain. So yeah, we fucked in his pool."

Brandon asked, "What happened to him?"

"He moved away right after that. It broke my heart at the time, 'cause, you know, he was the first guy I ever did it with. But if I had stayed with him, I might never have met Ryan. So it was all for the best."

Brandon asked, "So what's it like to have sex in a pool?"

Aaron replied, "Oh, man, it's amazing! The sensation of the cool water against your skin as you're moving back and forth feels awesome. And it's easy to wrap your legs around the other guy because of your buoyancy in the water."

Brandon said, "Sounds hot. Too bad we didn't have a pool at our house in Prairie Village."

Ryan said, "If we had a pool, how could you have fucked anyone in it without Mom or Dad seeing you? Besides, they don't have block walls separating the backyards like we do here."

"True. But remember, Mom died during my sophomore year. And Dad was never home. He had something going on at the church almost every night. Since he didn't have Mom to cook dinner for him anymore, he ate out a lot. So yeah, he was never there. I had girls over all the time."

Aaron shook his head and said, "Sounds like you were quite the high school whore."

"Hey, when you're the star of the basketball team you can get all you want. And those cheerleaders in their tight little uniforms... well, they may look all pure and wholesome on the side of the basketball court, but at parties after they get a little drunk..." He smirked. "And once word started getting around..." He glanced downward and grinned.

Ryan said, "Okay! Now we've gotten naked together, talked about having sex in the pool, and discussed your high school whoring. I'm ready to move on. What else can we talk about?"

For a moment, no one said anything. Aaron reached for his mojito and took a few sips to finish it off. Brandon said, "What's that?"

Ryan said, "It's a mojito. It's made with rum, limes, mint, and sugar."

"MMMmmm... I bet that tastes good."

Ryan took the rather obvious hint. "Would you like one?"

Brandon feigned surprise. "Oh! Well, I suppose if you're going in to make another one for you and Aaron, I wouldn't mind having one too."

Ryan rolled his eyes and said, "How kind of you to not put me to any extra trouble." He swam over to the edge of the pool and hoisted himself out. He walked around the pool in all his pendulous glory, toweled himself off to remove the excess water, and then disappeared into the house.

Brandon moved a couple of feet closer to Aaron, flashed a mischievous grin, and said, "You're a lucky man."

"Yes, I am, but for many reasons besides that."

"And he's a lucky man too. I'm really glad you two found each other. I can tell you guys make each other happy."

"Thanks. We do."

Brandon hesitated for a moment, then asked, "So, just curious... Can you actually get it all in?"

Aaron scowled at Brandon and took a step back. "Dude! Seriously?"

"I mean, you know... It looks like his and mine are about the same and... well... one time in high school I tried doin' it with a guy and he had trouble with it."

"Wait a minute. You fucked a guy in high school? I thought you said you were having girls over."

"That's right."

"But you also fucked guys?"

"One. And just once. He was one of the male cheerleaders. Like, all of them were gay. Not that there's anything wrong with that."

"I sure hope not."

"We had a bunch of classes together, and one time he suggested that we get together to study algebra. So he'd come over to my house after school. This was after basketball season was over and after Mom died. So yeah, we studied algebra, but I guess you could say we got to know each other a little better."

"Let me guess – you switched to studying anatomy."

Brandon chuckled. "Yeah, that's one way to put it. We started by watching porn on the internet and jerking off together. I let him blow me a few times. I mean, hey – a blowjob is a blowjob, right? And then one time he wanted me to try fucking him and... it didn't go so well. It was hurting him, so we stopped. We didn't have any lube, so I was using spit."

"Did you loosen him up first? You know, like work a couple of fingers in?"

"Dude, I'm not gonna put my fingers in another guy's ass."

"Why not? You were going to put your dick in there. You can't just shove it in. Especially not that thing. And especially not if it was his first time."

"I do that with girls."

"Yeah, but vaginas stretch more. And hopefully you got them moist first."

"What do you know about vaginas?"

"If you must know, I had sex with girls a few times in college. Remember, I only figured out I was gay last year. But back to you. So, basically, you'll fuck anything that will stay still long enough."

"Hey, I'm a hypersexual guy! What can I say? But I have my standards. Not everyone gets the Bauer Bone."

Aaron rolled his eyes.

Brandon said, "I don't get hung up about this gay-or-straight thing. I'm not into labels. People are people. If two people are hot for each other and they want to do it, fine! I mean, you're basically gay, but you've done it with a woman. I'm basically straight, but I've done it with a guy. Who cares?"

Ryan opened the sliding glass door and emerged carrying a tray with three mojitos.

Aaron said, "So tell us about your job at Food World. What do they have you doing?"

Brandon said, "They had me bagging groceries and gathering stray shopping carts for the first week. Now they have me restocking the vegetables in the produce section. Sometimes I restock the shelves in the center store."

Ryan set the tray down on the edge of the pool and slid in, being careful not to splash water into the drinks. "That's what I did when I worked at Price Cutter during the summers when I was in high school."

He handed mojitos to Aaron and Brandon and took the last one for himself. They all took sips from their drinks.

Brandon said, "MMMmmm..... this is awesome! You'll have to teach me how to mix drinks."

Ryan said, "That'll make you popular at school."

Brandon glanced at Aaron and smiled. Neither of them said anything.

The Rehearsal

Friday, October 20, 2017

Aaron drove to the airport at 2:00 p.m. to pick up his parents. After hugs and kisses, Martha said, "Oh, honey, I'm so excited! I can't believe the big day is almost here!"

Ralph asked, "How's everything going? Are you all set?"

Aaron said, "It's been going remarkably well. Almost too well. Everyone's told us to expect that something will go wrong. We'll forget something, or something won't happen on time, or whatever. But so far, so good. Ryan's been keeping track of everything on a spreadsheet. He's so well organized."

Ralph said, "Well, maybe some of that will rub off on you."

Aaron smiled. It was typical teasing from his dad, and he was used to it. Besides, there was some truth to it. "So, your hotel's pretty close to here. We'll stop there so you can check in and drop your stuff off. The rehearsal's at 4:00. The park where we're getting married is not too far away. Do you want to stop somewhere for lunch?"

Ralph said, "Sure. Just don't take us to that place you took us last year."

There was no way Aaron would make the mistake of taking them to an exotic restaurant like Kahuna's Tiki Paradise after last year's disaster. Kahuna's was one of Ryan and Aaron's favorite places and the site of their first date. Ryan had suggested Kahuna's for the rehearsal dinner but Aaron vetoed that.

Aaron asked, "How about Subworks?"

Martha said, "That's fine with me. Nothing fancy."

***

At 3:50, Aaron and his parents arrived at the pavilion he and Ryan had reserved in Papago Park. Martha ran up to Ryan and hugged him. Then she hugged Brandon.

Aaron introduced his parents to everyone else who was there. Then Ryan took over and proceeded to run down his meticulously organized checklist.

"Kent and Justin, you'll need to be here by 2:00. The rental place is going to drop off the chairs between 2:00 and 2:30. We're expecting around 30 people, so we rented 36 chairs, just in case. Please set them up in three rows, with six chairs on either side of the aisle. I brought these two chairs from home for today. This is where the two chairs on the center aisle of the first row should be. So there will be five more chairs on either side of them, and then two more rows behind them. Oh, and don't forget to hang the Reserved signs on these two. The one on the left side is for Aaron's mother. The one on the right side is for Eddie, who's going to set up his video camera and livestream the ceremony."

Ralph said, "Will we be walking up the aisle?"

Ryan said, "No, you and Aaron are going to enter from the left side, and Brandon and I will enter from the right side. After the ceremony, Aaron and I will walk up the aisle, then each of you will follow."

Ralph said, "Well, shoot. I thought he'd be wearing a wedding dress and I'd get to walk him down the aisle."

Several other people laughed while Aaron fumed. "Dad! We're two men. Stop acting like I'm the woman in this relationship."

Ryan added, "Or else we'll send you the bill for all of this."

Justin almost made an inappropriate remark, but Kent subtly elbowed him.

Ryan asked, "Eddie, did you bring your laptop?"

"Yes, I did."

"Good. Let's test the livestream. We'll have Aaron's grandmother, his aunt and uncle, and several of my friends watching." Ryan got out his phone to make sure he could view what Eddie's video camera was sending to the feed. "Cool. It works. Make sure you remember to charge your camera and your PC tonight. Okay, Rob, why don't you run us through the ceremony, starting with the four of us entering from the sides."

Rob took over and guided them through the entrance, the various stages of the ceremony, and the exit. The photographer took some pictures of the rehearsal and Kent shot some pictures with his phone. They went over the directions for the photographer. Kent reviewed the pictures he had taken and uploaded his favorite to his Facebook page. He tagged Aaron, Brandon, and Rob, and captioned the photo, 'At Papago Park for Aaron and Ryan's wedding rehearsal. Can't wait for their big fabulous wedding tomorrow afternoon!'

Then Ryan took over again. He made sure everyone who was bringing refreshments and setting up decorations was clear on what they were expected to do. Next, the photographer gathered everyone in the front and arranged them for a few group photos.

Finally, they had covered everything. People returned to their cars to caravan to Dick's Pork Pit for dinner. Martha remarked to Aaron, "When you said Ryan was well-organized, you weren't kidding."

Ralph said, "Does he organize your whole life that way?"

Aaron said, "No, he's not usually like this. But it's going to be the biggest day of our lives and we want it to go off without a hitch."

The Wedding

Saturday, October 21, 2017

It was a perfect day. The temperature was 83 degrees, but with the light breeze and 25% humidity, it felt comfortable. The sky was mostly sunny, with occasional puffy white clouds floating by. There was no chance of rain.

At 3:50, Ryan checked with the photographer. He was ready to go. He walked over to Eddie, who was sitting in his reserved seat on the aisle in the front row. "Are you ready to start the livestream?"

"Yep. I started it five minutes ago. Your friends Ted, Darnell, and Ricky, and Aaron's Aunt Caroline are already on. And some guy named Rocket. I'm just waiting for your grandmother."

"Okay. Let me know when she's on."

He walked over to the side of the concrete pad where Aaron, Martha, Ralph, Brandon, and Rob had gathered. "Are we ready?" Everyone nodded. "Ralph and Brandon, you have the rings, right?" They reached into their pockets and pulled out the rings. "Ralph, you have mine, and Brandon, you have Aaron's, correct?"

Brandon said, "Oh, shit. No, I have yours." Brandon and Ralph switched the rings.

At 3:55, Rob walked over to Kent, who was playing music they had selected through a portable speaker. Rob asked Kent to lower the music long enough for him to make an announcement. He turned on his wireless mic. "Good afternoon, ladies and gentlemen. We'll be starting in just a few minutes, so please take your seats."

Martha turned to Aaron and Ryan and said, "I'm so proud of you boys!" She kissed them both, then walked over to her seat on the aisle in the front row. Aaron and Ralph walked behind the chairs to take their place on the opposite side of the stage, where they would enter.

Ryan scanned the group of thirty friends that had gathered for this event. Most of them were people he met in the last year and a half. His life had changed so much in those 18 months. He realized he was richly blessed to be surrounded by so many good friends – not to mention his reunited brother, his new in-laws, and the man who would become his husband in about 15 minutes. Chris and Seth had traveled from Arlington, Virginia for the wedding. As Ryan scanned the crowd, he locked eyes with Chris. He smiled and winked. Chris smiled, but he had a slightly uncomfortable look on his face. Seth was focused on his cell phone.

Ryan looked at Eddie. A few seconds later, Eddie looked back at Ryan and gave him a thumbs-up, signaling that Grandma was now online. Ryan looked over at Aaron and Ralph and gave them a thumbs-up.

Rob walked to his place in the center of the stage. Aaron and Ralph entered from the left and Ryan and Brandon entered from the right, in perfect symmetry. The four men stopped in their designated spots and faced Rob. Kent faded the prelude music.

Rob began. "We have been invited here today to witness and celebrate the marriage of Aaron and Ryan. They are taking the first step of their new beginning; their new life together.

"The ability and desire for one human being to love another is perhaps the most precious and fulfilling gift that has been entrusted to us. It is an all-consuming task, a lifelong endeavor, the journey we've been preparing for all of our lives. Loving someone is a reason to stretch beyond our limits; to become more for the sake of the other. It is to look into the soul of your beloved and accept what you see. Loving is the ultimate commitment that challenges humans to become all that we are meant to be.

"As they join in marriage today, Aaron and Ryan are announcing to the world that they are welcoming this challenge.

"Aaron and Ryan, this new chapter in your journey will be, at times, richly rewarding. Occasionally, it will be extremely difficult. But, most importantly, it will be a journey you take together.

"Before this moment, you have been many things to each other: acquaintance, friend, lover, and teacher, for you have learned much from one another. But today, you are crossing a threshold together. From today forward, you will say to your friends and family and the world, 'This is my husband.'

"You are here today because you hold the highest respect, admiration, and attraction for each other. You each feel a profoundly personal joy from the mere existence of the other.

"Marriage is not a selfless act that requires you to sacrifice yourselves to each other. Your marriage is not a sacrifice, because the value you each gain from each other far outweighs any hardship you will encounter. You will help each other through tough times, not because you are obligated to, but because the happiness of the other is essential to your own.

"Your marriage is much more than your signatures on a legal contract. You are promising, in front of these people who matter most to you, that you want to be with each other and only each other for the rest of your lives, and that you will do everything in your power to honor the promises you are making here today.

"Now, I would like to invite Aaron's mother, Martha, to share some words of wisdom and advice."

Martha rose from her chair and walked up to the front, clutching a small booklet into which she had written her message, and which she would give to Aaron and Ryan after the wedding. She seemed nervous but determined to do her best. She smiled at Aaron first, and then at Ryan. She turned to face the audience, and Rob moved beside her so he could hold the microphone for her.

"This is marriage advice my mother read to Ralph and me at our wedding. It meant a lot to me at the time, and it truly made our wedding day special. More importantly, these words have stayed with me throughout our marriage. Once in a while, especially when times get a little tough, I get this out and read it again. It always seems to have the answer to whatever the current situation is. I have updated it a little bit to suit Aaron and Ryan, and to add a little bit of advice from me. Here goes.

"Always remember that when you marry someone, you are marrying the entire person – not just their attractiveness and their good qualities, but also their faults and shortcomings. You have to love their faults as much as you love everything else about them.

"Love is a commitment, not just a feeling. Always remember that you love each other, even when you struggle to like each other. Always tell your spouse 'I love you' at least once a day, even when you don't feel like it.

"A marriage is like a bank account. Every act of kindness and every word of admiration or support is a deposit. You have to make deposits regularly for your interest to grow. Every fight, every bit of resentment, and every careless word spoken is a withdrawal. Whenever necessary, deposit a little extra so your balance remains healthy. You must never overdraw your account.

"Remember that an argument never results in a winner and a loser, it results in two losers. You are partners in everything, so you win or lose together.

"Your marriage is more important than whatever may be stressing you out, so don't take your stress out on your partner.

"Remember that marriage is not a 50-50 proposition. That's what divorce is. Your marriage will only thrive if you both give 100%.

"Don't expect your spouse to read your mind. Communicate your thoughts and feelings clearly, and ask your husband for his. And even when you think you know the answer, ask the question.

"Love your spouse more than you love your career, your hobbies, and your money. Those things can't love you back.

"No matter how busy your lives become, always set aside time to spend together. Never stop going on dates.

"And finally, it takes more than sex to build a strong marriage, but it's nearly impossible to maintain a strong marriage without it!"

Martha smiled as if she was surprised she made it through the reading successfully. She turned and kissed Aaron, then Ryan. She whispered, "I love you both." As she walked back to her chair, the audience clapped.

Rob announced, "Ryan and Aaron have written their own vows to each other. Ryan won the coin toss and elected to have Aaron go first." The audience chuckled. Rob handed the microphone to Aaron.

"Ryan, until I met you, I never believed there was such a thing as love at first sight. But all that changed on Sunday morning, May 22nd, 2016, when I showed up at the gay running club – at 7:00 a.m. no less – and saw this tall, blond, handsome man. I was immediately smitten. As we ran, it was all I could do to keep up with you. In many ways, that's still true. But as I watched you run with such beauty, power, elegance, and grace, something deep inside told me you were the one."

Right after Aaron said, 'Something deep inside,' Ryan heard Brandon snicker. *Don't you dare laugh out loud. Don't make me turn around and smack you.*

Aaron continued, oblivious to what had just happened. "Over the past 17 months, you have proven over and over that my inner voice was right. You *were* the one, you *are* the one, and you will always *be* the one. The first three months were kind of rough, but that only made us stronger. We learned how to communicate, how to solve problems, and how to deal with conflicts. Now, I'm certain we can deal with anything that comes our way. Ryan, you are strong, smart, determined, multi-talented, generous, principled, dependable, loving ... and let's not forget downright sexy. You are everything I could ever want in a husband.

"Ryan, as your husband, I promise to care for you, trust you, be responsive to your needs, communicate my feelings, and behave in a way that shows my love and respect.

"I promise to let you play your jazz music in the house anytime you want.

"I promise to feign interest while you tell me all about the life history of whichever jazz musician you're listening to at the time." Several people chuckled.

"And I promise to always install a new roll of toilet paper in such a manner that the end sheet passes over the top of the roll, not out from the bottom." Everyone laughed.

"I say these things because I love you, and want to live out the days of my life with you."

Aaron handed the microphone to Ryan. He saw tears running down Ryan's cheeks.

Ryan wiped his eyes on his sleeve and sniffled. He turned to face the audience and said, "I wanted Aaron to go first because I thought he would be the one who was more likely to break down and cry. Now look at me." People chuckled.

Ryan turned to face Aaron, took a deep breath, and began. "Aaron Bradbury, to say you've changed my life would be a vast understatement. After some of the things I've been through, relationships have been difficult for me. I had reached the point where I was convinced I would spend the rest of my life single. I surrounded myself with a nice home and material things, thinking I could live a comfortable life by myself, with only a few close friends.

"But when you came along, I realized that as nice as all that was, my home was empty. My life was too quiet – well, except when I put jazz on." Ryan cracked a smile and several people chuckled. "You have filled my life with positive energy, fun, hope ... and love. You convinced me to play my trumpet again, which brings me great joy. Thanks to you, Martha, Ralph, and your Grandma, I have a family again. And thanks to you, I am reunited with my brother Brandon. My life is now full and I am richly blessed.

"Aaron, as your husband, I promise to care for you, trust you, be responsive to your needs, communicate my feelings, and behave in a way that shows my love and respect.

"I promise to let you play your music too..." Some people laughed. "...once in a while." More laughter.

"I promise to always laugh at your corny jokes – a quality you have inherited from your wonderful father whether you'll admit it or not.

"I promise to always watch Ohio State football games with you and to always cheer for the Buckeyes – even if they play UCLA."

Brandon whispered, "What about ASU?"

Ryan shot a glance at Brandon and said, "And ASU." He turned to the audience and said, "We picked today for our wedding because Ohio State is off this week." Everyone laughed. He turned back to Aaron. "And I promise to do everything in my power to console you on the rare occasions when they lose.

"I say these things because I love you, and want to live out the days of my life with you."

Ryan handed the microphone back to Rob. He saw that Aaron was barely holding back tears. He held out his hands and Aaron placed his hands in Ryan's.

Rob smiled, turned to Aaron, and said, "Aaron, do you take Ryan to be your lawfully wedded husband, to have and to hold from this day forward, for better or for worse, for richer or for poorer, in sickness and in health, in joy and in sorrow, to love and to cherish, and to be faithful to him alone, for as long as you both shall live?"

Aaron gazed into Ryan's moist eyes and said, "I do."

"Ryan, ditto?"

Ryan nodded and smiled. "Ditto." Everyone laughed.

"But seriously... Ryan, do you take Aaron to be your lawfully wedded husband, to have and to hold from this day forward, for better or for worse, for richer or for poorer, in sickness and in health, in joy and in sorrow, to love and to cherish, and to be faithful to him alone, for as long as you both shall live?"

"I do."

Rob turned the page in his notebook to the next section of the ceremony. "Wedding rings are a symbol that, even in your uniqueness, you have chosen to be bound together. They symbolize your commitment to your marriage.

"Your rings are precious because you wear them with love. As you wear them through time, they will reflect not only who you are as individuals, but who you are as a couple.

"When people look at you, they will look at your hand and notice the ring on your finger. They will know that you are committed to someone special and that someone special is devoted to you.

"Every day for the rest of your lives, every time you wash your hands or reach out to touch each other, these rings will be there to remind you of the great love you share and the promises you made to each other today. May we have the rings, please?"

Brandon reached into his pocket and handed the ring to Ryan. Ralph made a show of frantically checking all his pockets as if he couldn't find it. Ryan and the audience chuckled. Aaron was not amused. After Ralph had milked the moment, he handed the ring to Aaron.

Aaron and Ryan extended their hands, holding their rings in their right hand and extending their left ring finger. They each placed their ring around the fingertip of the other's ring finger as they had rehearsed, ready to slide it on.

Rob said, "Aaron and Ryan, please repeat after me. I give you this ring..."

In unison, they said, "I give you this ring..."
"as a symbol of my love..."

"as a symbol of my love..."
"and lifelong commitment to you."

"and lifelong commitment to you."
"I ask you to wear it as a sign to the world..."

"I ask you to wear it as a sign to the world..."
"that you are my husband..."

"that you are my husband..."
"and that you may wear it..."

"and that you may wear it..."
"as a reminder of my love for you."

"as a reminder of my love for you."
"With this ring, I commit my life to you."

"With this ring, I commit my life to you."
Aaron and Ryan slid their rings onto the other one's finger simultaneously. They resumed holding hands.

Rob smiled and proudly announced, "Aaron and Ryan, you have

each chosen to be joined in marriage today. In my presence and the presence of your family and friends, you have exchanged vows and made promises. You have opened your hearts to one another, declared your love and friendship, and united yourselves by exchanging rings. Therefore, it is my honor and pleasure to now pronounce you husband! You may now suck face!"

Rob quickly stepped aside so he wouldn't be photobombing the photos of their kiss. Ryan practically lunged for Aaron. They kissed enthusiastically while the photographer furiously snapped photos.

After about ten seconds, Ralph said, "Guys... get a room!"

They pulled apart a few inches and gazed into each other's eyes. Ryan whispered, "I love you."

Aaron whispered, "I love you too."

Aaron and Ryan turned and faced the audience with wide grins on their faces. Everyone was cheering and applauding. Kent started playing the exit music. Ryan scanned the crowd and spotted Chris. Tears were running down his cheeks.

Ryan and Aaron joined hands and walked down the aisle between the rows of seats. When they passed the last row of chairs, they stopped and kissed again while the photographer snapped a few pictures. Brandon exited next, then Ralph. Ralph paused when he reached Martha's seat. She stood up, and Ralph escorted her the rest of the way. Rob announced, "Ladies and gentlemen, please help yourself to water or soda and snacks. Feel free to mingle or watch as we sign the marriage license. In about 45 minutes, we will leave here and head to the restaurant for dinner."

Eddie ended the livestream and started putting his video camera away. Ryan, Aaron, Rob, Brandon, Ralph, and the photographer gathered around a small table that had been set up for signing the marriage license. Rob asked, "Who has the marriage license?"

Ryan and Aaron turned and looked at Brandon, who seemed to be caught off-guard.

Ryan said, "Please don't tell me you forgot the marriage license."

Brandon said, "No, no... I'm pretty sure it's in the trunk of the car. Hang on."

As they watched Brandon scamper toward his car, they spotted an unfamiliar car with a man sitting in it. When he saw Brandon approaching, he quickly started the car, rolled up the window, and drove away.

Brandon found the light brown envelope containing the marriage license in his trunk and hurried back to the wedding party. Ryan said, "I wonder who that was and why he was here."

Brandon said, "That was Dad." He instantly regretted saying that.

Ryan exploded. "WHAT THE FUCK!!! What the hell was he doing here? How did he even find out about it?" He glared at Brandon.

"I didn't tell him! I promise! I haven't even told him you live here or that we're back together."

"Well, then, how the hell did he find out? Who else could possibly have told him?"

Brandon had no idea what to say. Ryan was getting angrier, and the others feared he might turn violent. Everyone else stopped to stare at the commotion.

Aaron said, "Wait a minute." He pulled his phone out of his pocket and launched Facebook. He scrolled through the posts for the past 24 hours. "Here's our answer. Kent posted a picture he took at the rehearsal yesterday. He tagged Brandon, Rob, and me in it."

Aaron showed Ryan the picture. The caption read, 'At Papago Park for Aaron and Ryan's wedding rehearsal. Can't wait for their big fabulous wedding tomorrow afternoon!'

Ryan turned to Brandon, "So you're friends with him on Facebook."

Brandon nodded.

Aaron said, "And he saw that photo because Brandon was tagged in it. It showed up on his news feed."

Ryan was livid. "Goddamn fucking Facebook! Now you know why I don't want anything to do with that shit." He looked around.

"Where's Kent?"

Aaron stepped in front of Ryan and said, "You need to calm down. Kent didn't do anything wrong. He didn't know your dad would see it. There's no reason he would even think about it."

"Don't you fucking tell me to calm down! Besides, if he saw this sometime in the last 24 hours, what did he do? Fly out here just to spy on us?"

Brandon replied, "He lives here now."

"WHAT??? Why the fuck didn't you tell me?"

"Because you don't want to know anything about him."

Aaron said, "He's right. You don't want to have anything to do with him. So don't blame Brandon for not telling you. Besides, you've said over and over that you don't consider him to be your father anymore. Well, if that's the case, then so what? Some man – no one in particular – just happened to pass by. No big deal." Aaron paused to let that sink in. Ryan had no answer for that. Aaron continued. "Or is it? But put yourself in your dad's shoes. He's scrolling through Facebook, and he sees this picture of you next to Brandon. This is the first time he's seen you or heard anything about you for ten years. Don't you think maybe he'd want to see you?"

Despite all the logic being presented to him, Ryan was still seething. "GODDAMMIT! Hasn't he ruined my life enough already? Now he picks today, of all days, to show up and ruin my wedding."

Aaron had enough. His stare penetrated Ryan's eyes with an intensity Ryan had never seen before. "No. NO! You listen to me, Ryan Robertson." Ryan was about to snap back, but Aaron shook his head and kept glaring at him. "All he did was park his car over there. He didn't get out. He just watched from a distance. He didn't interrupt anything. And now he's gone. *He* hasn't ruined anything. No, Ryan. NO! *He* didn't ruin your wedding. YOU are ruining your wedding. That's right. YOU." Aaron forcefully jabbed his finger toward Ryan's face, stopping just a few inches shy of contact. "And you need to stop it. RIGHT! NOW!" Aaron paused to breathe. "He showed up, and he left. You can't control that. But you can control how you react to it. And you're doing a pretty shitty job."

Ryan scoffed. "Thank you, Buddha."

Aaron ignored that. "Let it go. Just let it go. This is supposed to be the happiest day of our lives, and you're the one who's ruining it, not him. And either you get over it or I'm going to tear that marriage license up into a hundred tiny pieces and we're through."

Aaron, Brandon, Ralph, and Rob stared at Ryan, waiting to see what he would do. All the other wedding guests were standing at a distance, watching. For one tense moment, no one said anything.

Ryan took a few deep breaths and willed himself to calm down. Then he smiled. "Well, then, let's sign that paper and get this party started!"

Everyone breathed a sigh of relief.

Ryan hugged Aaron and whispered in his ear, "I'm sorry. I love you."

Aaron whispered, "I love you too."

Ryan and Aaron signed the marriage license, with Brandon and Ralph signing as witnesses. The photographer took a flurry of pictures and then gathered the wedding party for more photos.

After taking what seemed like hundreds of photos, the photographer dismissed everyone. Ryan looked around. Kent, Jordan, and a few of their other band friends had collapsed the folding chairs and placed them back on their carts so they would be ready for the rental company to pick up. Ryan glanced at his watch. "We have about ten minutes before we need to head to the restaurant. Why don't we mingle with our guests for a few minutes?"

Ryan saw Paul standing nearby, so he walked up to him to chat.

Paul said, "That was really beautiful. Congratulations!"

"Thanks! Hey, I hope you don't mind me asking, but I was wondering..."

"...if your mother was here? Yes. She's gone now, but she was here for the whole thing. In fact, right before you guys walked in from the sides, she walked up the aisle spreading flowers, like she was the flower girl."

Ryan chuckled. "That is so sweet! Thanks!" He gave Paul a hug.

Then he walked over to Eddie and said, "Thanks again for livestreaming the wedding. Did it go okay?"

"I think so. Everyone was still on at the end."

"Cool. And it will be available to watch later?"

"Yeah. And I'll download it and burn a DVD for you."

"Thanks!"

Meanwhile, Chris excused himself from Seth for a moment and walked over the Aaron. "Congratulations! That was such a lovely ceremony. I think it's great that you held it outdoors."

"Thanks. I'm really glad you and Seth came."

"Me too. Thanks for inviting us. And of course, it's a chance to see his family too."

"I'm glad you and Ryan are back in touch. I know that means a lot to him. And after all our chats on Facebook, I feel like we're friends now, too."

"So do I!" They hugged each other. "I'm happy for you. He's a wonderful man, and I'm glad you two found each other. And... well, I probably shouldn't say this, but... I'm a little envious of you."

"Really?" Aaron could guess why, but he wasn't going to say anything.

"I love Seth and everything, but there was a time, many years ago, when I dreamed Ryan and I would get married someday. Of course, back then, gay couples couldn't get married in most places. But a guy can dream, right?"

Aaron had no idea how to respond to that. He just smiled.

"But obviously, that didn't work out, mostly because of his father. But anyway... I have Seth now, and I'm glad the four of us are becoming friends. Someday, we'll probably end up living out here. I can tell he's getting tired of Washington and all that comes with it. So yeah, we'll probably move out here sooner or later."

"That'll be great. It will be fun for the four of us to hang out and do stuff together. And you both play sax, right? You could join our band!"

"Yeah, there is that. God, it's been, what? At least five years since I've touched my sax."

"Trust me, it all comes back. So, I forget... Are you and Seth married?"

Chris sighed. "I wish. I can't get him to do it. He just doesn't see the point. He says that's something straight people do, and he doesn't need some piece of paper from the government to tell him he loves me. Maybe after seeing this, he'll change his mind."

"I hope so."

"That's another reason I'm kinda envious of you." There was more Chris wanted to say, but he knew he probably shouldn't.

Then Ryan called out, "Attention, everybody! It's time to head to the restaurant. I've printed maps for anyone who needs one. They're over on that table."

People started heading toward their cars.

Aaron hugged Chris, and they held each other for a few seconds. Then they rejoined their respective partners.

***

In Kansas City, Trevor and Rocket watched the wedding in Rocket's apartment. After the livestream ended, Trevor said, "Wow. That was really nice, wasn't it?"

"Yeah. Now I wish I had gone."

"I know what you mean. The livestream was okay, but it's not the same as being there."

"It would have been nice to see Ryan again in person. And Chris."

Rocket didn't get up from his chair. He continued to stare at the screen.

Trevor said, "You know, it's amazing that they could get married. Hell, when we were all in high school together, a lot of states were passing constitutional amendments to ban same-sex marriage."

"Yeah, especially backward states like Kansas and Missouri."

"It's amazing how much has changed in ten years. Anyway, I'm glad they can do it now. I'm really happy for them."

Rocket nodded and let out a barely audible, "Yeah."

It was just after 6:30, their time. They had shared pizza and beer before the wedding. Trevor wanted to go out and do something on Saturday night, but Rocket seemed moody.

Trevor looked at his buddy and said, "You still have a thing for him, don't you?"

Damn. Busted. How the hell did he know? What should I say? What the hell... He's my friend, and he's already figured it out. "Yeah, I guess. We talked about it in therapy. Like, I don't think I'm gay – not that there's anything wrong with that – but... I don't know. There's something about *him*."

Trevor put his hand on Rocket's shoulder. "It's okay. I won't say anything."

"Thanks. I'd really appreciate that."

There was more both of them could say, but they didn't. Trevor took his hand off Rocket's shoulder and stood up. "Hey, you wanna go out and do something tonight?"

Rocket stood up. "Nah, I'm not really in the mood for anything. Thanks, though."

Trevor nodded. "Okay. Well, I guess I should be on my way then." He turned and headed for the door. Rocket followed to let him out.

When they reached the door, Trevor said, "Thanks for having me over to watch the wedding. I'm glad I got to see it. And thanks for the pizza and beer."

Rocket hugged Trevor and said, "Thanks for being my friend."

The Meeting

Sunday, October 29, 2017

As usual, Brandon came to the house to join Ryan and Aaron for their weekly Family Night dinner. Brandon was excited that his second season on the ASU basketball team had just gotten underway. His first home game had taken place on Thursday evening. Since Ryan and Aaron had band rehearsal, Brandon invited his father to use one of his comp tickets.

After telling them all about the game, Brandon said to Ryan, "Dad said he would like to meet with you sometime soon."

"No way. Seriously. I have no interest in ever seeing him or talking to him again. And I still can't believe he showed up at our wedding."

"He said he wants to apologize for everything he did."

Ryan said nothing.

Aaron said, "Now that he lives here in town, you're going to run into him sooner or later. C'mon, go talk to him and get it over with."

Brandon said, "He's a changed man, Ryan. He's not the arrogant, self-centered, power-hungry man we grew up with. He's broken. He's been brought down. He's trying hard to be humble and rebuild himself into a better person. He's lost his job, his book deal, and his reputation. His whole world came crashing down. He moved out here to get a fresh start and to be close to me."

Ryan said, "Well, boo fucking hoo. Whose fault is it that his world came crashing down? His, and nobody else's. May I remind you that in July 2007 my whole world came crashing down, too – all because of him?"

Aaron said, "Listen to you. You sound so stubborn and cold-hearted. I've told you this over and over, Ryan. This anger you've been carrying around for years is eating you up. And trust me, it's not a good look. It's not harming him, it's harming you. So let it go. It's been ten years. Time to move on."

"I *have* moved on. A long time ago. I think I've done a damn good job of creating my own life after everything that happened."

"Yes, you have. It's one of the many things I admire about you. He's not a factor in your life now. So go meet your father. Hear what he has to say. Maybe even forgive him. Sounds radical, I know. And I know what the next thing you're going to say is. 'He doesn't deserve to be forgiven.' Well, maybe or maybe not. But why not forgive him anyway? Be the better man."

Ryan sighed. "Oh, all right. I'll meet with him. Once. In a neutral location. I'm not going to make any promises about forgiving him."

Brandon said, "He'd like to take you out for lunch or dinner. You can pick the place."

"No. I don't want to be with him that long."

Aaron said, "How about meeting him at the pavilion in Papago Park where we held our wedding?"

Ryan said, "Yeah, that would work. Brandon, go ahead and contact him and ask when he's available."

Brandon pulled out his phone and texted his father. "He says how about Saturday morning, at around 10:00?"

"Sure."

Brandon texted his father, then said, "Okay, it's all set."

***

Saturday, November 4, 2017

At 10:00 a.m. Ryan pulled into the parking lot next to the pavilion where his wedding took place three weeks ago. Brad had already arrived. He was sitting on top of one of the picnic tables in the pavilion, with his feet resting on the seat, facing the parking lot.

Let's get this over with, Ryan thought.

As Ryan approached, Brad stood up. He smiled as he took a few steps toward Ryan and extended his hand for a handshake. Ryan did not extend his hand, so Brad let his hand drop to his side. Obviously, a hug was out of the question.

Ryan spoke first. "Okay, Brad, let's hear what you have to say."

Brad frowned when he heard Ryan call him Brad instead of Dad. *I guess I deserve that*, he thought.

"Hello, Bryan. No, wait... Brandon said you changed your name to Ryan. I'll do my best to remember that, but I might slip and still call you Bryan."

"That's okay, you can call me Bryan." He almost added, 'My friends call me Ryan,' but he stopped himself. "Whatever." *It's not like you're going to have any opportunities to call me by either name.*

Brad took a few steps back toward the picnic table, thinking they would sit down. Ryan didn't move from where he was standing. Brad decided to remain standing too. They stood a few feet apart.

"Okay, then." Brad took a deep breath and began the conversation he had rehearsed in his head dozens of times. "Well... The first thing I want to say is, I'm sorry. I am so very sorry. I now realize what a terrible father I was and, well, what a terrible person I was. It's been a little over a year since I got caught attending that event and lost my job at the church. This has been the most difficult year of my life. I've had everything taken from me. For the past year, I've been doing a lot of self-examination. I've reflected on my entire life. I've questioned everything I've ever believed. And I've discovered I was wrong about almost everything."

Ryan said, "Before you go on, let's clarify something. You said you had everything taken from you. Like someone else did that. Like you were the victim. But no, *you* lost everything. It was all your fault. And the most tragic thing is, you were the last one to lose. Everyone else suffered before you did. I suffered because of what you did. Mom paid the ultimate price for what you did. Brandon suffered too, because he lost his older brother, then his mother, and you were never around for him."

Brad lowered his head and stared at the ground. "Yes, you're right. You're absolutely right. As I said, I now realize I was a terrible father."

Ryan asked, "Did you even want to be a father? Did you even want to be married to a woman? Now that we know you're gay, was it all just a sham, so you could have your big, massive church with thousands of adoring fans?"

"I loved your mother. I truly did. And I truly wanted to live a normal life. A good life. A godly life. I didn't want to be gay. I didn't think it was what God wanted, and it certainly wasn't something my parents would have tolerated. I wanted more than anything to be straight, and I thought if anyone could make me happy being in a straight marriage, it would be your mother.

"And as for the church, I believed that if I could become a good enough Christian, a good enough servant of the Lord, then He would deliver me from my constant temptation. But the sad thing is, it was never enough. No matter how big I built that church, no matter how many souls I saved, no matter how many books I wrote or sermons I preached, I never stopped feeling a desire for men.

"But when I met your mother during my senior year of college, something – I thought it was God – told me she was the one. She was the one who could lead me away from all this. I had been fooling around with my roommate. I knew I shouldn't be doing that, but I did it anyway. I'd feel guilty about it afterward and pray to Jesus for forgiveness, but then I'd turn around and do it again. So I told him we couldn't fool around anymore and I married your mother instead."

Ryan said, "And that was Dr. Babcock, the so-called counselor you made me see to try to make me straight."

"Yep. That was him. We were roommates for our sophomore, junior, and senior years."

"Sounds more like boyfriends than roommates."

"Well, I wouldn't say we were boyfriends. Maybe roommates with benefits. He's the one who initiated it. I mean, we were horny college boys, and we knew we weren't supposed to have sex with a woman until we were married. We kept it a secret. But yeah, we experimented. Ron wanted us to be a couple. He wanted us to move to someplace like Atlanta, Los Angeles, or San Francisco, where they have large gay communities, and become part of all that. But I just couldn't do it."

"Three years is a pretty long experiment. You would think the results would have been pretty conclusive after three years."

"You would think. Actually, it was conclusive for Ron. He lived the homosexual lifestyle for five years before he finally decided to leave it and marry a woman."

"Yeah, he told me his 'Road to Damascus' story at one of our counseling sessions. I could tell he was still gay, though. He even admitted that he had to pray each morning for God to get him through the day without yielding to temptation. He said it was that way for most gay people."

"Yeah, that's what we believed."

"My head's about to explode. So you spent three years in college having sex with this guy, you knew people couldn't really be cured, and yet you forced me to go into counseling – with the guy you fucked during college!"

"At the time, I thought it was the right thing to do. I knew you had just started to have feelings for that other kid. I thought if we got to you soon enough, we could prevent it from taking hold with you."

"What a bunch of bullshit! And what about what I wanted? I didn't want to be so-called cured. I was okay with being gay. I loved Chris and I wanted to spend my life with him. But you didn't even let me have a say in how I wanted to live my life."

Brad paused and looked off into the distance. "Like I said, I was wrong about everything. I feel terrible about it now."

"Well, that's nice to know, but it doesn't really change anything."

"No, I guess not. But look how you turned out! Last Thursday, when I went to Brandon's basketball game, I took him out for pizza afterward. I asked him to tell me about you. He said you graduated from UCLA..."

"Magna Cum Laude, by way. And I had to work hard to pay for it."

"Yes. I'm aware of what you had to do to put yourself through college."

"Who told you?"

"No one. I saw it. They played porn videos at those parties I went to."

"OH MY GOD! You've seen me in porn? You were watching me fuck while you were fucking? Shit! How can this possibly get any more fucked up?"

"I don't hold that against you. It's what you had to do to support yourself. But today, you have a good job, a lovely house, and a nice man to share your life with. And you're playing your trumpet again! I'm so glad to hear that. Your mother always talked about how talented you were."

"Too bad you never came to my concerts to hear for yourself. There was always something going on at the church that was more important than your kids."

"Well, maybe I can come and hear your concerts now. Oh, and Brandon spoke very highly of your partner, too."

"*Husband.*"

"Yeah. Husband."

"You should know that. You invited yourself to our wedding and watched it take place."

Brad said nothing.

"But yeah, I've done well – despite you. Even though I got separated from my boyfriend and couldn't go to college with him and spend our lives together as we planned. Despite not having any contact, let alone support, from my mother or my brother. And despite landing in a big city all by myself and not knowing anyone. So yeah, I did all that myself – no thanks to you. But let me tell you something. When all that happened, I told myself two things. One, I was a survivor. I was a fighter. I was bound and determined to make it on my own, whatever it took. And two, I was gay and proud of it. I didn't care who knew or what they thought of it. I was going to be honest and true to myself and live my life the way I wanted to. So now, as you're doing all this soul-searching about your life and contemplating what you're going to do next, maybe that's what you need to do."

"I'm working on it."

"So, what are you doing now?"

"I've got a small apartment in east Mesa. I've tried to build a network with some churches in case they're looking for a pastor or they need a sub to fill in or something. But it seems the news about what happened traveled farther than I thought. In the meantime, I got a job delivering packages for UPS so I have some money coming in. And I've been working on a book about my experience. I'm writing it myself this time instead of using a ghostwriter. I'm still shopping it around to publishers, but I'll publish it myself if I have to."

Ryan said, "So you're going to try to profit from this sordid story?"

"That's not really the point. I hope I can reach some churches, or even some individuals, to try to get them to change how they treat their gay children. Maybe I can get some speaking gigs so I can spread the word."

"Good luck with that. Do you really think very many churches are going to be interested in hearing that message? They attract a lot of followers by preaching homophobia."

"Not the hard-core churches, but maybe some of the more middle-of-the-road ones. But I figure, even if I only reach a hundred people, it will be worth it."

"So am I going to be part of this book?"

"Well, you are a significant part of the story."

"I really don't want to have anything to do with that, but I guess I can't stop you. Just make sure you refer to me as Bryan, not Ryan. And don't say anything about where I live or anything else that might identify me."

"Agreed."

Ryan glanced at his watch. "Well, I'm going to be on my way."

"Bryan? I mean Ryan? There's one more thing I want to say. So, I've already said I'm sorry for all the mistakes I made and all the bad things I did. I know, maybe saying I'm sorry won't change anything, but I want you to know I'm owning up to my mistakes and trying to become a better person. As part of my healing process, I want to make amends with everybody I've harmed."

"Sounds like part of a twelve-step program. Is there a Homophobes Anonymous?"

"Maybe there should be. Anyway, I stand before you today, humbled by my sins and my failings as a father, knowing you've turned out to be a better man than I'll probably ever be. I would like to ask if you could find it in your heart to forgive me."

They stood and looked at each other in silence while Ryan contemplated how he should respond. He took a good look at his father. He was older now – 52. He was showing his age. Ryan remembered his father from ten years ago, proudly standing on that giant stage in front of several thousand people in his congregation. He wore perfectly tailored suits, every hair was in place, and he exuded confidence and charisma. He was a masterful speaker and he commanded the stage. Today, he looked haggard and worn down. Gray hairs were starting to outnumber the light brown ones. He was a shell of the man he used to be.

Ryan decided that even though his father was still a fucked-up mess, he was genuine in his desire to apologize for everything he had done and request forgiveness. He recalled the numerous times Aaron had pleaded with him to forgive Brad, saying he would be doing it as much for himself as for Brad, for it would allow him to finally release his pent-up anger and move on.

Ryan took a deep breath. "Okay, Brad. I forgive you. Go in peace."

Brad smiled and his demeanor improved. "Thank you, son. You have no idea how much this means. Now we can begin the process of reconciliation and make up for lost time." He took a step toward Ryan, like he was about to hug him.

"No. I said I forgive you. And I mean it. I forgive you. But I didn't say I want you back in my life." He paused for emphasis. "Because I don't."

Brad looked to the ground. He couldn't think of anything to say.

Ryan said, "I hope you do well with your book. I hope you get back on your feet and find your way again. But just like me on the day I arrived in Los Angeles, you're going to have to do it on your own."

He turned and left.

Afterword

Thank you for purchasing and reading this book. I hope you enjoyed it.

This is the fifth in a series of six books called "Gay Tales for the New Millennium" that follows Ryan as he finishes high school, goes to college, launches his career, forms relationships, and comes to terms with his past.

I invite you to subscribe to my newsletter. I'll keep you informed about my upcoming books and offer them to you at a discount. I'll share background information about the stories and the writing process. From time to time, I may solicit your input which will help make the books even better! To subscribe, visit my website: AuthorDaveHughes.com.

To thank you for subscribing, I will send my short story, *Cruise Virgins.* In it, Ryan (as a young adult) and Ted experience their first gay cruise – and confront their feelings for one another.

Now, I have a small favor to ask.

As a new, self-published author, it's incredibly difficult to get my books noticed in a world in which hundreds, if not thousands, of new books are released every day. It's challenging to build an audience for my work. If you enjoyed this book, please consider posting something about it on your social media platform of choice. All it takes is something simple, like 'I thoroughly enjoyed reading *Karma Train from Kansas*, by Dave Hughes. Check it out.' Also, please consider leaving an honest review on the website where you purchased this book.

Thanks! I truly appreciate it.

I would like to thank my launch team for their thoughtful reviews and support of my books: Tom Bogardus, Gary Brenkman,

Aaron Chavez, Jeff McKeehan, Paul Phillips, and Mike Triggs.

Thanks to my email subscribers for their loyalty and support. I've made numerous decisions based on their feedback. And thanks to the Chandler Public Library Downtown Writers Group, led by Andrew Flynn, for their encouragement, support, and constructive feedback.

Special thanks to Gregg Edelman of Exposed Studio & Gallery. His charming art gallery is the perfect location for my book signing events. Thanks for all you do for the community!

Very special thanks to Mark McNease, prolific author of LGBT-themed mysteries and short stories (see MarkMcNease.com), for his priceless support and friendship. Mark hosts podcasts, writes on Substack, runs a website and Facebook group called LGBTSr, and promotes my work through all those avenues.

Most importantly, I would like to thank my husband, Jeff McKeehan, who has supported and encouraged me every step of the way, provided great ideas and valuable feedback, and tolerated all those times when my mind was immersed in the world of my characters. Every spouse of an author knows exactly what I'm talking about.

Other Books by Dave Hughes

Fiction

Gay Tales for the New Millennium
Maybe Next Year
Instant Adult
Open Books, Closed Sets
If I Seem Quiet...
Maybe <u>Now</u> (September 2024)

Retirement Lifestyle

Design Your Dream Retirement
Smooth Sailing into Retirement
The Quest for Retirement Utopia

AuthorDaveHughes.com

About the Author

This is Dave Hughes' fifth novel in the "Gay Tales for the New Millennium" series. The last book in the series, *Maybe Now*, is scheduled for release in September 2024.

Before writing fiction, Dave wrote three retirement lifestyle planning books, *Design Your Dream Retirement, Smooth Sailing Into Retirement,* and *The Quest for Retirement Utopia.* Dave created the website RetireFabulously.com, which enables readers to envision, plan for, and enjoy the best retirement possible. In addition to writing hundreds of articles for RetireFabulously.com, Dave's writing has appeared on US News & World Report, LGBTSr.com, Medium, Yahoo! Finance, CNN/Money, Next Avenue, Tiny Buddha, and others.

Aside from his writing, Dave is also a jazz musician. He plays trombone and steelpan in various bands in the Phoenix area. He owns an embarrassingly large collection of jazz, Brazilian, exotica, steel band, jazz/rock, and vocal ensemble CDs and videos.

Before retiring at age 56, Dave was a software engineer for 34 years, working for companies such as Intel, Computer Sciences Corporation, McDonnell Douglas Space Systems, and NCR. Throughout his career, his assignments included software development, customer support, training, course development, and management.

Dave resides in Chandler, Arizona with his husband Jeff and their dog Maynard.

Dave is available for interviews, book readings/signings, speaking engagements, and panel discussions. You may contact Dave at Dave@AuthorDaveHughes.com.

Visit AuthorDaveHughes.com to learn more and subscribe to his newsletter.